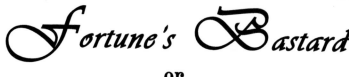

Fortune's Bastard

or

Love's Pains Recounted

A swashbuckling adventure of lust, learning, and love.

Escaping the religious hysteria of Renaissance Florence, young Antonio leaves his family and fate behind to find a better life. Misfortune, betrayals, friendships, and unexpected favors toss him around the Mediterranean as he makes his way as a pirate, an itinerant actor, and a fugitive before becoming a notable merchant of Venice. Inspired by Shakespeare, author Gil Cole reimagines Antonio as someone different of his time—a man who openly desires the love of another man.

"Hold onto your codpiece—Shakespeare has never been hotter. Gil Cole's lusty yet literate *Fortune's Bastard* is a thrilling, imaginative, and above all romantic homage to the great bard."
—Wayne Hoffman, author of *Sweet Like Sugar* and *Hard*

"*Fortune's Bastard* is a thrilling tale of manly virtues tested—love, loyalty, honor and physical courage—and manly desires given their fullest and freest expression. Gil Cole's adventure is epic, operatic, and Shakespearean. He writes with complete confidence (another manly virtue!) as he rolls out a grand pageant of heroism and love on the fifteenth century Mediterranean. On every page I found fresh surprises that kept my pulse racing."
—David Pratt, author of *Bob the Book* and *My Movie*

Gil Cole graduated from the Julliard School and acted in several plays of Shakespeare, as well as in many classic and contemporary plays. He currently resides in New York City where he works as a psychoanalyst.

Fortune's Bastard

or

Love's Pains Recounted

a novel

Gil Cole

Chelsea Station Editions
New York

Book design by Peachboy Distillery & Design
Cover design by Peachboy Distillery & Designs from art images by re_bekka, pavilla, and Viktoriya, Shutterstock

Author photo by Steven Mays Photography

Published by Chelsea Station Editions
362 West 36th Street, Suite 2R
New York, NY 10018
www.chelseastationeditions.com
info@chelseastationeditions.com

ISBN: 978-1-937627-01-0

Library of Congress Control Number: 2012956433

First U.S. Edition

Fortune's Bastard

or

Love's Pains Recounted

Part I

Florence

I remember the moment so precisely because it arrived with an acute thud to my chest: the moment it was clear to me that dissembling would no longer work. When it was clear to me that although I had hoped to be able not to notice that I had objections, my objections would no longer be overlooked.

The moment came on the evening when Virgilio Speziolissi was the guest of my father. The dinner to which he'd been invited was convened to confirm a plan, nothing out of the ordinary, just an expectable part of doing business. Virgilio Speziolissi had a daughter, Marianna, quite young, thought to be fair by most who beheld her, in sooth a lovely girl. There was nothing objectionable about her. To the contrary, she brought with her the business interests of her father, and these nestled neatly with the business interests of my father. A wedding was necessary to weld these interests, and for a wedding to take place a groom was needed. There was nothing out of the ordinary in such a plan. It was so ordinary, in fact, that when my father had first broached the idea to me, I felt no objection stirring at all. I felt nothing because this was simply how marriages worked. Marriages founded in the interests of family businesses made the life we recognized happen. There was no reason to give this plan a second thought. That I would have a wife was no reason to think my life would change in any way that I would feel keenly. At least this is what I told myself in order not think on it any further.

But when the moment arrived thoughts—objections—overtook me. The chamber stifled. Torches and guttering candles cast wavering shadows on the tapestries that lined my father's banqueting room. The table was strewn with the remnants of a meal that was too heavy for the season, but my father knew well Speziolissi's appetite and ordered accordingly. The meal had done its work and the men smiled on each other with the special affection inspired by sufficient amounts of wine and visions of mounting wealth. The two men pushed back in their chairs to ease their tight bellies.

"Once more, a toast to the marriage that will link our houses, and make us the strongest dealers in the finest stuffs that Florence has ever seen," my father nearly sang in his excitement.

His gestures, like his speech, had grown more expansive with each toast. Speziolissi let forth a resplendent belch. I cast a glance at Marianna, the frightened fifteen-year-old girl who was to be my bride, and suddenly felt a pang of sympathy for her discomfort. My hands quaked. Rivulets of sweat dripped from my brow and down my back. An enormous mistake was about to be made, and only I could avert it.

Speziolissi spoke. "Marco, the brightest days lie before us, and before you, my new son." He leered in my direction. "My Marianna is a precious jewel to be cherished. You will promise me that, won't you boy, to cherish my child?"

"Antonio knows just how precious a gift you've bestowed on him, my friend. As do I. Don't you, my son? Stand and address your new father-in-law."

The smoke, the heat, and too much wine made my head swim. I stood and lifted my glass, intending to raise it to this man and speak warmly about his daughter. She was not more than a child, really, and I knew very little of her other than that our destinies had been decided by our fathers. What was there to say about her? I opened my mouth and naught fell from my lips. I set my cup on the damask cloth, bowed to the old men before me, turned, and walked out of the chamber. Speech may have failed me, but not my legs. Action took the place of words, and my actions were joined to the thoughts that would no longer be ignored. I could not go along with this plan, with this life that was mapped out for me. I could not overlook what I knew to be true. I pushed open the wooden doors, stepped out into the courtyard, strode across the stones and opened the outer gate to the street. The dark retained day's heated embrace. My heart pounded with an insistence that would not be calmed by mere walking. My body demanded that I hasten. Strides were not enough. I fell into a headlong rush, and as I ran the burden of what I was leaving behind began to fall away. I raced all the way to the little Square of Saint Cecilia before I stopped, doubled over, hands on my knees, and gasped deep draughts of the heavy evening air. The grip of the ordained tightened round me. The work my flight began was far from finished. Escape was required, but just how it might be completed was not at all clear, only that I had to act. My father had decided that my marriage to Marianna Speziolissi would bring forth prodigious issue: the most advantageous partnership in the history of Florentine fabric merchants. How I felt about the matter wasn't important in the least.

This was not unusual. Marriage for my father, as for most men, was not important beyond the getting of children and the forging of good business alliances. Love had nothing to do with it. Love was a matter for art, for enjoyment, and few men in Florence made a marriage for love. It would have been odd indeed if my father didn't expect me to carry on in this style. He was certain that I'd take over his business, when he'd finally exhausted himself. That eventuality, I was sure, would not occur very soon. My father showed no signs of slowing. No, his fervor seemed inexhaustible and he saw in the alliance with Speziolissi a promise of greater wealth beckoning with irresistible allure.

My father was a dealer of linen and silk whose prospects were not flagging. He made for my mother, my two younger brothers, and me a comfortable life. We had servants and tutors, grooms and cooks, private rooms and entertainments fashioned for our amusement and education. To these comforts I gave little more than the most cursory inventory. That my inattention might have been insulting to those whose labors I ignored I could not know. I wasn't home much and I was a heedless youth, I will confess it. From my boyhood I had strayed from the bosom of my family because I hated the idea of being a dealer of linen and silk. Of counting bolts of cloth, and worrying the threads between my finger and thumb to judge their quality. Of counting bags of money traded for those bolts, and wondering whether I'd been cheated, or if my customer would figure out that I'd cheated him.

My grandfather had been prosperous and my father intended his children's lives to be more prosperous, each generation exceeding the last. We were raised to be prominent, embraced by the zenith of Florence society. We wore the finest of the linen he dealt in, and slept in big soft beds, and our cellar held fine wines from many places. Such were the entitlements to which I was born. But the comforts of this life choked me. I felt coddled and caged and longed for an escape, though just what I wanted to escape and how was obscure to me.

I knew I wouldn't live the life my father wished for me, though I was not ungrateful for what he provided. Even as a youth I understood that I wouldn't be a father—wouldn't stand at the head of a family in the way my father did. It was true that I was good at the things a young man ought to be good at. Skilled in the ways of the athlete—riding and archery—and I had an avidly hungry mind for studies in Latin and mathematics. But it had always been clear to me that I had no wish to cultivate the arts of dalliance with ladies and certainly no desire for marriage. A woman's form did not rouse me. I knew that a wife was necessary only for the continuing of our blood and our family's acclaim. She would be someone for whom I was to provide accoutrements of our station, but certainly she'd not be a partner for my thoughts or for my passion. Hadn't that been the manner of my father's behavior with my mother? The pretense of marriage, of love, that a man swore some oath of constancy to a woman, was only part of my objection to such vows. Few men I knew took this pretense to heart; men had wives and families but reserved their passion for their young lovers. It was with them they surrendered to love's blandishments, displayed their charms and truths. My own father, I knew, still saw his Pietro as often as he could. This was the open secret, the way of men in our world. Most of the men in this world could live in this manner, preserving the pretense that guaranteed their social and economic advantage. This was not a solution that could work for me—this dual existence, this tacit acceptance of one life in exchange for another. It wasn't deception, for all was known. It simply was not spoken aloud. And because it was never spoken my objection to a life lived in this manner wasn't an idea that I had found a way to articulate. There was no need to articulate it until I turned to bestow some words of affection on the girl I was to marry. In that moment it became a discrete particle, something I could think. Before that night it was as if this custom, this structure, lived me. There was no choosing something that lived me. There was hardly even the recognition of it. It was clear in the outward form I was to comply with, but not available to consideration in my mind.

Oh, certainly there were those who sought to guide our lives through faith, or, rather, the velvet-clad iron machinery of religion and its politics. The Church's robed enforcers sought to shape and cage and crush with ever changing, ever elaborated rules, behavior they found necessary to control. But I never respected, let alone feared, a god, particularly when he so often was understood to be clearly interested in the political fortunes of one man. This I know is a risky admission, and so I did not make it aloud. My most private thoughts I'd never spoken. How many times I saw how men and women alike developed the elaborate skill of appealing to a god to justify their selfishness, their ambition, greed, and small mindedness. I knew better than to give my trust away so freely. I trusted my wits, my strength, and even before my beard was more than palest, sparse velvet, I knew quite well that my beauty gave me leverage I could use to my benefit. I wasn't a delicate beauty, no Antinous, but to some tastes, I was catnip.

Whether I loved men or women needn't have mattered, as I would do as I please, beyond the restrictions of religion and society, just as most men I knew did as they pleased. Because I was still only eighteen, the question of marriage was new, even premature. It was the custom then for men to marry when they were past twenty-five, finding a young girl not past fifteen from a family successful enough to bring a prodigious dowry, advantageous connections, or property. It was to be preferred, of course, that the sacrificial bride bestowed all three on her husband. For the sake of my father's business, the question of whether I would wish to be married was beyond consideration, and the question of whom I'd wish to love had even less to do with my marriage than that.

Most men in our city, my father included, found pleasure of

greatest heat with boys. Youths would meet their lovers at taverns, at the public baths, or at a shed beside the building site of a new cathedral. That detail always pleased me, and I found a special enjoyment in swallowing a handsome man's seed where a marble pulpit would rise one day, beneath an image of that naked man stretched out in a passionate agony for our worship. That was communion indeed. I had taken to adventure of this sort with ease since I was fourteen, excited by the fervor my rhetoric tutor showed for me. He'd taken me to the shop stalls that lined the Old Bridge one evening. It was there I found that sharing the pleasures only a man's body offered was like recovering a self I did not know had strayed. To the Old Bridge I returned, knowing I'd find there the comfort I needed to strengthen my defiant resolve.

The heft and hairiness of men a good deal older than me excited me far more than the cool ivory of a girl's countenance. This I had always known, but until that night, knowing it had not required an action that disrupted life. But that night was different. That night a future marked by decisions became explicit. That night it was clear to me that a disruption was coming and was necessary. I was certain that I could not carry off the double life that was expected and never named. Squeezed between my father's expectations and the real dangers that faced those like me, I had to find a way to think, to find a hope, a thread, a plan to escape. I found my usual spot midway across the Old Bridge, between a leather dealer's stall and a goldsmith's, to wait for Franceschino. Franceschino would know the necessity that drove my decision. He would understand. I could stanch my worry in his warmth.

$$\oplus$$

Since the death of Lorenzo life in our city had become more and more difficult, and particularly so for those who remained bachelors too long. The friar Girolamo's ferociously skillful sermons had so raised people's fears that more and more often men and the boys they loved were denounced to the Office of the Night. This was the bureau that provided that particular kind of surveillance. They had always been part of our city's machinery, but the extent of their power could wax and wane as politics demanded. The Night Officers knew all the likely places where boys and men would find one another. They knew precisely where to look because they had sought those shadows, too, enjoying the pleasures that it was now their pleasure to police. The Night Officers kept copious records of all who chafed and scoffed at the laws proscribing sodomy. If you looked with care at their lists, you'd find the names of all the great families in the city, those famous for public works, thriving businesses, and handsome children. Despite the influence of those prominent names recorded on their lists, the vigilant presence of the Office of the Night resisted any effort to abolish it. As if finding general consent, the making of a list of sodomites seemed as important to the life of the city as the making of money. One might well surmise that policing men's pleasure and generating power were inextricably linked. For years, the Office of the Night played capriciously with men's fates. Inconsistency enhanced the fear they sought to evoke. Many a time to be apprehended or denounced brought with it only the inconvenience of paying a negligible fine, or, if the apprehended were scandalously prominent, they suffered a temporary exile from the city. Most men became accustomed to this elaborate dance and all knew the steps and kept time.

But Lorenzo's death brought change. Fanatics daily called for sodomites to be burnt, a death penalty even for the first or second conviction. Fanaticism's fears could be contagious. My friend, Niccolo Guicciardini, from a family well situated in the new regime, grew more and more alarmed. He told me he was afraid; that sometimes he felt he could believe what he heard the friar preach at the new Saint Mary's, that the terrible storm that set fire to the roof of the church was divine punishment. He quaked to hear Savonarola thunder, "God sent this scourge so that we would repent of our sins, especially sodomy, which he wants to be done away with, and that if between now and August we don't correct ourselves these streets will run with blood."

Apparently this madness was irresistible. The Dominican friar actually recruited younger boys, beauties who just last month enjoyed the best favors and fucking their lovers could give them, into a band of noxious little vigilantes. Incredibly, our governing authority, the nine men who make up the Signoria, had found it expedient to exploit Friar Savonarola's influence to consolidate their power, and his political faction was now writing the laws for our city. More than one of Savonarola's enemies were dragged before the Office of the Night and accused of sodomy. Some awaited execution. Emboldened by the irresistible intoxication of doing God's work, and the power to enforce drastic new penalties, the friar's boys became a life-threatening menace.

⊕

Franceschino was thirty years old, broad and dark, and I knew him by his silhouette as he approached me through the mist that had settled over the Arno. He cocked his head, appraising me. His right hand reached over and grabbed the left side of my chest, and he squeezed. "Antonio, my handsome boy." Then his hand slid down the front of my doublet and found the pouch where my cock was already straining against the embroidered cloth. "As eager as ever to see me. And as I am to see you." He leaned over and kissed me, holding tight to my cock. I reached around his neck, holding his mouth against mine.

"Oh, how good it is to kiss you," I said. "To feel your arms." I pulled my head away.

"What is this trouble that clouds your brow?"

"What I dread is come. Tonight my father intended to announce my betrothal. What I thought I could do, I cannot."

"Oh, my boy. This is an impediment only, not a disaster. What can have changed? You were prepared for this yesterday and it was hardly unexpected. It is unwise to bolt, given the mood of the city, this you know well. Who was the unfortunate intended who you'd deprive of such a catch as you?"

"I wish not to speak of it. Let me have you. I want you so."

He pulled away, murmuring, "My impetuous handsome one, can you not pause a while. I've brought you something."

Franceschino enjoyed giving me gifts, though they meant little to me. I exulted in his interest in me, not in what he brought me.

before me, just what kind of life I wanted with Franceschino. It was far more than what we'd known before that night. Far more.

As if to soothe me, he said, "Oh my handsome one, it is so. It must be so. You play me like a virtuoso, and you give me great pleasure. We've enjoyed each other so much, don't part from me so petulantly."

"I'm not only angry. I'm frightened. You saw these boys. We've not seen the worst, I think." He was silent. "You think I merely play with you—you don't see how I want to be with you? That I wish not to stray from your side—nay—not for a moment?"

"I see that you want a great deal, and I have no doubt that you will find a way to get what you want. I may not be here to provide it, but I'm confident you will find another who will. Good luck to him, and to you."

"Franceschino—I—"

"I'm not as cold as I sound. I do fear for you in this city, but you are young, and if you play the game, you will survive. Marry, and carry on. It is a game. My presence, though, can no longer be tolerated. I will be disposed of one way or another. Oh, my Antonio, I will miss you, you know. You do mean so much to me. I want you to be safe. Perhaps, when this spasm of political maneuvering has been exhausted, I may be able to come back. Just do not waste any time waiting for me. That I could not stand."

"When do you go?"

"Tomorrow." He held my head between his hands and covered my mouth with his. I breathed in his warm breath. I wanted to inhale him, to keep that flavor, that scent, with me always. It was true that I had toyed with him, that I came to him for pleasure, but now, kissing him goodbye, I knew that he was more to me than an amusement. I'd never imagined the lack of him.

"So this is our parting?"

"Unfortunate that it was dominated by these boys' zealous fervor, but, yes, it is."

"And now, what is to become of me? My father has arranged a marriage for me, a marriage that I cannot think of even for a moment. You would leave me now, at the worst possible time? I cannot stay here either. I can't. I won't. But—"

"Antonio, stop. You'll triumph, you will. I know you will. This madness will pass, you will simply be more careful. You still captivate most of the men in Florence, men whose power will protect you."

"That's not true. You must know that. I've gotten older, you know, these years I've been with you. I'm nearly nineteen. It is boys my brother's age and figure that captivate. My beard is thickening. You've held onto me too long to notice."

"I will not fight with you, and I will not take you with me. Just know how it hurts that I'm going to leave you now. Right now. How will you make your way home? Not across the Old Bridge."

"No, of course not. I'll walk up to the May Bridge. Franceschino, stop—" Suddenly, as if for the first time, I knew that something I didn't want to happen was happening, and I was powerless to change it. This was impossible. Incomprehensible. What was I feeling? I had always known that I wanted him. Now I was losing him, and it was if I was sinking through the stones of the square. He held me again, tightly, with his left hand on the side of my face, looking into my eyes. We stood that way for I don't know how long. Then he turned south toward the building site of the new Pitti Palace and disappeared into the night.

⊕

I walked along the Arno to the bridge that would lead me to my father's house. I was shaken by what had happened within me. How I could not understand what I felt about Franceschino until the constancy of his presence was denied me? I had simply come to believe that I'd always have him. The idea of giving him up had never crossed my mind. In our city, a passionate romance like the one we enjoyed was commonplace; it was well known that they occurred, but it was also well known that they would not last. A beloved youth grew older and became the mature lover to another youth. This was part of our social order. And now this order was condemned.

Even before the friar's madness had set the city afire, a romance like Franceschino's and mine, one that lasted so long, was rare. We met and enjoyed each other, shared our cares and our love, for nearly four years. We drew attention to ourselves by failing to conform to the custom, the form. If most men in our city failed to conform to the law, they conformed to the custom. Everyone knew this, but everyone also chose not to know what they knew.

But there were moments that this choosing could not stand, when a general acknowledgement was made. Such a time as this, when the Signoria decreed that we had to be stopped, the city purged of corruption, arrests made, executions carried out. Before the rise of Friar Girolamo, enforcement was a half-hearted attempt, a nod to convention. The Office of the Night, though established years ago, had always been toothless, really. A pretense. The older men paid a fine and after a few weeks we were left alone to find one another again. This was simply how younger men of my class became known to the society of adult men. Along with their cocks and cum, our lovers gave us advice, introduced us to the ways of doing business. But it was also expected that all of these younger men would successfully marry and have families. That in their turn they'd fall in love with a younger man who needed to be initiated into the hypocrisy of the kind of adulthood that would guarantee the stability of our world. These romances seemed to promise a way of straddling a life lived both inside and outside, but of course there was no outside of a system that encompassed both the passionate love between an older man and a younger and the necessity of creating families.

That night Franceschino—the idea of the absence of him—forced me to realize that I was different. I'd thought I'd always have him, or a man like him, and that I'd never have to take my place in the order of the family. Suddenly it was clear to me that living that hypocrisy would tighten around my throat like a noose. For the first time I understood that Florence would no longer to be my home. That my home had become dangerous to me. I had to leave.

⊕

By the time I reached my father's house, the band of friar's boys had already paid a visit. They were truly in rare form that night. My father had been roused from his stupor by the boys' chants and was seething. He heard me push the gate open, and stood before me in the courtyard.

"I'm surprised you dare to come home this time. You press me, Antonio. You press me beyond my endurance. On the very night your betrothal is discussed. The very night. You insulted Speziolissi, and humiliated that poor child. And now you come back? You defy me and expect to slink back to safety under my roof? What teems through that fevered head of yours? You strain my patience past my bounds. You do. I have forbidden you to go to the Old Bridge. You know it is far too dangerous now. What, did you find Franceschino? I'm amazed he's still in Florence, that he hasn't been assassinated. The friar's boys have just left. I fear for you, my boy. I do. And I cannot help you now. You will be denounced. One of them knows you?"

"Yes, Timotheo, who is saving himself by denouncing others."

"That is not my concern any longer. You have deliberately defied me."

"Well, it is hardly the case that I told you I wouldn't, is it?"

"Antonio, this cannot continue. This will not continue. Are you stupid, are you doing your utmost to ruin your life? To get yourself executed? Surely you see how things are different now. Not only because of this demented Dominican friar. My business, my opportunities at this moment are ripe. Your behavior makes your contempt clear. That is inexcusable. I will not have it."

"You'll not have to have it, then."

"What is that supposed to mean, you ungrateful fool?"

"I do not mean to be ungrateful, Father. I know, I really do, how much privilege you've afforded me. And protection. But I came to understand something tonight, clearly, and for the first time. I cannot live as you expect. No, as you demand. I will not. I must make my own way. I know now that I must leave."

"Where do you think you can go?"

"I'm not as helpless without you as you'd wish me to be. Do you really think I cannot survive without your—it is help you intend to give me, but I can—I must—do without it. I don't know where I'll go. I'll take my chances. What other choices do I have?"

"You might ask me if there are choices. I'm not entirely without feeling for you, my son. You delight in turning away from me, from all I offer you."

"What delights me should not be your concern, but I assure you that seeing you in a rage does not delight me. Father, you've always made your expectations for me very clear. Your help always binds me closer to you. What you offer as help becomes a burden. You know it not, but your help, your expectations are for yourself, not for me. You cannot see that I am not you. So, I turn away."

"How can help be a burden? Antonio, listen. You will need to find a way to live. What do you—"

"Father, let me try to find my way. Let me at least try."

"Try first to listen to me. It may be good to leave the city. In that you are thinking. We'll send you to Genoa. You can use my name there, with the shipowner I deal with, you know him, Vincenzo Battista. I will write a letter in the morning that you can present to him. Perhaps he'll find a way to use you somehow."

I had no idea whether this would suit me any more than another plan. But I was tired, and I wanted to sleep. I wanted not to feel the twisting stab in my guts that Franceschino had left there. I wanted this night to be over.

"All right, Father. I'll do what you say. I'm too tired to struggle tonight. Can we just stop now? I know that again I must thank you. Always, when I've most displeased you, I find myself in the position to thank you. I don't understand—why this sudden care after your fury?"

He stood silently for a moment. We were only shadows in the courtyard, in a silvery blue light. His hand quivered, as if wishing to grasp something.

"No, you really don't understand, do you? You say you are not me, but you are, you know. You're my oldest son. You are my son."

"You sound like you are talking about something you own." I saw a spasm of anger cross his brow. "No, I'll not start fighting with you. I don't want to fight any more. I will just thank you, and leave you."

And so, at the end of the week, I did.

The Pirate

Father's choice, the last one he made for me, was right: Vincenzo Battista put me to work learning the management of his shipping trade. His fleet traveled as far to the east as the Black Sea, and as far west as England and the Low Countries, and his business was growing. In the two years that I worked in Genoa there were mishaps, of course, when ships with their holds full were lost to the fury of a storm. There was the constant annoyance of privateers, who sometimes relieved a ship of their goods, but left its crew in peace. Pirates were worse, often caring little if lives were lost as they plundered. But Battista's losses never overcame his gains. Fabrics, grain, spices, leather, wine, most anything that could be supplied to dealers along the rim of the Mediterranean was carried by his ships.

There was satisfaction in learning the shipping business, but few responsibilities were conferred upon me. Battista's manner led me to believe that he trusted me but my tasks were limited almost entirely to bookkeeping. The only interruptions to my sedentary occupation came when he sent me on the odd errand. It was a meager start to a man's career, but it was my own.

I lived in rooms to the back of his offices, near to the quay. Being far from my family quieted the squalls inside me. My father's insistently solicitous plans could not intrude on me there. Danger was not so nigh, since Genoa was not caught up in the religious madness that made life in Florence so difficult. I found diversion in seeking out men in this new city. I learned the signals and the places, the ways of the port and the docks, the pleasures to be found in the shadows and stalls. In all that time, I encountered no man I wished to tarry with for more than one night's enjoyment. Whether the fault was mine I cannot say. I did not seek to assign fault. I simply kept searching. I was restless. I could not say for whom I searched or for what. Truly I think I cared not. It was the search only that drew me.

The ache of Franceschino's absence eased in time, though there were moments when I longed for him with the old urgency. I learned that all of his family was exiled from Florence when the mad friar took power, and I wondered how we'd find each other, if ever I'd see him again. Alone, truly alone for the first time, I found a different Antonio within. I felt the paltry extent of my solitary reach, certainly, but I also glimpsed the possibility of grasping something for myself by myself. Lacking my father's protective indulgence showed me what might, in time, be required of me. There was some comfort in feeling the necessity of my own strength, but I could not deny how sorely solitude left me yearning.

The winds had begun their shift to the north and on a clear day freshened by the hint of autumn I saw the man who would push me farther than I had ever been. I had seen him before, and had always felt a quickening in my chest when I did. He had a way of skirting the edge of the square that fronted the harbor, casually but with dispatch, never lingering, as if he intended not to leave a trace behind. But his face and silhouette lasted, and left a disturbance that stirred me greatly. I finally learned his name from Emilia, a beaming grandma who seemed never to be out of sorts, and who sold her meat pies in a shop at the edge of the harbor square.

"My beautiful mama, what have you for me today?"

"Ah, you are just in time, you rogue. I have two savories left. I thought Rodrigo would buy all my wares today, but your breakfast is safe." She chuckled as she handed me the small packet, marked with a faint spread of oil.

"Rodrigo? The man who passed out of here a moment ago?"

"The same. The handsome phantom who appears as suddenly as a whim. And you, my boy, what—no time for me today?"

I had laid my coin on her table and dashed to the door but he was nowhere to be found.

"Pardon, mama. I must—" I was already in the square.

In my confusion I didn't know what I must.

Rodrigo was an infamous pirate who dared to enter port cities to restock his ship, trading what he plundered from the merchant ships he preyed on for the supplies a pirate vessel needed. He was a handsome roughneck who was known as much for his daring attacks as for his handsome square rigged caravel, the *Black Phoenix*. He was notorious, as much for his method as for his success. He sought never to harm the crews of the ships he plundered. The legends grew about him like the garlands of a wreath of victory. Admiring fame announced that his form and skill conquered the stout hearts of many and that his crew, a happy few, was a steadfast band of brothers.

I saw him the next afternoon, a day shining brilliant as if the breeze scrubbed the light. I was loitering near a market stall looking for the ripest peaches in the vendor's basket.

He was overseeing the sale of his latest haul, fleeces and hides he'd relieved from Ragusan barges loaded at Varna on the Black Sea, making their way west. We'd heard about the piracy; news traveled fast among the shippers. The Ragusans' business thrived, but their boats were cumbersome and slow, no match for the nimbler, faster *Black Phoenix*, a ship that Rodrigo himself received from Ottavio, his former master. Ottavio had been killed in one of the few sea battles that overtook the *Black Phoenix*, when ships of the Venetian navy had their one chance of good luck and surprised them at the mouth of the Brindisi harbor. Piracy was almost routine, and presented a problem for the merchants who'd made Venice the Queen of the Adriatic. Pirates could swoop down on the cumbersome barges and balingers as swiftly as a falcon, unburden them of their wares, and fly back out to the open deep where the coastal vessels, small, with shallow drafts, were unsuited to the rougher water. They made their mercantile way hugging the shore, from port to port.

"Boy—yes you, handsome one," Rodrigo called out to me. "When you've tired of dallying there, bring me some of those and I'll tell you why you'll not be sleeping at home tomorrow night."

My neck flushed hot. I thought I was so subtle, staring at him from a discreet distance, pretending to occupy myself with the fruit I fussed over. He read precisely not only what my next move was to be, but that I couldn't take my eyes off him. After picking three peaches and paying for them, I turned a corner into the market square, and somehow there he was, standing in the shadow of the colonnade. He was dark, nay, burnished by wind and rough weather. The sun beyond the shade where he stood polished the shine in his eyes and as he stepped in front of me he smiled broadly. His face was scored with lines that made him more beautiful. His smile cracked my heart. I couldn't breathe for a moment; my feet were lead. I, who dared to be proud of my certain equipoise, was a gibbering fool. He saw me down to my toes, and I was nailed. He chuckled softly as he leaned over, grabbed me by the shoulders, drew me back into the shadow and kissed me, hard, on the mouth. The peaches fell to the cobblestones. His tongue pushed through my lips to meet mine, a mixture of clove and salt, and in a timeless moment, he set me firmly on my feet, his laugh a low rumble.

"Yes, my beauty, incomparably good. I do know you, don't I?" He reached down, picked up the bruised fruit, dusted it off, and held one out to me. "And you know me, don't you, though this is our first meeting. I'll see you again, if you're not careful, and then you'll be glad."

I was speechless. My arrogance was shaken and useless. I thought I could always rely on my ready wit. Those two years I was away from the safety of my family had taught me that if I played the part of the one in charge, I'd be treated that way. It was how I had made my way in Genoa. But now my guts were turned to jelly. I couldn't have played a part if my life depended on it. My excitement was pointing due north, and clear to anyone who cared to look at me.

"I—I do know who you are," I stammered.

"Of course you do. And now you know who you are, too." He wiped the juice that ran down his chin, and put the fruit to my mouth. I bit. "An invitation, then. Dawn, at the quay. I need a new boy. I want you. I think you want me. It is up to you."

He wiped the juice from my mouth and sucked it from his fingers, his dark eyes riveting mine to his. Then he turned, drew back into the shadow, and was gone. I skulked back to Battista's office, too full of something queasily new even to think of eating. I did know that the moment had arrived when I truly could make my escape.

My sleep that night was fitful, marred and wonderful by turns. I was visited by an insistent dream. At its start I was shackled to the desk I knew, the one in the next room, but in the dream stacks, nay, towers of ledgers loomed over me. Suddenly the ceiling opened and my shackles dropped away. I felt myself lifted skyward with a giddy heave. At that moment I woke with a start, certain that I was about to fall from a great height. I groped about for something to grab, to break my fall, and in a panic I tangled myself in the sheets. I heard nothing but the pounding of my heart, squinted about in the dark, and after I could reassure myself that I was only on my narrow cot, I tried to settle back into repose. As I lay there hoping sleep would overcome me once again I conjured Rodrigo's face before me. When I slept again the dream returned, three times, maybe four. My fears and my desires wrestled through the night. Surely I knew that to cast my lot with him was to turn away forever from the safety I had always known. Just as surely I knew that safety seemed a meager portion to my vaunting appetite.

I woke at dawn with a gnawing hunger, but I couldn't imagine putting anything in my stomach, it was churning so. My mind, though, was as clear as the lightening sky. Without a thought I made my way through the warren of narrow streets to the open square before the harbor again. I didn't have a plan; I didn't feel the need to think of a plan. It was as if I were following instructions.

Approaching the square from an alley opposite to the quay, I crossed into the sharply slanting light, and saw a single skiff bobbing on the waves in the harbor. To my left, from under the awning newly opened over a carpet seller's stall, Rodrigo called out to me.

"A fine morning made finer to see your handsome face, boy. Take this sack from me, and put it in the skiff that waits for us, while I get our breakfast." He slung the sack across my shoulders, and then held my face between his hands as he spoke to me. Their roughness made the look he gave me more precious. He did not expect me to speak, which was lucky, because I could not summon any words. I simply let myself fall into his care. For that is what it was. It was clear that his lust for me was strong. But his caring was as true.

There was a sailor in the skiff whose knowing look said that he expected me.

"Ah, the youth Rodrigo has found. Yes, he was certain you'd come. You're surprised? Ever been to sea? No, doesn't look as if you have. But you'll take to it, I think. You'll have to." His laugh was a low rumble. "Yes, lad, you are just as he said—rough, ready, and needing some handling. Oh, good, you smile through your blush. That is a good sign. I'm Rodrigo's second, Matteo. Give me that, and hold this line fast till your new master's finished. He's crossing down now, there—" he said as he nodded across the pier. Rodrigo was striding toward us carrying a smaller sack in his arms.

What was happening to me? Was I being kidnapped—abducted? I watched myself as if from a distance. There I was, standing on the quay, holding fast the skiff that belonged to one of the most notorious pirates on the Mediterranean as he made his final preparations for a long time at sea. Certainly I understood that I was about to become his. Or perhaps it is better to say that this was my wish. I couldn't tell if I was following orders or answering an invitation. I felt no fear. The trembling I saw in my hands and felt at my knees was excitement. But across my chest warmth spread that felt like relief.

Rodrigo tossed the smaller bag to Matteo, jumped lightly into the skiff, and looked up at me. "Now, beauty. This is the moment. Which is it?" He opened his hand to me expectantly. My heart thumped. I breathed in the cool salt air and then I jumped down, and dropped the rope into the small boat. I looked over at Rodrigo. His face was kind but serious, and he nudged me into place manning the oars. I was to work for my breakfast.

"That was the right decision—boy—I—blast me but I haven't asked your name. I wonder what you thought of a man who'd snatch you up without knowing your name?"

My name seemed the least important thing, considering what it felt to me he did know about me. "Antonio is my name," I murmured.

"We have another Antonio aboard. I'll call you Tonio. The others will call you 'Boy' but you won't mind, will you? Get to it, Tonio, we have no more time to waste, and put your back into it."

The water was calm and the current gentle, so rowing us out to the *Black Phoenix* was not beyond my power. Rodrigo pulled a meat pasty out of the sack, bit off half of it, and pushed the other half into my mouth. "Not too greasy. You probably know the granny who bakes these—Emilia? My favorite here. More?"

He was so easy to fall in with. He set the rhythm and the terms so I needed to do little but watch and learn. All was mystery to me, yet it felt completely natural, as if I was doing just what I ought to be doing.

The skiff was loaded with other sacks of provisions, and there were four hogsheads of something they were sitting on, they must have been water and wine, but even so, the rowing was easy. The sun climbed before us and threw a brilliant light on the city as it shrank with our progress. I didn't even know we had reached the ship when a voice called down to us.

"Captain, the breeze is coming fresher, you've finished not a moment too soon." The voice belonged to the man who tossed a hemp ladder down to us. When I looked up at him he fixed me with a look I could not read there was so much in it. His beard was red and lush, a man in his young maturity. The other voices I heard were shouting instructions to hoist the last of the provisions aboard and stow them below decks.

"Tonio—take this to my cabin—the men will show you where," and Rodrigo tossed a small canvas bag up toward me. "Then come up and find Matteo, and he'll tell you what your duties are to be. You'll tend to me later."

I struggled to climb the rope net that had been tossed down to the skiff, holding the salty drawstrings of a bag in my teeth as I clumsily fitted my feet in the squares and pulled myself up hand over hand. There was a sound like the rushing of water, or like shouting in my head. With each handhold the moments left for me to change my mind ran scarcer and scarcer. What if I jumped into the brine and swam back to land? For all its tedium, it was a life I knew. With each new foothold I cast my lot with I knew not what. Was I a rogue or a fool? The wind blew more steadily, the chill stiffened the back of my neck. And still I climbed, my body obeyed while my brain buzzed in argument. When I got to the rail, the younger man with the red beard grabbed me by the belt and hauled me over.

"You'll want to know where Rodrigo's cabin is. I am Tomasso.

My place was once where you will be making yours. Just as one day another will take your place. Here—you see there, go down those stairs there, and straight back. Rodrigo's cabin is the middle door. The big one." He held my shoulder and looked into my eyes, hard, as if he was trying to find something. He brushed the hair off my forehead. "Go on."

The severity of Tomasso's greeting silenced the argument in my head. It was good to have a task, it was simple and clear and I could do it. I stumbled down the steps he had pushed me toward. The sudden dark of belowdecks bedimmed my eyes, and I groped my way forward like one who has lost his sight. I pushed against the biggest door and light poured out as I fell into a large cabin. The whole wall in front of me was a row of big windows across the stern of the boat. There was a large sea chest at the foot of a bed that stood against the wall to my right, and a carved oak cabinet inlayed with ivory and stones flanked the opposite wall. Next to it was a small table with an ewer and cloths on it, and in the middle of the cabin, right in front of me, a desk covered with charts of the seas that make up our part of the world. I set the bag down on the chair that sat ready in front of the desk.

What had I done? This was not playing, this was an actual, important decision that I had made or, rather, *not* made. And not making this decision formed me. I felt my edge, my limit, more sharply than I'd ever felt it. This time there would be no going back. There was only pressing on. But still my fretful brain teemed. Would I ever be able to get word to Battista, who had welcomed me like another son? What new sorrows would my reckless act visit upon my father and my silent, neglected mother? But hadn't I fought to make my own way? Didn't I want to break free of my meager days hunched over a desk? The argument among my thoughts started anew, regret bit me deeply. What kind of fool is this, firstborn to a wealthy merchant, to thumb his nose at what fortune puts in his way? How I envied the illegitimate, the bastard, freighted with neither name nor position. Such a one has no choice but to set his course by his own lights. Such a one had no time for arguments like this that jangled inside me.

Suddenly my stomach heaved. I turned and ran back up to the

deck making for the side to vomit. But as soon as I hit the morning air, my stomach lay back down. Scores of sailors were climbing up the two masts and across the booms. They unfastened the ropes and with a thwacking whoosh big square sails dropped open, stuttered a moment, then blew big bellied as the wind found them. Sailors streamed down to the deck again. Men were shouting at each other, two were cranking a winch that wound the rope of the anchor onto its spool. My paltry argument ran dry. I knew I had made the choice. That it was mine alone was all. I searched—I couldn't count how many faces—for Rodrigo's. He was standing back at the big spoked wheel up on a deck above, Matteo next to him, talking into his ear as he held the wheel steady. Matteo glanced toward me, and beckoned.

⊕

By the time night fell on my first day aboard the *Black Phoenix* I began to learn what my duties were. Mostly preparing my master's meals, looking after his cabin, and being ready for anything else he might wish me to do. The men looked at me with a mixture of amusement and benign interest. Because I was Rodrigo's boy, and because the men loved Rodrigo, I felt safe enough. This was an atmosphere I had never imagined could exist. There must have been at least three score men aboard, but I couldn't be sure. Men who lived only with other men. Gradually it dawned on me that all of these men felt about themselves as I did, that they'd rather love another man than any woman.

On this boat, on this my first night on the sea, I was beyond the reach of the expected. I was free of the demand that I carry on as the world wished. Here I was free to belong to my master; a freedom I could only begin to fathom as he called to me that first night.

"Tonio—Tonio, what the devil are you at?"

Matteo had told me I was to serve Rodrigo's dinner and wash his things after, and I was wiping the last dish with the greasy cloth that was all I could find in the galley.

"I'm here—just—I'm here." I dropped what I was doing and dashed the few paces to his door. He was leaning out as he looked for me.

"Ah. There's the lad I want. Get yourself in here. You've done well,

not called criminals."

"You speak of men of business. Now you are their enemy. Tell me—your former master's customers—you knew them, you made their acquaintance?"

"Some. When they couldn't avoid coming to Genoa."

"Did you see enough to choose with open eyes to leave that life?"

"My whole life I knew the ways of business. Greed and brutality thrives among all men, whether called criminals or no."

"And whose greed will blot out all trace of a man's honor? The shipper's? The trader's? Or the pirate's?"

"I know not how to answer you. How can I know what I have not lived? Have I in word or action betrayed any hint but that this is my choice?"

"That is not enough. You must know what you have chosen."

"I cannot know that. No man can know that. But how I can choose more strongly?"

He turned his face away for a moment.

"My boy. My Tonio. You are right. I will gainsay you no further. You see how my care for you exceeds my reason."

He stood with his eyes closed for a moment.

"My boy. My Tonio." He held me close.

I lowered my voice to a whisper. "I can be of real use to you now, can't I? You need someone to handle the spices in the Marseilles market. Let me do it. I'm certain I can find a buyer. Battista shipped to a merchant there often, a man I never met, a Spaniard called Garcia. I've overseen the other side of this many times. But won't the traders you relieved of this treasure be looking for it?"

He pulled his head back and grinned at me.

"First of all, most of it was bound for Messina, the rest for Naples. Months ago. Second of all, we change the weights and the packing. This boy has found his voice and he means to use it. This boy is very bold to think I don't know my business." He cuffed me on the cheek. "A few months working in Genoa and he's a seasoned businessman. And what if Battista's clients have heard that you suddenly disappeared? You assume that no one is likely to be looking for you. You must think I'd be willing to put you in danger. You have been among those ruthless men who think of nothing but money for too long. Pirates appreciate life far more than that rabble. The deal is not nearly as important as the pleasure to be gotten as a benefit of the deal. That is why we persist in our success. Our willingness to forbear, when life is made better by forbearance, keeps us safe. No, Tomasso and Pato will move the load. A young, inexperienced trader may not be just the person who can trade this lot. You can accompany Tomasso, if you like, but you are to stay with the goods."

This was a sudden turn, and my heart danced now that he saw the uses he could put me to. More than a mere cabin boy, but one who provides as well as receives.

⊕

Since the *Black Phoenix* couldn't make an appearance in the port, moving the load of spices required three trips. I was to wait on the quay with each portion. We started well before dawn, so as to avoid notice as much as possible. Once all of the goods were ashore, I was to act the part of the merchant's clerk, accounting for the shipment, a role I knew that I could play.

Pato stayed with the skiff, and Tomasso went to find a buyer. The morning was nearly wasted when I saw Tomasso approach with a round little Frenchman toiling behind him. He'd bought the lot, and wanted to be sure he wasn't being cheated. I wasn't supposed to talk at all, that Rodrigo and Tomasso had made clear. But Tomasso wasn't the shrewdest businessman. The Frenchman began arguing, and I could see that Tomasso was losing patience. Bargaining's skills eluded him and he took no pleasure in the transaction. The Frenchman was growing belligerent and turned as if to walk away.

"Sir," I began, braving Tomasso's sharp look, "you can see, you can measure, you can weigh for yourself. You have sampled, and know the quality we provide you. A better price you'll not find this week. It is late in the season for these goods, the winter presses upon us, and you know your customers will pay a premium for spices at this time of year."

"For such a young person, you have an insistent approach.

Insistent but winning. Have I seen you before? What house do you work for?"

"For the house of my master, and you've not seen me before. At the beginning of my career, sir, and I'd be glad to work out a regular arrangement with a merchant as discerning as you clearly seem to be."

"Very smooth, young man. That is a possibility. I wish to sample again"

By this time, Tomasso was red with anger, but he saw that chastising me would spoil a deal that was underway. He paced along the edge of the quay, trying not to speak and glaring out toward Pato bobbing in the skiff. The Frenchman was untying the ropes around the canvas-covered bales. He reached in and brought out a handful of cardamom, inhaled its perfume and rubbed it between his palms.

"Not bad. Not at all bad, young man. Yes, You've found a buyer. The price, as your boy told me before, is only a little too high."

"The price, as my partner quoted to you, is the price you'll pay. And we'll have done a good day's business, monsieur—?"

"Millepieds. My shop is at the north end of the market square. When next you are in Marseilles, come directly to see me. You, not your partner, as you say." He handed me a pouch heavy with coins. I handed it to Tomasso, who hadn't stopped pacing. His face was white by this time, with the effort to keep silent. I shrugged. The deal had been made, and we got the price Rodrigo expected. In the end it was very easy.

Millepieds's boy came with a wagon to pick up the load and we were to buy provisions and return to the ship as quickly as we could without drawing attention to it or to us. But by now it was nearly noon, and it would be another two hours before the midday lull would slow business at all. And the size of the shipment had already made us an object of interest to others along the quay.

"Straight back to the ship?" I asked.

"What do you think? Or do you assume that you are in charge, now?"

"Look, I know but, well, he assumed that I was a man of business. Can I help what another assumes about me?"

"You can help by doing as you are instructed. This is finished. But don't think that Rodrigo won't know."

"What Rodrigo will know is that the shipment was sold at the price he wished, and that we bought the provisions we need."

"What he'll know is that you act for yourself regardless of what you are told. That is not what is expected from a new cabin boy."

"Tomasso, your anger outweighs my offense. The situation demanded action; there was no time for consultation. Our aims are the same."

He was silent. We had much to do, and we both knew it. And we both knew also that there was much more between Tomasso and me than he was willing to say.

Pato rowed the skiff round the bluff to where the *Black Phoenix* lay anchored. I knew better than to speak, and Tomasso's eyes could have drilled holes through the boat's hull.

⊕

Rodrigo had planned our route from the port of Marseilles so that we could take advantage of the approaching winter weather. When the mistral blows, the crossing due south, to the coast of Africa, is swift and effortless. In fact, the mistral is so powerful that it is usually impossible to navigate any other course. The wind took us to a deserted bay between Djidjelli and Collo where we were safely beyond the patrol of the ships of those kingdoms searching for the *Black Phoenix*. After six days, we were able to sail to the island of Tabarka, where we found a secluded cove. There we had time and resources to wait for better weather.

The ship required maintenance. Pirates rarely have the opportunity to rest in dry dock. The only safe port was Algiers, held tightly by Barbary pirates. There it was possible to find the skilled laborers and supplies to last the year at sea. There a captain could find the caulkers to fill a leaky hull, the canvas and rope to refit a battered ship. But it also meant submitting to the whims of ruthless corsairs who thought nothing of selling an entire captured crew into galley slavery. Forever hunted by the Venetian Navy, and notorious throughout the Mediterranean, Rodrigo took pains to pilot us to a secluded spot that was truly safe. This small island was home to the *Black Phoenix* and her crew through winter weather to rest, to repair, and to plan. There was cove that was deep enough to approach quite close but then disclosed a broad shallow that was a good spot to run her aground so the hull could be scraped. We set up camp on the beach, and lived in seclusion for as long as we needed.

To beach the ship, we first had to unload our supplies to the shore. The ship was anchored close, and we worked with the tides. These are small, but Tabarka is near enough to Gibraltar and the larger sea beyond it to give the tide enough lift to beach the hull. Once the hold was empty and the decks cleared, Matteo steered her toward the wide beach at a sharp angle. Empty and light, she listed all the way over as she tilted to a halt in the sand. Run aground, the entire crew hauled her farther up the beach with ropes all along the rail.

Secured there half her hull was exposed to the air. Then the process of cleaning, caulking, and repairing could begin. Most of the crew worked at this. We'd dangle down the side of the hull on ropes, rappelling as we cleaned and scraped. Once she was clean, we'd descend again, filling her seams with tar, and make her ready for another season. When one half of the hull was finished, we'd wait for the next high tide. We hauled her back into the water, and Matteo would run her into the sand at the other angle, beaching her so as to expose the other half. The job lasted weeks. Once the hull was cleaned, the rigging and the sails were thoroughly worked over. Tears in the canvas were mended, weak places in sheets rewoven and made strong.

It was a different life, in that camp at the edge of the beach. By this time I knew well what my responsibilities were to Rodrigo; I worked like any crewman on repairs to the ship. I helped in the camp kitchen, a long narrow tent with cook fires, stacks of our stores, hogsheads of wine, and the trunks of felled trees for men to sit on.

On this beach the rhythm of our life slowed to an easy pace. Work on maintaining the ship took most of our days, but the empty hours of the evenings brought other occupations. Affection and lust men freely expressed, but enmities there was no time for on the sea flared too. I saw men turn on their mates, snarling in fury over a slight that would have passed with hardly a look. I could never understand what insult lit the fuse. Once alight, fists pummeled work-hardened bodies, noses were bloodied, and feuding factions emerged. But like the fires that shine most brightly they were soon burnt out, or doused by our captain's sure and steady voice. At most of these squabbles, Rodrigo laughed. He would brook no ready danger to any of his men.

Winter's difference offered me a new vantage. I could observe from a distance and mark what could not be noted so near to my crewmates. There were pairs of lovers, certainly, but each pair seemed to decide for themselves how they wished to be a pair. Many of the men did not pair off, but shared a bond with any and all of the crew. These ties were consummated often, loudly, openly, as the men freely enjoyed each other. In our camp on Tabarka, men joined together in groups of threes, fours, in heaps of more, as if their muscles hadn't strained against the ropes and the work of repairing the ship enough, they strained against each other as if they could not pull their comrades close enough, as if they were trying to pull their mate into themselves.

I saw that Tomasso often spoke with Rodrigo, close and alone, in a way that was different from the way Rodrigo spoke with anyone else. It was as clear as spring water that Tomasso was jealous of me, but it was also clear that Rodrigo still held him close. I didn't know whether to be wary or to trust that Rodrigo's attention to him would salve his wound. On those rare occasions when Tomasso had some reason to speak to me, mostly to tell me what I was doing wrong, there was a searching look in his eyes. He looked like a man trying work out the answer to a problem.

Tomasso's nights were spent in the company of Matteo and another senior crewman, the Portuguese called Pato. One night on the beach I watched their play begin. Tomasso nuzzled Matteo's chest, lingering over each nipple as he hungrily nibbled at them with his teeth. Matteo growled his pleasure as Pato embraced Tomasso from behind, reaching around his chest to tweak each of his nipples with his calloused hands. There was something frantic about the way Tomasso threw his head back with a sharp intake of breath. I couldn't take my eyes off of the men. They were naked, the flickering of a candle in a lantern casting a yellow light over their bodies. Tomasso's still rounded muscles bursting through the softness of youth into the hardness of maturity; Pato's body heavy, dark red from the sun, ponderous with thickened muscles of years on the sea and a hard belly rounded with sack. Matteo, taller, his chest and shoulders furred with black hair that turned silver at the center of his breastbone, his forearms as thick as the haunch of smoked pork hanging in the mess. From where I crouched, awestruck, watching, their bodies entwining together as one, their massed flesh was like the still beating heart of a bull I had once seen thrown to the floor of the butcher's shop at home: distinct chambers, connected, working as one, pulsing with life.

Suddenly Matteo lifted Tomasso on his back up onto a bale of canvas waist height, and pressed his legs back. He buried his face in Tomasso's butt. Tomasso arched his head back, his eyes rolling up, as Pato cradled him against his chest, still pulling on his nipples. Tomasso made sounds that were like a frantic animal; as if he were trying to forget that he was a man. Matteo licked at the rosebud of Tomasso's bum, opening him firmly wider as he hungrily dug his mouth and chin into him. Pato leaned down from in front of Tomasso and kissed him, their tongues playing against each other through the red and black of their beards, their breaths deep, each guttural growl announcing that they would never be sated.

Matteo lifted his head and joined their kiss, three mouths hungering together, a salt and pepper beard mingling with the red and black, and he pushed his thumb deep inside Tomasso, who gasped and shook for a moment, then grabbed each of his lovers firmly by the neck and looked deeply into their faces, from Matteo to Pato, and growled. He lifted himself from Matteo's palm, turned around, onto his knees, as Matteo wetted his cock with spit. Pato knelt in front of Tomasso, who rooted in his crotch till he found his prize, licking first the head, then the arching, straining shaft, then taking all of Pato down his throat. Matteo eased his cock into Tomasso slowly, Tomasso, grunting, pushed back against him greedily, as if he couldn't wait to take both of his lovers deeper inside of him. Over the bridge of Tomasso's torso, marbled in the candle light, Pato and Matteo, mouths joined, eating each other's beards, inhaling each other's breaths, as Tomasso worked both of their cocks with his hungry body. Tomasso's juice dripped from him as he rocked and bucked against the older men's bodies, all three gleaming with sweat. Matteo held Tomasso's hips as he pushed deeper inside, Pato's hands on either side of Tomasso's cheeks, as if gently cradling him. Then suddenly both of them arched back as they shot their stuff deep into Tomasso. All three groaned long and deep.

The older men pulled away from Tomasso and gently lifted and carried him to the pallet they shared on the sand. With his arms around their shoulders he let his head loll against each of their chests as they set him down. As they knelt beside him, he pulled their heads to his and the three kissed again. Pato slid down and took Tomasso's cock in his mouth while Matteo gently traced circles around the tips of his nipples. Tomasso gasped quietly, and stretched long against Matteo's hairy body, wrapping his legs around Pato, who was sucking deeply. Pato took Tomasso deeper and deeper, massaging the shaft with the muscles of his throat until Tomasso exploded, crying out. Pato greedily lapped up the pearls of his juice that oozed out. Then, shifting slowly, they settled their bodies against each other, ready for sleep, inhaling the combination of smells their bodies made as if it was intoxicating, sending them into dreams no one could imagine.

Life at Sea

I was not sleeping. I gazed at the silhouette of my master next to me. Though now it had been many months since he had rescued me from the dull ache of my career, my chest still tightened, my breath quickened, when I let myself look at him. This night that quickening came with a thrumming dread from a source I could not divine. Shipboard life offered much that I'd sought. Here the restless discontent that the city's infinite choices nursed into a fussing clamor no longer troubled me. Here in our floating world men loving men was solely a matter of our own disposition, not subject to laws or sermons. Here pairs made up of loyal friends, lasting lovers even, formed among the crew, but these bonds were pledges, not boundaries, and rarely impediments to keep a man from enjoying the passions of a moment with any other man, if they were moved to enjoy each other. A jealous flame might leap up between a pair, but once ablaze it was easily doused, for each knew what kept all of the men here: the love among pirate-brothers.

But Rodrigo saw only me; he hadn't left me alone for a single night. He rolled over and reached for me.

"You are wakeful this night."

"Yes." My voice limped with hesitation. "I wish to ask you something."

"You know you can ask me anything, and I will seek to satisfy you."

"When first I came on board, Tomasso told me that he'd been in my place before."

"Yes…and? …There is more matter here, I think."

"I—I don't understand. He was special to you? He was your boy?"

"Of course he was. He always will be. My attachments are strong, and they are not easily severed."

"But now, it is you and me, isn't it? It has been that way. I see it and I know it. But I do not understand. What becomes of your love for Tomasso? And of Tomasso's love for you?"

"I love Tomasso as strongly as ever. If you look, really look, at what I do, you will see that. Our circumstances are different now. You are important to me and you know that. But my attachment to you is not to a possession; I do not feel that I own you, though I think you like to think so."

"I do belong to you. That is how I feel."

"You belong to no one but yourself. I do not claim you. I offer you my love. That is all. You make your own shackles."

"I do not feel that I am shackled. I feel more free than I've ever been. It is the belonging to you that gives me that freedom. I wish to belong to no one but you, and I do—I do belong to you."

"You may wish it, and it may excite you to feel that way, but one day you will have to know that you do not belong to anyone. I think that may come as a shock to you."

"I don't understand."

"No, I see that you don't. Come here, Tonio." He wrapped his arms around me. "Feel my hold. Do you feel it? Here I am. Right now. Take this in. You make me feel many things, many good things. But I have no wish to claim you for my own. I am attached to many, and I will become attached to many. But I will always be attached to you, too."

"But what becomes of those who love you as deeply as I do?"

"They are still here, some are. And some have gone on to other ports, new lives. But the love I feel for them does not go away. I love them still, whether they chose to stay near to me or to go. That is up to them, because they are free."

"But surely, Tomasso wishes he were in my place—in your bed—*still!*"

"Does he? You'd have to ask him. And he may share my bed again and share you with me. He is a wonderful lover. You would have a fine time with him."

"Even should I want that, any fool can see that Tomasso would that brings lesser dangers."

A look flickered between Matteo and Tomasso. Rodrigo only laughed.

"What bold plan does my boy hatch?"

"No plan. But if there be a port where we are not known as pirates, then it is a place ripe for dealing of another nature. Perhaps new traders who seek a shipper for western ports"

"Tired of the pirate's life so soon? This from the boy who wanted to learn to fight," Tomasso spat. "A taste of the saber and the boy quivers. Why is he here?"

Rodrigo shot him a look. "Enough, Tomasso. This I do not expect from you. What is in your mind, Tonio? Speak out."

"The questions worth asking are whether there are places and times to find new ways to do business. To move goods that we do not steal, perhaps we are paid for the moving of them. These are merely questions."

"You have not the stomach for adventure such as ours?"

"I have the stomach for knowing what is possible."

Tomasso snorted, "He is a faint-hearted cur."

"Peace, Tomasso. A faint-hearted cur would not appear on the deck in his first encounter with the Moors. No, his is a restless mind, not a cowardly one. What kind of life do you wish to see?"

"I wish only to serve you, in every way I can. Is it cowardice to ask if any port may yield opportunities unknown to us?"

"My fame, I fear, precedes me even to the east. Sailing on the *Black Phoenix* marks us all. But, Matteo, mark our course toward Alexandria. There is no harm in exploring the port. And when we draw near, you, Pato and Tomasso, see what fortune waits there."

"But I am the newest and so the least known man of your crew. Why cannot I be of the party?"

Tomasso made a fist that Matteo instantly covered with his meaty hand. Rodrigo turned to him.

"Yes. Tomasso and Tonio. You will make the excursion with Matteo. I need both of you to be my eyes and ears. Perhaps we will come to know the quays of Alexandria, and I may be with you to see what you have found." He turned to Matteo, "The strife between the

Sultan and the Spanish may be cover enough for a good season."

✦

In the evenings Matteo taught me the art of steering by the stars. That night was clear and fine and he showed me how our course was set according to the heavens. When he went aft to find Pato, Tomasso approached me.

"Learning your lessons, boy?"

I looked at him a moment before speaking. "It is a fine night. Matteo says we'll be past the Barbary waters in another day."

"I wonder what are you playing at, boy? What are we to find at this Levantine port? You seek to trade our corsair's boldness for the slinking slowness of the merchant? That is not the way to keep Rodrigo. And even your dewy newness will fade. If you do not like our life, you can leave it."

"Tomasso, I do not wish to leave it. I bear you no ill feeling. Rodrigo loves you still."

"It will be better to speak not of Rodrigo's love if you seek to soften the air between us. I'll count you as a brother when you cease your pushing."

"I offer my hand in peace, Tomasso. Though you doubt it, I believe I can offer things you know not of, which can better us all."

He laughed. "I know that well enough, just as you pushed a better bargain in Marseilles." He smiled as he faced me. "Yes, you are quite a master in your way. You got the better of me then." He shrugged and cuffed me on the shoulder. "Pardon, brother. My heat is like that of the older brother who likes it not when the younger shines more brightly than he can. A failing of mine. Come, embrace me, then?"

This turn was welcome, but seemed as sudden as the lightening, and as trustworthy. He caught me in his arms and found my lips. I felt the soft curls of his red beard and the warmth of his breath.

"Ah, Tomasso, I—"

"Come, beauty, we'll be comrades." He reached round and grabbed my haunch.

It is true that his grip set a stirring in my groin. "You are a fine

"Go, Tonio. Tomasso, come here." He grabbed Tomasso's neck and drew his mouth toward him. They kissed a moment. "You two should be more together. That would please me a good deal. Show Tonio the way the stars will move as the summer wanes. He likes learning about the stars, don't you?" He drew me close to the two of them and our three mouths came together in a lapping kiss. "Go on."

Tomasso led the way, and I looked back to Rodrigo on my way out.

"I'll be asleep when you come back, I'm finished for this night. So, come and don't wake me when you crawl in."

I turned and followed Tomasso up the steps. He'd already poured a mug of sack for us both and was leaning against the rail, looking out at the night sky. "Here, you'll like this," offering it to me.

"Thanks." I drank half of it off.

"Look you, we speak little, I know, and when I do I chide you roughly. But we have worked as brothers since our time in the Levantine seas, have we not?" If he meant that we did not quarrel openly, I could not but agree. "I cannot hold a grudge. It doesn't make sense anymore—it is so long ago. We're brothers on this ship, and we should make the best of a good life together. What do you say?"

"I say that this good life is to be made the most of. And that if we can be better friends, I am glad of it."

"You love Rodrigo deeply, don't you?"

"Yes. I do. You do, too."

"Everyone loves Rodrigo. He loves everyone. He loves having the many who love him circling around him. And we are content to circle, aren't we?" He pulled me close and held my face between his hands for a moment. Then he kissed me, urgently, pushing his tongue insistently into my mouth. I pulled away.

"I—I'm confused. What do you want of me?" I asked.

"I want us to know each other better. I want to know your fine young body finally, after all these months."

"But you're with Matteo and Pato, and I'm with Rodrigo. That contents me now."

"Drink up, my brother. I know very well how you are feeling. I've

61

felt that way myself. But you can enjoy my kisses, too, you know."

"I'm sure I could enjoy them if I wanted to."

"Your famous candor again. Well."

As Tomasso spoke a dizziness came over me. For a moment I thought I was ill. I stumbled back against the rail.

"Whoops, there, steady, Tonio. A long day you've had. Here, drink some more. Fortify yourself for the night ahead." He held the mug against my mouth and tipped my head back. I drank more, hardly knowing what I was doing. Drowsiness crept up behind my eyes, and the night sky swirled and blurred. I inhaled, trying to rouse myself, but couldn't fight the oblivion that overtook me.

It was then that Tomasso must have bound me, wrapped me in an old sail, and dispatched me in the little skiff. My wrists were not bound so tightly that I could not work the knots gradually. He'd meant for me to know something important. He'd meant for me to be terrified, and to know that Rodrigo was his. The knots loosened, I reached down in my sack to find the ropes around my ankles, slipped them away and rested again. Time was the one thing I didn't need to fight against. I had plenty of time; just not enough air if I exerted myself too hard. Gently, slowly, in the dark I felt round for a seam, an edge of canvas. As I slipped my hand through a fold, the canvas fell away. It hadn't even been bound. I was wrapped close, but without fetters. I inhaled the cool sea air and rested, relieved to see the stars again. I sat up, heard waves breaking on the shore, so I knew the skiff was nosing close to land, but I couldn't make anything out in the dim silver light. I sat up in the skiff and discovered a packet at my feet, I reached in and found it held food and a skin of water. I was to live. But I was to be abandoned, where I knew not.

I tried to think. The course Rodrigo had set was taking us back toward the west, but after a stealthy slide down the eastern coast of Italy. That was the closest land we'd pass. A steep, rocky shoreline. Perhaps I could find my way back to Genoa. But what could I possibly do there? Battista would hardly welcome me back. Surely Rodrigo would stop as soon as he found me missing. Surely he'd turn back, maybe put in at Ancona to look for me, or Bari, but where was I? Or perhaps I could make my way to the ports where I knew he'd be later in the autumn. It would be months before the *Black Phoenix* made its way back to Marseilles. It was a risky route through the Adriatic, slipping past the Venetian enforcers. It was out of the question that I follow, the *Black Phoenix* was to stay in open waters. It would probably take me as long to make my way back to his regular ports, Genoa or Marseilles, as it would take him to get there. But I couldn't make a plan before knowing where I was. The only thing I felt certain of was that I had to be with Rodrigo again. He was my only lodestar, and his ship was sailing southward, to the narrows at Otranto. For all I knew far beyond me now.

My immediate problem was reaching dry land without being smashed to bits on the rocky shore. But the sea was gentle this night and I was not to be smashed to bits, perhaps only scraped raw and bloody. The skiff bobbed closer and closer. I had no oar, little rope, and there was not enough light to see an opening in the crags. I gathered the canvas wrapping and, as a swell drew me alongside a rocky shelf, I tossed it over and held the skiff there long enough to straddle the gunwale and steady myself. I gathered the pouch, and drew my other leg onto the rock. I tugged the skiff along and wedged it into a crook in the rocks, and pulled it up as far as I could. I didn't imagine I could use the skiff to get myself anywhere, but it seemed foolish not to make every attempt to preserve all my resources.

The moon was a crescent, hanging low in the sky. I could see no light on any horizon, and I was so disoriented I had no idea what time of night it was. I picked my way gingerly across the rocks away from the water. I'd rest on the canvas till light. Morning would bring a sign, anything, that would lead me to that which had to be next.

I lay in the dark thinking about Rodrigo. How long could it be before he missed me? Not until morning? We had shared a bed each night since he rescued me. Could he imagine that I shared Tomasso's bed that night? Could Rodrigo believe that of me? I couldn't help but see Tomasso in Rodrigo's bed, and my heart raced. This must be jealousy. This terrible icy thrill that made my heart thump and turn cold. This was the earwig of doubt, gnawing away at what I'd known was certain. I crumbled so easily I was ashamed. It was I who wanted to own Rodrigo. I'd dressed it up and turned it around, but it was I who made the claim. What I'd thought was a lover's gaze I cast on him was an owner's vigilance. I wanted to be held close so I could do the holding.

Here was panic indeed. I was alone, and accompanying me was someone I did not want to recognize but was unmistakably me. Sleep did not come easily that night.

Settling in some soft weeds, I drew the canvas around me. My heart raced. I put my hand on my chest. I tried to bring Rodrigo's face to mind. As well as I knew that face, as many times as I'd studied it, searched every line, every plane, I could not summon it. Each portion I could recall dissolved. Terror undid each particle of progress my memory could claim. I pulled the canvas over my head and prayed for oblivion.

The Comedians

A sound like no other I'd ever heard, piercing, harsh, insistent, split open the morning quiet.

"All I am saying, begging, really, is that you do not kill the laugh that you know is there, and that I've set up so beautifully." A young woman's voice, shrill, screeching like a crazed parrot.

"Just what is it you'd have me do?" The voice of an older man, loud, exasperated. The veins must have been standing out on his neck. It was past dawn. I had been sleeping near the rutted path their horse-drawn cart was slowly bouncing over. Banners dangled listlessly at the top of their canopy in the morning stillness. I could just make out from under my covering that the cart was loaded with trunks, some biggish rolls of painted canvas, and a few pieces of furniture. They were dressed with the tattered exaggeration of traveling players.

"Do exactly NOTHING." Her voice could strip rust from an iron bar. "Stand still. The crowd will laugh. Then we go on to the next bit, where you look under the bed and the Doctor pushes you over.

"I won't have you speak to me in that manner." He pouted with the plummy sound of the truly deluded.

"'In that manner'—how grand you become when you know just how foolish you are. You know as well as I do that crowds do not come to look at you. Without me, you'd be lost."

"You, the pathetic, filthy little whore I found, who I trained, who I turned into a decent player, you can turn on me like this." He nearly choked he so enjoyed his pathos. "And for what? What terrible thing have I done to you?"

"For a start, you had us cross these godforsaken lands to try our fortune, no, no, how did you put it? To bring our art to this withered and friendless coast. God's balls, you picked me up because you loved the way I sucked your cock. I know it, you know it, we all know it." And now I knew it, too. "That I am a girl men love to look at was another benefit to you. Lord, how you enjoy working yourself into a state." She adjusted her billowing breasts as she spoke, always aware the old man couldn't seem to take his eyes off of them. "I was merely asking you not to ruin the laugh that we both know I ought to get when old Pantaloon finds me safely locked in the house where he left me. We both know that the lazzi I've embroidered with such care get a laugh, except when a vain old fart can't stand it that the crowds are bored to death by him."

"Lazzi you've embroidered with such care. The pretension. As if you knew how to develop a lazzo. That posing and flouncing you insist on including looks like the flailing of an idiot child." He snorted. "You say the audiences would be bored to death without you. If they are so bored by me, why do you think audiences hearing that I am coming crowd around our stage? How is it that you've managed to survive these months since I took you on?"

"Oh, so it is you they come to look at. Of course. A fading comedian with a spreading big fat ass is who they come to look at. Not the girl whose tits are about to fall out of her costume, whose tits you can't take your eyes off of, by the way. Of course."

"How you can speak of yourself in this manner. We are comedians, it is true, we travel from village to hamlet to city. We perform the comedies of our invention to crowds whose dreary lives and mournful spirits are lifted by our talents. We are a reviled lot, but necessary. And we must still respect ourselves."

"Again with 'in this manner.' Have you noticed what we've been eating lately? Or rather, not eating? Have you noticed where we sleep? Do you notice anything, you swollen gasbag?"

"Please, please stop, the two of you. You're actually making me sick." A third voice, a man's. "No, I'm not joking, Catarina, the birdlike musicality of your fluting voice is going to make me vomit." A head poked out from under the canopy, face patchy, eyes bleary. "Catarina, maneater of Tuscany, your delicate charms set the loins of every man on fire. You are their only desire. It is true. We all know it. Luigi, you are the greatest comedian, peerless from Trieste to Reggio. And all the world knows it. Unless either of you can open your mouth to tell me that we have something to eat, I beg of you to keep those gaping maws closed." Luigi pulled up on the reins, and the cart stopped a few yards from where I was lying. I wasn't sure whether this was the crew who could rescue me, or if I needed rescuing now more than ever.

The old man struggled down off the cart's bench to relieve himself against a tree.

Catarina turned on the younger, "Giovanni, dear heart, are you still living? You, my wily lover, you look as if you've just been forced to eat a mattress and wash it down with horse piss."

"My darling, your wit is limitless. How did I survive before you came into our lives?" He rolled off of the cart onto his knees, retching. "You see, I was right. You've finally accomplished it. The sound of your voice and the sight of your lovely personage have actually made me vomit. Now I've truly lived, and can die a happy man."

"Yes, why don't you take yourself off and die?"

"Catarina, delicate flower, I couldn't really die in peace knowing that you needed protection from this fearsome and dangerous world."

"Giovanni, Catarina, my young colleagues, we simply must press on if we are to reach Bari for the beginning of the market. The crowds may be generous there. Bari has been good to me before, I've had a following."

"Luigi, dear old, old man, your dreams of a following are touching. Deluded, and touching."

"Uncle, let me take the reins, you rest in the cart. How much farther to Bari, do you think? You are sure the others will meet us there?"

"Giovanni, you are very thoughtful. Yes, I am certain that our comrades will be there, as they've promised. Have they ever failed us in that way?"

"They've failed in so many ways that one loses count. But no, they haven't abandoned us yet. How much farther?"

"A full day at least, probably a full day and a morning. We'll be set up in Bari for the end of marketday tomorrow. Is there anything to eat in this cart?" He struggled to hoist himself into the back.

"Perhaps a rind of cheese, but I can't swear to it. Catarina, are you ready to join us, or has Holy Mary interceded and inspired you to make other plans for the duration of your entire life?"

Catarina had wandered off to squat and piss in the bracken near me. I lifted my head as she rearranged her skirts, and when she saw me her eyes widened as if they could eat me.

"Now you, young man, are the kind of man an audience would come to see. What are you doing in those weeds? You like watching young girls piss?" She cleverly tossed her skirts to offer me a view of her crotch. This close I could see that the term "young" was a euphemism.

"I—I apologize, I hardly meant to disturb you." I scrambled to me feet. "My story is, well, a bit complicated, but it is simplest to say that owing to treachery I washed up on shore in the middle of the night, and made my way this far inland before I fell asleep. Your approach awakened me. My name is Antonio."

She accosted me with a sly smile and tried to tickle my chest with a long piece of grass she'd picked. Apparently she thought she was irresistible.

I continued, if only in an attempt to defer her heated pursuit.

"I couldn't help but hear that you make your way to Bari. I must find my way there, too." I stooped to gather up my bundle, and avoid the hands that were already appraising my chest. "I have some small supply here, with me, dry crackers and water, which I'd gladly share. Can you guide me?" As soon as I said it, I knew I'd chosen the wrong word.

"Young man, I can guide you to delights you've never known."

"I'm absolutely certain that I've never known what you have in mind. And I can say with confidence that I never wish to know them."

She emitted a sound that might have been a giggle. "Luigi," she shrieked, "I've found our new romantic lead. Look at this face, just look at him. He'll drive the young girls wild. Giovanni, you can rest your sorry behind, and work up the old Servant's lazzi. We've got my new love interest."

Though my throat was as dry as ash and my head thick as a sopping mop I knew I had to interrupt this notion. Her look was steady and eager. I held my hand up as if to slow a child running headlong into danger.

"Pardon me, miss, but I'm not a comedian. I'm far from accomplished in your skills, and would never make a success at it. I'd be a liability to your troupe."

"Antonio, you overestimate the requirements for a comedian's success. A man who looks like you need trouble himself no further. The eloquence the part of the lover needs will come. A few rehearsals, a few performances, and you'll be fine. I'll coach you in our craft."

I hesitated and she pressed on.

"Come, sit with me and tell me everything. There is no need to be on the road alone. Besides, these are terrible times. When we were in Brindisi we heard that Charles has taken the Pope at his word and means to make good France's claim to Naples. He is sure to invade. A single traveler may be in grave danger."

The old man took up the suit. "Young man, your polite manner is most refreshing. I would be honored to have you join us on our way to Bari, and beyond, if you'd care to join us. Our numbers are reduced, it is true, and we are in need of more comedians to perform our art more effectively. Catarina is perhaps correct in thinking that you could become a valued part of our traveling band, and we may indeed offer you a measure of safety." He bowed floridly, as if we were in court.

"Sir, I am indebted to you, but I must find my way back to my ship. The best, the only place I can think to start, is Bari."

"Very well, no need to decide today. Catarina, you and this young man sit up front, Giovanni and I ride in the cart." Did he actually think her methods of persuasion would work?

Giovanni leaned over and whispered, "Catarina, heart of my hearts, see if you can manage not to devour him before lunch."

She ignored this, wrapped her arm around mine and led me to the cart. In spite of myself I welcomed her keen attention. I was in no position to push away any hand outstretched in sympathy, and there was life in her eyes, there was no gainsaying that. I handed the bundle of canvas and the skin of water to the old man, and climbed up to the bench. Catarina stood and simpered, waiting expectantly for my hand to help her up. A ravening harpy one minute, a demure little princess the next, as soon as she was seated next to me, her hand found its way to my codpiece. I firmly put it aside, and snapped the reins.

Fallen among mad comedians, I was on my way to Bari.

⊕

"So, Antonio, how is it you were sleeping in the weeds along this dusty, godforsaken road? You really are such a good-looking boy. It is hard to imagine how you'd come to be in such a place, and with nothing." The wagon rocked and lurched as we made our labored way down the road. I held the reins in one hand, and steadied myself on the bench with the other.

"If I knew the answer to your question, I'd be a happier man. All I can say is that I was aboard my ship last night when I went to sleep. A sleep heavy with drink, it is true, but no more wine than what I've had many times. I fell into a ponderous sleep, and the next thing I knew, I was wrapped in canvas, in a skiff that was washed against this rocky coast."

"Apparently someone wanted to get rid of you, which is hard to imagine."

Speaking quietly to me, she became agreeable, even sympathetic. Her interest warmed me at a time I needed warming. Her hands stayed wrapped around the bench, and her smile was gentle. Gratitude lightened the desolate heaviness in my breast. I turned to her and saw friendship in her eyes.

"I think you are right. And I think I know who did not want me." I felt a blush spread across my brow so I looked straight down the road, into the sun that already felt hot on my face.

"You poor boy. This is about love, isn't it? A jealous lover put you ashore. What sort of ship do you serve on? Or were you a traveler?" She looked at my clothes. "No, you are a sailor, aren't you? Or are you a pirate?" She giggled again, this time with a sound that was more nearly like a girl.

"I serve the captain of a merchant ship."

"Then why were you so mysteriously put ashore? There is something odd about this, you know. I think you were on a pirate ship, and I think you were punished for something. I think you've been a very naughty boy." She pinched my cheek hard, then leaned in and kissed me. I pulled back.

"Miss, I—please, I...." Suddenly tears sprang to my eyes, surprising me, and I turned away. I couldn't tell if Catarina noticed.

"What, you don't like the taste of my kisses? Well, it is first thing in the morning, and we've run out of cloves days ago. The last time we saw Bartholo and his little Adela, I think. And I think they made off with my supply, the fiends. They are the second leads, our Brighela and Columbina, and not very good, I can tell you. Really more trouble than they are worth. They tell us we'll see them in Bari, and I'm not going to hold my breath. But we hardly have a troupe as it is, and we can't perform properly without them. I haven't the slightest idea what Luigi thinks we're going to do when we get to Bari. So you see, we're all in very sorry states." She looked over at me, without the smarmy leer of the voracious maneater. "Oh, Antonio, you are very sad. A very sad boy. You can talk to me, you know. Who is this lover you have lost? I'll stop. I know I am ridiculous, but I also know that many men like me to be ridiculous. You've been very nice to me. I think you are a very likable boy. So, if you wish, you can tell me all about it. Or not."

We rocked down the road for a few moments. Finally I could stay silent no longer.

"I have lost the most important person. I must find my way back. My hope is that the ship has put into the port at Bari and they are looking for me."

"You still leave out the details that really interest me. You are very cagey. Who is this most important person? I think I understand. This most important person is your captain, isn't he?" Her smile was gentle, not the smirk I'd thought she'd taunt me with. "Beautiful one, a man has broken your heart. This is why we get on so well. We've both had our hearts broken by a man. Filthy beasts. I feel it. I know it. Tell me that I'm right."

"A man has betrayed me, that is true. A man, a young man, put me off the ship because he hated me. Not enough to kill me, I think he wouldn't dare to kill me. But I didn't understand that he hated me so much."

"And this young man was jealous of you, wasn't he?"

"Yes. I knew he was terribly jealous. But our captain couldn't— wouldn't see it."

I sat hunched over in misery. My chest felt hollowed out and I realized I'd stopped breathing. I straightened up and filled my lungs with air but with each breath stinging sadness clenched my heart.

"And you both love your captain, don't you. He must be a rare man, to be loved by such a boy as you."

"Yes. He is. And I do." I looked away. I was so hungry all of a sudden. My stomach felt as if it was eating itself. I felt her hand on the back of my head, gently combing through my hair.

"He is a lucky captain, I think. You feel things deeply, don't you, Antonio? Do you know that not everyone does? Some people are no more than stones. They try to make themselves into stones. Noisy stones. It is harder to be one who feels. We'll see if your ship is at Bari. And if it isn't, you'll stay with us. I think you'd do very well. You can start with the lover, since he wears no mask. Later you will learn how the masks work. What you lend to the mask, and what the mask grants you in return. You might even like it, you know. Audiences laughing, clapping for you. It is freedom, not an easy freedom, but freedom. I work for no man. I invent my own jokes, my own words. And I have all the men I want." She glanced at me and laughed her raucous laugh again, but it didn't hurt my ears. "You would be very popular. With the men as well as the girls. You think about it."

I said nothing, squinted into the sun that was higher in the sky, and prayed that Rodrigo would put anchor near Bari and come to find me.

The Comedians' Life

Rodrigo was not in Bari. No one from the *Black Phoenix* was anywhere to be seen in the harbor or the market. It would have surprised me if they were. Bari was far too close to Venice to risk putting in to shore. Knowing that didn't keep me from hoping that I'd see him.

That first day, after I had searched for any sign of Rodrigo or another familiar face, I had no reason not to watch the players' performance. It was perhaps the last thing I wanted to do, but even the slight familiarity of the three people I'd traveled with for the last day and a half drew me back.

When we rolled into the market square, Bartholo and Adela were there, waiting for us. Luigi drove his wagon to one edge of the square where he, Giovanni, and Bartholo set to work preparing their stage.

"Greetings, comrades," Bartholo crooned. "There is tremendous news. Have you heard? Charles's forces have taken Naples without a siege. Without so much as a shot, some say. It seems all people of the Naples are now subjects of France."

Luigi squinted, as if reading a message written too small to make out. "My friends, our art is needed now more than ever. At a time of war we must rise to heroism as we assure these simple people that their lives can retain a degree of civilization."

Catarina snorted. "Did you not hear, Naples has been taken without a shot. Alfonso apparently decided to learn the lessons of those cities that put up a fight when the French marched on them, and paid dearly." She looked at me and added, "Another reason to stay with us. A man traveling alone in times like these takes a graver risk than a tattered band of foolish players making their way across the frontier."

I looked to the brown packed earth of the square and was silent. She was right, of course, the safer way was with them. My heart ached in protest. I did not belong there. I was supposed to be with Rodrigo, not jouncing along rutted roads with squalling players. I was supposed to be at sea with my adventuring brothers, not dodging the dangers kicked up by constant wars. But there was no other course than to grasp the hand Fate offered.

Bartholo was blithely uninterested. "You'll be delighted to learn how quickly I've been able to discover a salacious bit of news fit for our use. Apparently some secretary to the governor here is putting pressure on the sister of a condemned prisoner to render up to him her most precious possession, the jewel of her virginity, to gain a pardon for her brother." Luigi's countenance lifted. "But wait, it gets even more delicious. This lovely young girl is a novitiate at the convent at the top of the hill. Since this young secretary is posing as a pious do-gooder himself, he's made some trouble for himself."

"You don't mean that there is hypocrisy in high places, here in Bari! I was hoping we'd found a place that finally would be safe for our vulnerable Catarina," Giovanni whined as he lowered the canopy. He turned to hang several painted canvas rolls from a bar that ran across the framing.

"Excellent nose, Bartholo. Work it into your first scene, and we'll have the crowd with us," Luigi chuckled.

Catarina opened a large battered trunk and lifted out their masks and a basket of properties. "Giovanni, dear heart, your concern touches me." She handed him one of the masks. Its brow and nose were grotesquely exaggerated; in an instant it announced a character. "Now, in our scene together, do you think you'll be able to remember that it is the third time you lunge for me that you end up on your ass? Or is your ass still too tender to play the comedy so that it actually entertains the crowd?"

Luigi was changing into the clothes of the old Pantaloon, and moaned through the tunic he was lowering over his head, "Please, please, can we have an end to your bickering?" He took the mask Catarina held out to him.

She and Adela turned away toward the curious townspeople

who'd begun to gather around the stage, and began to sing. Adela strummed a mandolin as if it were a washboard, and drew a gawking crowd. Catarina pulled her blouse down low across her breasts, so that they were nearly falling free. I heard some of the women in the crowd curse her for a harlot. This struck Catarina as hilarious. For them she and Adela sang with special delight a little catch about putting candles out with her farts.

"My lady and her maid, upon a merry pin,
they made a match at farting, who would the wager win?
They took three candles then, and set them bolt upright,
With the first fart she blew them out, with the next she gave
them light."

Their voices were not disagreeable, and they played the crowd skillfully. I was no less susceptible to their talents. I had never found the comedians my father favored at all amusing. They were cynics with a knowingness that blighted my enjoyment. But these players had a different power over their audience. Their joy was catching. Catarina especially seemed to cast a spell over the men. This effect was instant and, I came to learn, as consistent as the sunrise. And it was true that at a distance, she had an allure. With great art, she always set herself off to her best advantage.

As the crowd grew, Luigi stepped in front of the curtain to announce their performance and this prompted the women's quick exit behind the curtain. For a moment there was an uneasy grumbling from the crowd, as if they were unsure whether they had been duped. Then Bartholo stuck his head out between the curtains and began.

"Woe to the father of a willful daughter. Woe to the poor servant who works for the father of a willful daughter. And woe to the duke's secretary who can't keep it in his pants even when it is the veil of a novitiate that covers what he's after."

The crowd chuckled at this, and then he pulled the curtains open, revealing Catarina and Luigi, the young girl and her father, in the midst of a heated argument.

They all became different creatures when they performed, but

Catarina and Giovanni were truly transformed. As if lit from the inside, somehow. Their wits were faster than any I'd ever encountered. They could fashion new jokes, find a new way to fall down, find a reason to show her breasts, in an instant. Though they never seemed to stop bickering, once they set foot on stage, the heat of their pleasure in each other glowed. The plot was crude, something about a marriage that the old man wanted to arrange, but that his daughter refused. This seemed negligible. First I thought that the point of the play was to show off their wit and their tricks, but then I realized how naïve that was. The comedy was only a pretext. The real point was to take pleasure in each other.

At the end of the play, with another song, Catarina and Adela passed through the crowd with baskets imploring some reward for their pains. They didn't take in very much.

"So, what did you think of our little show?" Catarina ambled over to the spot at the side where I'd been watching the crowd and the comedians. She seemed so genuinely interested in what I thought that I was quite disarmed. She had gathered her hair up and held it in her hands, displaying her profile like a tatterdemalion queen. There was something so direct, even innocent, about her open expectation that it would bring me pleasure to look at her as she posed for me that I could not help myself. She earned my admiration, too.

"I'm not sure. You know how to make the crowd react just as you wish them to, don't you?"

"Clever boy. You see what is important in a situation, don't you? Audiences are generally very simple. They really want to like you, and you must find a way to tell them that they are having a wonderful time. It is usually easier if you are having a wonderful time. And I do, except when Giovanni is being a pig. Today he was not a pig. Today he was in top form. That always makes me ravenous. Come, eat with me."

Though she had my admiration, I hoped she would demand no more of me. She knew my affections lay another way, but even so, I hoped we each would not mistake the other. Her strength was unmistakable, and I did not imagine that she brooked disagreement with ease. But I was in a yielding state. How good it would be to have a friend. Perhaps a friendship would please her, too. She took my arm and we walked through the square toward a food seller's stall. She rattled the coins in her hand and shook her hair free.

"Now, since you've come back to our stage, I think you did not find your captain, or anyone from your ship."

I looked away. The orange afternoon sun cut a sharp angle across the stone arcade.

"Well then, I think you ought to take the part of my lover. In the comedies."

"But I haven't the skill. I wouldn't know the first thing about what to do."

"I will teach you. You are a very sensitive boy and you will pick it up fast. Also, the young lover is so insipid, a candlestick would do. You are much nicer to look at than a candlestick. That makes all the difference."

"I don't know. I...."

"Antonio. You did not find your captain, did you?"

I could not reply for what felt like the kick of a horse to my chest.

"I didn't think so. What else are you to do? Oh, you could get on another ship, and hope that at some port or other you find him again. Or, you could travel with us for a while. We will travel across through Salerno, then up to Rome and farther to the north as the weather grows warmer. You will stand as good a chance of having something to eat on a regular basis with us as on your own. Perhaps even better. You might even enjoy doing something different for a while. What a surprise that would be, to enjoy yourself." She stopped, turned to me and put her hand gently on my shoulder. "Your sadness is very clear to me, you know. I think you should stay with us and remember what it is to laugh."

Like a sister she turned and tickled me in the ribs and I could not but laugh, though my mind raced to reason out the choices. If they were to travel north, perhaps eventually I could make my way to Genoa when Rodrigo would be there again. That seemed to make more sense to me than chasing after him on another boat. But thinking couldn't help me. I was lost and loneliness made it impossible to think. I nodded to Catarina.

"Teach me. I'll learn how to be a comedian."

"Wise boy. I have a feeling you're going to be very good. And we'll find all the most attractive men in every town we visit, and we'll share them. Yes? All right. Now, are you hungry, too?"

⊕

It did not take me long to find my way into this new role. The first time I was oafish, stiff, and nervous. The troupe was to stay in Bari a few days, so the next morning Catarina rehearsed me for the afternoon performance. I certainly did not wish to be an actor. Being a rash youth I thought that leaving my father's house meant the end of dissembling, and here I was being trained in art of cultivating a falsehood. Catarina was a patient tutor. She explained what I was to do, and demonstrated the attitudes I was to adopt. It was so artificial and false. I felt a fool, posing in such a manner.

"No one would believe that I am this lover."

"That is far from the point. No one believes, but no one doubts either. Make your entrance again, and this time when you behold me, trace a wide arc with your hand as you bring it to your heart. Think of the shape you make in the air. It is not ordinary life we present. It is far more than that."

I stretched my arm out and the gesture seemed to find me, to make me into something other than what I was.

"Yes. Better. Much better. You see how the artifice takes you over, carries you. Now, when we are on the stage together, never settle for the ordinary. Heighten the urgency of the lover's plight and see where that takes you. I think you can do that. Remember that it is always terribly urgent for the lover. You will be fine."

Neither my lack of experience or inventiveness seemed to matter to our audience in that first performance. Catarina was right. As soon as I set foot on the stage, the young girls sighed for me.

She'd told me that I was to make my entrance after she said "Oh, my beloved Silvio, how I've missed you!" Catarina actually reached behind the curtain where I was waiting and pulled me out.

I did remember what she told me to say. "My love, how can we marry when your father means to marry you to Captain Metamoros?"

"Beloved Silvio, I have a plan. Scapino will help us, but you must agree to risk all and come away with me, you must come away with me."

"Do you doubt my ardor, beautiful flower?"

("Very good" she said, under her breath, facing away from the audience. "Now kiss me.")

I leaned in to kiss her, but she slithered out of my grasp and yanked on my arm. I lost my balance and fell over a stool. This was not in our rehearsal. I was dazed, and sprawled out on the deck. The crowd found this hilarious. I'll never understand why. But this was the first general rule of audiences I learned. The crueler the joke, the louder their raucous laughter. Pleasing them seemed absurdly easy. Catarina was enjoying herself, too, finding laughs because I couldn't. Through that whole performance she pushed and pulled on me, whispering to me how to stand, when to take her hand and sigh, when to embrace her and try to kiss her. I was black and blue when we finished. Was it the bruises that made me wince so, or was it being made to feel such a fool? The crowd's raucous glee made it hard to tell.

"Antonio, you did very well today. Now, tomorrow morning, we'll work out one or two new moves. All right, my love?"

"But what of the words we say to one another on the stage?"

"Your powers of invention will grow, I assure you. Soon your mother wit will provide well enough."

"Why not write the best of them down? Work the rhetoric and the logic; polish the argument to a fine luster. Then the play can be passed to others and its pleasures known more general."

"General pleasures known by the writing of words?" She sounded like she was playing before the crowd again, which made me still the fool. "I find my pleasures in the instant. Besides, you seem to think all comedians can read what might be written. That is folly enough. But far worse is to think that our inventions can be cast, like little bronze toys for others to play with! What kind of play would that make? What fun is there in that? What skill in a repetition of what is written?"

"The skill is in making it new each time."

"But it is new each time the way we play it now. So we need not concern ourselves."

"And the words—the words—what of the words?"

"Words, words, words. What matter is there? You mystify me. No, no, my duck, our comedian tradition is strong enough to serve us."

"I'm not sure I'll survive this. You didn't tell me this was to be quite so, well, so violent."

"My boy, how can I make you understand?" Her fingers played through her thick dark hair as she gave me an appraising smile. "You inspired me, and you, you really were very funny. Do you know that? You fall in a very funny way."

"That is something I've never had occasion to know. Must I fall in that funny way so often in every performance?"

"Find a way not to, and you won't." She grinned up at me. It was a challenge.

Playing a comedy with Catarina was a game, a very competitive game. And the game was different every time. It didn't take too long before I grew more confident. It wasn't as if there was much to learn, really. The names of the plays we performed varied, but the plots were all the same. It was the playing of the game that changed. This was her freedom. She dared the other comedians to play as roughly, as freely, as she did. She dared me to come alive with her in her game. And when I was able to forget myself, I began to be able to keep up with her.

⊕

After Bari, we made our way west through the Principality of Salerno. At each town, after our performance, I'd linger in the darkening square, looking for the place where men gathered for each other. After my time on Rodrigo's ship it was odd to retreat to the shadows in this way, but the shadows hold a certain pleasure, too. And I got to be rather good at noticing how each town's system worked. It was another game. I had learned how to play the game in Florence, in Genoa. Each town had a particular system that gave the game a particular flavor.

Usually, if the town were big enough, there would be a building project near the center, an improvement that the city fathers decided the town required. Such a project invariably included sheds and scaffolding that offered shadows and shelter. Late, long after dusk, the familiar ritual unfolded. I'd look for the man whose hold was strong enough, whose gaze was deep enough to make me feel his presence. But each man I found, each cock I sucked, failed to quiet my mind.

There were many. There were nights when I felt frantic with loneliness. When, after Catarina and I had taken a meal at a tavern, and she'd found a man for the night, I could do nothing but walk. I walked the narrow, stony streets of villages where no one stirred. I walked the cobbled squares of larger towns, where men who looked for boys found them. I found the men who were interested in a youth my age, and I tried to enjoy them. Surely my fervor impressed them. I was greedy and I was skilled. My greediness made me skilled. I wanted more cock, all the cock I could find. I wanted to feel every man in my mouth. I wanted to hold their need and their vulnerability in my mouth and please them. I wanted to take all of them in. I couldn't drink enough cum.

But I could see only one man's face. No, that's not right at all. I saw nothing but the absence of only one man's face. Kneeling before every man, it was his presence I missed. I could not summon his image. I traced the outlines of a memory, the one man I thought I knew better than anyone else, but he remained just beyond recovery. As on that first day under the colonnade at Genoa, I could make out only his shadow.

⊕

The rutted, rocky road west toward Naples made riding in the wagon nearly impossible. I walked alongside. Catarina walked with me, Luigi drove, and Giovanni slept, somehow, under the canopy of the cart. We made our way slowly. The sun seemed to grow hotter each laborious day. My thoughts filled only with images of the ports to the north and a ship anchored far enough from the harbor not to be noted.

"Sweet boy, you always look so distracted. So far away. How is it that yearning for one man can make you so miserable?"

"He's a man I cannot forget, but at the same time, I cannot bring him enough to mind. It is as if I can feel him, but can't find him. It is this constantly being reminded of the absence of him that hurts so much."

"You hurt yourself in this. You are here, on this fine hot day. With me, someone who despite herself has come to care about you. And yet you cannot enjoy this because you will not let yourself stop losing your captain. It is as if you keep losing him every second."

I shuddered and stopped walking. "Catarina, you are uncanny. That is exactly what it is like. How can you know that?"

"I have only to look at you. Your constant churning. No one could torture you as perfectly as you do yourself, you know. Come along, keep up."

"Have you never lost someone you could not bear to lose?"

"Of course I have. But I don't let my life come to a stop because of it. I had a husband once, who treated me uncommonly well. He was a rare man."

"A husband? I would not have guessed that. And who was the man?"

"Sweet boy, are you certain that you wish to hear my story of heartache? Yours is so endlessly luxurious."

"You are unfair, and if I didn't know you I'd swear you are unkind. Yes, of course I do."

"Is it unkind to be accurate? No need, love, to turn on me." She chuckled her low, welcoming chuckle. "So, I'll tell you my story. I was the elder of two daughters. My little sister was a great beauty, or so she was told, and so she enthusiastically believed. What young girl can resist that flattery? But she was a willful, sniveling little creature. She decided that she'd fallen desperately in love with an insipid youth, and begged our father and mother to let her marry him. The problem was that they had long ago decided to get rid of me first. Apparently it was some dishonor for their younger daughter to wed before their firstborn. For my part, I felt no dishonor. I wasn't interested in marrying simply for the sake of marrying. I didn't like what I saw of my mother's life. I didn't much like what I'd seen of life in our town. By this time I had developed a reputation for being, well, difficult. You'd never describe me that way, would you, sweet boy? People couldn't seem to stand it that I'd tell them just what I thought. I couldn't simper and smile the way my sister did. She was really the actress. She played my father like a lute. But he was adamant that a husband must be found for me before she could marry. All this was long ago, when my father had money. So the word went out that if a man could win me, I'd come with a considerable dowry. This was the truly humiliating part."

"To be auctioned off like that."

"It wasn't as if I was repulsive, you know."

"Only difficult."

"Oh, my boy, men are so often disappointments. Delicious, necessary, required, even, but so often disappointing. But then Ferruchio came to our town. He was assuredly not a disappointment. He was a remarkable man. Not handsome, at least not in the ways that thrill young girls. You would have admired him a great deal, judging from the men I've seen you with. How can I put into words what made him so different? Yes, it was that he liked to play. He liked to play a bit rough. Not in bed, as a rule. He wanted a woman who could meet him. I could. We played very well together. Like those days when you or Giovanni can really play with me, you know? We enjoyed each other so much. And I lost him. The bastard. He got himself killed, in a stupid brawl between the followers of two families who hated each other. A feud whose cause no one could remember. He hardly knew them. He happened to have been drinking with one of these vicious youths when it broke out. The crazy children with their daggers took him in a blazing noon in the middle of the town square. He left me with nothing. I didn't want to go back to my family. How could I, when I'd lived with my Ferruchio as we had lived?"

"You began to sell yourself then?"

"You needn't adopt so disapproving a tone. I know how many men you have had. At least in the month I've known you. Is that why we enjoy each other so much, because we both know how much the other enjoys men?"

"I enjoy you because I've never known anyone like you. You seem not to have to manage me, to manipulate me. I wasn't used to being treated that way. Rodrigo was like that, too. He never tried to manage me. He had no expectations that I change into someone other than who I am. He told me clearly what he wished, and how I could give it to him. I felt so firmly on the ground, somehow. No sense of having to translate some mysterious code. My family seemed always to have expectations that they were leading me toward but they pretended it was all up to me. And they acted as if I couldn't tell that they were leading me. Aren't you getting tired of walking? You want to ride for a while?"

"No, I'm happy as I am. We're not playing tonight. Or tomorrow. This is the dreary part of our journey. But once we reach Salerno, we'll be back to playing. What do you mean by your family's expectations?"

"Oh, everything about how I was to live, it seemed. How I was to act to my father's business partners. How I was to dress, which people I could consort with. Especially that I'd take over my father's business. That I'd marry and produce issue. That I'd comply. That I'd keep quiet about what was more important to me. I was once very good at that. I remember once when I was a little boy my father praised me for being so tactful. It was disgusting, really, praising a little boy for learning so early how to manipulate his elders. It is a skill that I've put to good use; there is no doubt about that. But it is corrupting. Rodrigo rescued me from that corruption."

We walked in silence for a time. Catarina went to the wagon and pulled a wineskin out of the back, and drank, then offered me some.

"You are too pure for this world, Antonio, I think. To talk of corruption. We are all corrupt. We can't help it."

"But we can notice it, can't we? We don't have to pretend so much, do we? Surely you of all people don't pretend."

"I pretend constantly. I put my gift for pretense to use. I couldn't survive if I didn't pretend. But you're right, I don't pretend that I don't pretend."

"That is why I trust you so."

"I wish you could have known Ferruchio. You'd have seduced him, no doubt. He would have liked you very much."

"You'd have stood by while I seduced him?"

"I'd have joined you, silly boy."

"Of course. What a treat. So, tell me, what next, how did you become a comedian?"

"Oh, Luigi found me in a brothel. Yes, I turned to whoring. No pretense. I love men, men love me, and I was good. And the mistress of the house was good to me. She was a bit overdone, you'd say, but she was vigilant about the welfare of girls she liked. Vicious with those she didn't, unfortunately. Luigi saw something in me, and took me with him. And I like this life even better. I'll never have what I had with Ferruchio, it is true. But that isn't a good enough reason to stop. Or to worry. I've had nothing, and I've gone on. One does or one does not. It is very simple. I have a big appetite. I go on. If you don't mind my saying so, I think you should pay more attention to your appetite."

"I'm surprised to hear you say that, since you know better than most that my appetite for cock is quite healthy."

"You're starving yourself in other ways, my sweet. And you know it. It won't bring Rodrigo to you. You'll just starve."

"I can't make a meal where I find no nourishment."

"You don't have to be so fussy."

"Oh, that's very good, coming from you."

"And in just what way am I fussy?"

"I won't even hazard to begin. Look, up the road, is that an inn, or a farmhouse ahead, do you think? I wish I could sleep on a bed tonight."

"Maybe we'll find one with someone to keep us company. We live in hope, sweet one."

It was a farmhouse, and we slept in the barn, with the cows. And the oldest son was not at all interested in either one of us. We kept each other company again that night.

Found

It had been just about two years since I was in the harbor at Genoa. Under the arcade where Rodrigo first spoke to me, first kissed me. I wagered all on Rodrigo being a man of habit, which is very foolish indeed, since his interest would have to be to avoid routine, in order to evade capture. But there is a certain routine built into maritime trade. Crops and goods must come to markets in their own time. The seasons set certain rules on the sea that sailors must abide by if their voyages are to be profitable. There were few ports that Rodrigo put into routinely. Marseilles, of course, because it was so easy to distribute pirated goods there, and the mistral took us to our winter quarters so swiftly. But if his raids along the eastern shores of the Mediterranean were to be effective, he couldn't be predictable. I knew he'd been in Genoa's harbor before the time he found me. After all, he'd said that Emilia's meat pies were his favorites. Genoa was a good market for the goods they'd have plundered in the east: fabric and leather. I bet my happiness on the likelihood that he'd be in Genoa again in the late summer, when he could trade spices from the east and the furs and cured hides from the Ragusans for the hogsheads of ale and wine the crew of the *Black Phoenix* needed for the winter.

In the time I had been away from the city, Battista had died. A competitor had taken over his business. No one had bothered to look for me for months. My father would have long since consigned me to the remote suburbs of his memory as a thoughtless rogue, unworthy of my name—that is if he hadn't given me up for dead. It seemed no one in the city bothered to know me. I played with Luigi's troupe for four days in the market square, and scouted the harbor every spare moment.

The fifth day we'd been there it was a foggy dawn, odd for September. I walked out to the quay. I stood looking south to the sea. Slowly the morning light dissolved the opalescent wall of fog into an iron-gray sea studded with brilliant diamonds. In the distance, a skiff emerged from the shimmering cloud. My heart thudded double time. There were two men in the little boat. One rowed, the other sat in the stern with his head in his hands. As they drew closer I would have sworn that the broad back and thick heavy arms rowing belonged to Matteo. The man in the back looked up as they drew close enough to spot the shore. Suddenly he straightened up as if struck sharply in the back and I knew that he saw my figure on the quay, I knew that he saw me. He shielded his eyes from the morning sun rising beyond the city. I would have been only a silhouette. He hardly moved as the other kept rowing. I started to walk farther out along the dock, breaking into a run as I realized that what seemed to be happening was in fact really happening. Rodrigo dropped his hands. They were close enough now to the quay and our eyes locked. We said nothing. No words came to my lips. Matteo looked up at Rodrigo, saw his transfixed look, and turned to watch over his shoulder. He broke into a broad smile when he spotted me. Gulls wheeled over my head. The waves lapped gently at the side of the dock. Without a word, Rodrigo tossed the hemp rope to me and I tied it off on the block at my feet. He reached his hand out, and I pulled him up. I felt his arms close around me, pulling me into him, his rough cheek next to mine, damp now with tears, I felt his chest heave, I smelled his smell again, so familiar that all my senses felt keener, I felt his mouth on mine again, his dark, spicy breath filling my nose, my lungs. I couldn't take him in fast enough. Our tears mingled on each other's cheeks. No words were possible. He held me and rocked gently, one hand at the back of my head, the other fast around my back. When we were both sure that we were not dreaming, we could pull our faces back enough to look at each other. He held my face in his hands, the same way he had that first day, and looked deeply into my eyes. Tears filled his as he smiled. I couldn't stop crying.

"I'm going to have to keep much better watch over you, my boy. Much better watch. I have found that I can't do very well without you. I think that will please you. You knew that I'd be in Genoa in September, didn't you?"

"I bet all my happiness on that."

"I bet all on my boy knowing that I'd be here to find him.

"Tomasso—?"

"Is no longer aboard the *Black Phoenix*. I know everything, my love. He told me everything. He was sick. Some invisible worm poisoned him, and now he is no longer part of our lives."

"That invisible worm was his yearning for you."

"No, it was not that, not that alone. But we needn't talk about Tomasso now. We've come ashore only to buy wine and ale. We'll put out at noon and hope for good winds to take us to Marseilles."

He grabbed me and buried his face in my armpit and inhaled deeply.

"All the perfumes of Arabia are as nothing to the scent of you, my Tonio."

Matteo had hoisted himself up to the dock by this time. He took both of us into his huge embrace. I wiped my face on the gray sleeve of my shirt. Matteo handed me a kerchief.

"Blow."

"But how did you make your way here? By my reckoning, you must have made landfall near Bari."

"Yes, a day and a half's walk out of Bari. I'd hoped you'd put in there and come to find me."

"The Venetian proxies were swarming. We had a devil of a time avoiding them. We had to tack so far to the east that we skirted the Greek coast. But tell me, what have you done these months?"

"I've been a comedian."

Rodrigo snorted.

"No, really. I've gotten to be rather good, actually. Can you come to meet someone? She's the one who taught me the art of the comedy. And she was the one person I could tell my sadness to. She would like to meet you."

"A comedian?"

"And a whore. And a free woman. And very kind. And my friend these terrible months."

"Then I insist on meeting her."

We were walking into the inner harbor on the quay, and the morning stillness broke into the activity of a busy port on a workday. The crowd grew around us, and though Rodrigo's striking face drew admiring looks from all who passed, we were unimpeded.

I knew Catarina would rise late. She'd found a new lover in Genoa, a huge, handsome blond Lombard. She stayed at his chamber east of the harbor near Saint Francis of the Village.

"How much time do we have?"

"You know I cannot linger here. Only enough to complete our business with dispatch. Where is your friend?"

"Catarina is with her new lover. His chamber is on the other side of the Grimaldi Palace from here. Not too far."

"Well, quickly, then. The morning wears." He held me by the neck with the crook of his arm and we set out. His presence and the pressure of his arm gave me a lightness and a strength I'd not felt in too long. In a headlong rush I told Rodrigo as much as I could about my time with Catarina.

The streets from the harbor east toward the Grimaldi Palace were not crowded that early in the day. One could reach the Saint Francis by a nearly direct route, not like most of the city, a winding warren of little, crowded streets folded in on one another. It took us only a little time to reach the chambers where I'd left Catarina in the care of her conquest. The shutters of the house were bolted. I walked round to where the bedchamber's window was, pounded on the shutter below and called.

"Catarina. Wake up. Antonio is here, with news. News from the harbor."

A shutter opened and her head emerged.

"But soft, what noise is this, you handsome lunatic—Paolo will— oh, you must be—Antonio, you found your captain. My love, you have been found. Marvel of marvels. For this auspicious moment your Catarina rises with the sun." The shutters swung closed.

After some moments the main door swung open. Catarina was wrapped in a bottle-green velvet coverlet that she clutched at her breast, her hair a tumble of thatch that she tossed away from her face as she held one hand out to me.

"Get yourselves inside, and quietly. Paolo is foul tempered when he is disturbed in the morning. Dear heart, you are glowing, a child of the watery moon casting a silver glow. And you, I need hardly ask, are Rodrigo. I know all about you. And Antonio was right."

"Right about what?"

"Your power to captivate in a moment. Your hand, sir. We have a common interest, and that is the well-being of this beautiful, charming young man."

"In that you are right. And I am grateful to you for tendering such care on Tonio these months. Your grip is firm, but your skin is soft."

"The demands of the life on the stage. Your hands are rough and strong. Hands that are meant for entanglement. You, sir, are a man I could tarry with."

"Energy wasted. You have my gratitude. That will have to satisfy you."

"And you," she turned toward Matteo, "Antonio told me about a man as large as he is kind. You are Matteo, are you not?"

"I am he. I spare few words. You, my lady, have my thanks as well. Tonio's friends are friends of mine.

"Such a wealth of beautiful virility in one meager chamber—my head begins to swim and I grow giddy. Antonio, embrace me. I fear I know what this means. You are leaving, are you not?"

"At the earliest possible moment. Rodrigo cannot tarry here." She wrapped me in her arms and held me fast. "Catarina, you know all I can say to you. You are my sister now. I shall always feel your lack."

"Antonio, sweet boy. You have talent, you know. Great promise. Kiss me and then get you gone, or I shall cry, and my face will be quite out of order."

"No weeping. I've been returned to the man I longed for, and you have a new conquest. We should be content. I shall never forget you."

"And you—" she addressed Rodrigo over my shoulder—"take better care of him, sir. If you treasure him as I think you ought, take better care."

Rodrigo grinned at her, took her hand, bowed and kissed it.

"I regret only that I cannot enjoy one of your performances on the stage. Here in the intimacy of your chamber, the skills Tonio told me of are extravagantly plain. You will, in all ways, be obeyed, my lady."

"Impudence from one so handsome is only slightly easier to bear than impudence from a toad, so have a care."

"Oh, your reputation is known to us. I see no reason to strike any sparks on the flint of your famously difficult nature. We take our leave, grateful servants to a queen of players."

Before she could take up the game with Rodrigo, I kissed her one last time.

"We must go. Remember the brother you found on the road to Bari. And fare you well."

My eyes welled up as I turned toward the brightening morning beyond the open door. I felt her hands groping for my sleeve, signals of how moved she was by this parting. I stumbled over the sill and Rodrigo's arm was there. He steadied me a moment.

"Ready yourself, now. We have no time. I will not willingly lose you again, you know. Here's my hand. It is yours for good and all now." With the other, he grazed my face. To be able to look into the dark eyes I'd feared I'd never see again was overarching joy.

"I am ready. Which wine merchant?"

"Gattopardi. Closest to the harbor. Have you eaten?"

I'd not eaten since the night before. We stopped at Emilia's as we crossed the square before the harbor. Matteo headed for the skiff and Rodrigo and I made for the wine merchant's. Our tasks made the months that had separated us wither into nothing. We fell into our familiar rhythm as if we'd never been out of joint. Life made sense again.

⊕

Rodrigo had always taught me much about myself. But on our first night together after the terrible separation, he led me past anything I could have recognized about myself before.

"Come here to me, boy. My Tonio, we have much to make up for, and I think you will like what I am going to do for you this night. I have something new to teach you." He had a kerchief in his hands. "You have not seen me for many months, and I have not seen you. But I have carried you in me all this while. You will not need to see me now."

"No—I want to look at you. I want to see you. All those months, I looked for you and always your face melted just beyond my grasp. Let me look at you now."

We sat on the bed.

"Look at me, my boy. Look well. Trace every line, mark every fold. Now look here. Keep your eyes on mine."

He stood up, stepped to the table for a moment where he picked up a length of rope, then took the two steps back to where I stood, motionless.

"Now I'm going to bind you as we are bound together. As you are bound to my heart."

He took my right arm and looped a rope around my wrist. He worked with care, telling me what he was doing at every moment. After he pulled the hempen rope around my right wrist, then the left, he drew it tight enough so that it dug into my flesh if I tried to move, but not so tight that it hurt me. He spoke quietly as he bound me. After each knot was complete he stroked the sides of my face and kissed me.

"You've given yourself to me, haven't you, my Tonio? You're giving me your trust, right now, in this moment, and I'm showing you my trust by accepting yours. You can feel my love as I bind you, can't you? You feel the depth of my trust in you, my wonderful boy, don't you?"

His voice was soft and dark, breathing in my ear. He drew my wrists together behind me so that my shoulders were held back with my chest pressed out. My stomach fluttered, my breath was light and quick. His breath mixed with mine as he kissed me and told me that he'd next bind my ankles. I felt the rope tightening around them as he finished tying the knot.

"Stand very still, boy. Feel your breath. Feel the rope I've bound you with. I've bound you because you are my very special boy, so important to me that I must bind you close. Never will you be far from me again."

He reached to the table and picked up a kerchief.

"You have looked upon me. Take that in. Take what you saw deeply in." He raised the kerchief to my eyes. "I'm going to bind your eyes, now. I am in you, as you are in me. Keep me there. Feel me there. Talk to me."

"I feel you with me. I feel you in me, as I've carried you with me."

"Good boy. I see that you are excited." It was true. Simply giving myself over to him always made my cock stand straight up, nearly dripping. I couldn't help it. He gently stroked my cock and kissed it.

Now I felt a new sensation. A cold, hard point pressing at the soft place where the throat meets the chest. I recognized it as the blade of a dagger. He slowly, softly drew the blade down my chest, then under each breast, tracing smaller and smaller circles around my nipples. Thousands of stars seemed to flash in front of my eyes.

"That's right, my beautiful boy. Stand very still. You've given yourself to me haven't you? You trust your master because you know that he loves you beyond measure. And you know that he trusts you so that he can reveal all of himself to you. And you want to please him. Let yourself breathe, that's right. Let your breath go."

I was nearly panting, my breath shallow, quick. My excitement beyond any I'd known. Each stroke of the blade sent shivers through the length of my body. I had to take a deep breath, and as I did, I felt my arms strain against the ropes. Waves of shimmering sensation throbbed up and down my spine. He covered my mouth with his hand and breathed into my ear.

"Yes, my boy, you are a very remarkable boy. My very own. Let yourself breathe. Let us breathe together."

His mouth covered mine and he held my nose with the fingers of one hand. He breathed into my mouth and lungs, filling me with air that had been inside of him. And I breathed out as he sucked the air that had been inside of me deep inside of him. And again, what had been inside of him filled me, and what had given me life, gave life to him.

I heard the dagger fall to the deck.

"Can you kneel, boy? Kneel for me. Show me that you honor your master."

I fell to my knees with a soft thud.

"That's right, my Tonio. Now I'm going to give you a gift. Can you tell me that you are ready to receive this gift from me? Tell me. Tell me, boy, that you are ready to receive what I'm going to give you."

"Oh my master." I could hardly speak through the shuddering waves of sensation coursing through me. "I've never felt anything like this. I hardly know what I'm feeling. I hardly know what I am. I know only that I am yours. That I want to be yours, always yours."

"Yes, Tonio, you are mine in this moment, because your trust in me and my trust in you binds us together. Now I'm going to give you my piss. Do you want my gift? Do you want my piss?"

Behind the kerchief covering my eyes, I'd begun to cry, though I didn't understand why. I wept for joy. But there was no me anymore. I had dissolved into the bond between us.

"Yes, master, I want your piss. Please give it to me. Please give me your piss."

"My Tonio, I want to give it to you. Open your mouth, boy."

His warm nut-bitter piss splashed across my face, into my mouth and I drank as he filled it, as the hot piss fell down my chest, running to my cock that was straining with excitement. As he pissed into me, as I drank, I felt myself coming. My cock shot a stream of cum up on my belly as his stream of piss ran over me. Next I felt his hard cock in my mouth, the head of his dick. He pulled on his cock until he shot his cum into me, he fed me and I hungrily lapped up his cum.

"My beautiful boy, how you love the gifts I can give you. Can you have any idea how much joy that gives me, to see how greedily you love what I have for you? Do you have any idea how greatly you please me?"

He knelt down and rubbed his cum, his piss and my cum over my chest, over his chest, and covered my mouth with his. As he kissed me he untied the kerchief.

"Here are my boy's eyes, those eyes that have depth with no bottom or compass. Never has a boy pleased me so much. Now I'm going to untie you, but our trust will not so easily be loosed. I am right to believe so, aren't I?"

I could only look into his eyes and nod. When he'd untied my wrists, I threw my arms around him and buried my face in the hair of his chest. He held me tightly until my breathing slowed down. He pulled his face away and smiled.

"I fear I shall weep. My joy in you makes me weep. We know something rare in each other, don't we?" He stood up and untied my ankles. Standing before me, he licked my chest and belly clean, and I licked him clean. Then he brought a flagon of sack to me, and we drank it off. We fell into his bed and I slept as I hadn't slept in over a year.

The African Prince

Gentler seas of spring signaled that it was time to leave our winter haven. Stores were depleted and the men restless for life at sea, The *Black Phoenix* was righted and ready to take sail again. We began an eastward route along the Barbary shore toward the Levant. I had risen with the dawn and was above deck while Rodrigo charted our course at his table below. The early morning watch called out an alert.

"Vessel ahead on the starboard side"

Matteo, who was at the wheel raised his glass.

"A very small vessel. And a large man, waving his arms. He looks to need aid. Go—find out the captain."

Lupo swung down from his perch on a lower boom and loped toward the rearward hatch just as Rodrigo attained the maindeck.

"News, Lupo? Do I hear an alarm?"

"No alarm, Captain, but something new. Mark you, a man." Lupo pointed, turned and clambered back to his aerie.

"What ho, Matteo?"

"A man, a princely looking man, alone on a vessel of rushes, one that looks none too seaworthy, seeks our aid, I believe. See for yourself." He handed Rodrigo the glass. "His boat is too frail to conceal a trap I think."

"And so do I. Tonio, drop the net down to him as he comes along side."

The man's boat neared us. Rodrigo called out, "Hail, fellow! How do you?"

The man, close enough now to hear us and to speak to us, responded, "Naked and alone come I to your ship. Permission to board, captain."

The man's voice was deep and sonorous. His skin was dark as ebony and his form was mighty. A princely man surely, and yet a castaway foundering in a boat made of reeds.

"Hie you, climb aboard before you taste the salty brine," Rodrigo urged. "We are just in time, to judge by the condition of your ship."

The reeds, bound by hempen rope, broke apart and spread across the gently lapping waves. The man had to hurl himself toward our hull to catch his handhold just as the gunnel of rushes fell away, breaking apart as he left it. He climbed swiftly and with skill, swinging his body onto the deck noiselessly. He stood a moment, casting his eye on the three of us standing before him, and bowed.

"I give you my thanks. When I saw you approach, I dared a desperate hope that my luck had changed. And when I saw your ensign, I knew my fortunes had risen truly." He faced Rodrigo. "You are known, sir, even in my country, and I thank you for your aid. I am called Adjullo. Of late I was a prince in my land. Now I am an outcast. Condemned. It may be that I would have lived another day, to find another way toward rescue, but for aught I can tell, you have saved my life."

"Your noble bearing would move a laggard to action, and since I am no laggard, I offer my heartiest welcome. Here is Matteo, my next in command, and my boy Tonio. We bid you welcome."

He bowed to both of us. "I give you my thanks." His voice seemed to set the deck to reverberate with his burnished tones. He took us in with an open appraisal. "I am not a seafaring man, but such is my condition that I must needs become one, if you can take on another man. You will find me an avid student."

"All that will unfold. Tonio, take Adjullo to my cabin and bring him sustenance. When you are refreshed, sir, we will see how our mutual fortunes might be mingled. Go and eat. I will come to you anon."

Adjullo silently turned toward me. His face fell into repose and revealed a beauty that had been obscured by the extremity of his state. His eyes gleamed with pleasure as he looked at me.

"Come, sir, and rest."

⊕

I fetched him a plate of cheese, the rounds of flat unleavened bread that had escaped mold, some cured pork, and a tankard of sack. I found him gazing out the windows of the cabin on the churning wake. Our sails had found the morning's freshening breeze. I set the plate and the mug on the table.

"Some food, sir. Sit you down and eat." My stomach fluttered in a most unwelcome way, and my voice betrayed me with a falter.

"I give you thanks, and ever thanks." He lifted the tankard a moment, but set it down. "Forgive me my custom, but is there any plain water aboard? I take no fermented drink."

"Certainly." Fortunately, we'd restored our freshwater supply from the spring that flowed on Tabarka. I poured a goblet full from the pitcher on the cabinet. My hand trembled as I handed it to him.

"I am most grateful." He glanced at me, then spoke with his head diverted, as if to grant me respite from the blaze of his eyes. "Your captain says you are his boy, but you are a man in the full bloom of maturity, are you not? How come you to be called his boy? Please forgive the forward nature of my speech."

"I have not yet twenty-three years on this earth, yet I have seen much. It may be that I appear older than my time. I am called Rodrigo's boy because we see fit to have it so. He is my master. As he is master of this ship, and commands the love of all aboard."

"I do not mean to rouse you to defend yourself." I'd hardly known I was doing so. "Your master is famous not only for his reckless success, but, at least among some of us whose lives are made better for knowing such things, for the succor he offers those like us." His face broadened into a smile. "It is for this reason that I count myself among the most blessed. In my kingdom such a man as I, a man who loves other men, is put to death. And because I was son of the king, my egregious state was a double damnation and I in double danger."

"Then know this, you are safe and you are welcome."

"To be welcomed by such a one as you is all I need to hear."

His eyes frankly lingered as he cast his gaze up and down. I had been regarded thus many times in my life, though not since returning to my lord. I had nearly forgotten the pleasure of finding my form so admired by another man. And I had never beheld a man like this one.

His skin gleamed as if polished with care, with a depth and a smoothness that asked hands to confirm its reality. His features were strong and straight and fine, but with a delicacy that hinted a wealth of feeling. His head was finely proportioned, and poised nobly on a neck well muscled. He was wide and thick at the shoulder, then tapered to a narrow waist. His arms and legs looked as if they might burst with power. I had to break my gaze away, so potent was his power to fascinate.

"I disturb you, do I not?"

"You do not disturb. It is myself. I rarely have beheld a man so finely made as you."

"Nor I one like you. I rejoice that our fates have brought us close. But fear not, I will not insult the captain's generosity, nor your gentle nature with any importunity. I—"

The cabin door swung open.

"Tonio, you have made our guest most welcome, I trust."

Adjullo answered, "Most welcome, sir. And most content."

"You have hardly touched your meal, or your drink."

"I eat not of the pork, but the bread and cheese have restored my strength, as your fine visage has restored my soul. The teachings of my land forbid fermented drink and the eating of pork. I do not mean to be churlish."

"Think not of it. Tonio, is there something more we can offer our new friend?"

The black man held up a huge hand. "I need nothing more than what your boy has provided." He smiled at me. I stepped back.

Rodrigo sat on the chair across from Adjullo.

"Now, sir. Can we speak of our mutual needs and benefits? How might they be joined so all may flourish? You are one of the finest men ever I saw, I confess. I know not when we make landfall again, nor at what port, but surely we can find a way that our fortunes bend together."

"I am alone and free to follow my fortune where it leads me. I am at your service if you can use a man like me. It is true that I am not a sailor. I am an able-bodied man, and eager to learn."

Rodrigo looked at me and smiled.

"Your words are most apt. I'll put you under Matteo's tutelage, and he'll make you a sailor fit for any vessel. You will find our men most welcoming. But that, I think, you know already."

"You see in me more than I have spoken."

"Your eyes speak for you, sir. And with an eloquence that needs little elaboration." He stood and walked toward Adjullo, who rose to face him. They embraced. Adjullo broke away.

"Captain, you must allow me my tremulous folly. I have lived so long in a place where my affections are forbidden that I am quite overcome now I am in a place where they are valued." He wiped his eyes. "My temper is not like a maid's, despite mine eyes' betrayal."

"There is no shame here, handsome one. Tears are welcome. When you are ready, come above decks and find out Matteo. Tonio, let us leave our fine Adjullo in peace a moment. More, much more of this anon. Come."

⊕

With Adjullo on deck, Rodrigo gathered the men and spoke:

"My hearties, this day the sea brought us a new man, and a rare one. Adjullo, newly plucked from the waves, joins us, and I bid you all welcome him as one of us. As some of you once were, he is new to life on the sea, but if you have eyes, and can use them now, mark his noble figure and know his strength."

Lupo, from above, called out,

"Hail to you, beauty."

The men guffawed and shouted their welcome. Adjullo, his arms opened wide, bowed his head in thanks.

"I will repay your welcome as best I can with work—"

"That's not the only way, I'll wager." It was a voice from the knot of men furthest away. More laughter rose at this, and hoots and nodding heads.

Rodrigo stepped between Adjullo and the men, but Adjullo put a hand on his arm.

He rumbled, with a smile, "I'll not be trifled with, nor will I toy with you, at least not unless you wish me to. Know me, first, before you heap me with derision. Let us know each other." The laughter waned, but the men did not take their eyes from his massive form.

Rodrigo called out, "Hie you back to your posts." He turned to Adjullo. "Deftly done, sir, deftly done. There will be no derision, but much desire, and that may cause many a collision. We all enjoy each other's favors on this ship, and it is clear that you will be sought after. That will demand more dexterity, which I think is yours to command."

"I am a quick study, captain. My desire has already been roused, and right glad I am to still feel its stirring." He looked at me. "Now, you, sir," turning to Matteo, "I think it is you who are to make me a sailor. I am yours to command."

Matteo grinned with delight. "Ah, my son, come with me, and I'll show you the measure of the *Black Phoenix.*" He clapped his arm round the other man's broad shoulders and walked toward the stern, deep in discourse all the way.

⊕

It was night. I lay in our bed awaiting my master. He sat at his table, a candle casting a fluttering light across the charts he studied. Suddenly he turned to me.

"You are troubled, my beautiful boy. I see it. What troubles you? Your face is as a book wherein I may read of many things. Methinks the arrival of our new man disturbs you."

"I am troubled. I know not how or why, but I am. I wish to say all that is in my thoughts, but I cannot find the way to speak them, so changing do I find myself."

"Speak calmly, then, and slow. There is nothing you could say that would harm me, that I know."

His eyes rested on me as if there was all the time in the world.

"You told me once that I was free. That you do not hold me. But I do not want to be free. Not free for others. I want only to be for you."

"Yes, my boy, I know it. This is the old churning, is it not? You say you don't wish to be free for others. You insist on it with such heat that methinks my beauty doth protest too much."

"Too much? No, Rodrigo. What mean you—?"

"Ah, my Tonio, I see you. I see how you discipline yourself. This is the reason you take so well to my discipline. It relieves you of an onerous job. And we are joined, so finely and truly joined that way, perhaps joined even more closely than when our bodies are joined. When I discipline you, I am following the orders you give me. Not in words, but in signals that I read because I love you so well. When I discipline you I play a role that you kept for yourself for so long. To keep you held. Like a prisoner. You wish to be held prisoner because of the tight grip that feels so sure, so lasting. You keep yourself prisoner to feel that grip. And when I can hold you fast, you no longer have to. I can do this for you. This we do together and it gives us a pleasure beyond imagining. This is a play of our devising that comes into existence even as we play it. But seek not to make a prisoner of me. I hold you freely. I heed your silent orders because I love you well. But know that I take on this task freely, not because I am held, and not because I expect you to be my prisoner. I expect us to be able to know ourselves. Not to be slaves to ourselves. Look at me, Tonio. My love, look at me."

I had hidden my face in the bedclothes. I knew from the heat that seared my face that I was burning red with recognition. It was as if he put a maggot in my mind: did I protest too much? Rodrigo saw so much of me. Nay more, a bright-eyed creature stirred inside of me and I quickened with the question. All he said was true. All he said sounded as if I had known it already, yet I could not have known it until he told it of me.

"I do not know if I can be the free man you wish me to be." Tears coursed down my cheek.

"That I wish you to be? But what of you? You need not know it now. The readiness is all. It will never come to pass unless you wish it. And you must know what I can do, and what I cannot. This prince has disturbed our peace because you want him, and he wants you. He is a prince worth wanting. We all know it. We cannot help ourselves if we seek not to know what we know. Oh, my boy, I am happy, you are safe, we are together. The danger is inside. Once you know that, it loses its strength."

"I depend on your strength."

"It pleases you to think so. It pleases you to lend me your strength so you can be weak. Would it trouble you to know that I do the same? That I need to be weak sometimes, and find the strength in you? You must love me for my weakness, too."

"I never look at you and see weakness. Never. I feel so tired. I cannot speak. Can you pardon me?"

"Think well for whom that pardon is needed, my boy. It may be that you must pardon me for saying what you had wished remained unsaid. Rest you awhile." He blew out the candle and slid into our bed beside me. "Kiss me and sleep, and let go that grip. We do not need it."

⊕

The ship's course made for the east, to try our luck with the Levantine traders, then up toward the Ottomans and the richly laden merchant ships burdened with leather and carpets and furs. Night's mantle fell on the third day since Adjullo came to us, and I found him on the deck, looking to the south, from whence he'd come.

"Look you homeward?"

"Ah," he turned. "You caught me out. My thoughts did range that way. But my home is far away."

"Tell me of your country."

"It is a place better imagined than lived in, I fear."

"Even for its sovereign?"

"This sovereign never knew his throne. The death of my father at mine uncle's hands, for it was he, I am sure of it, pointed to my demise. He spread discord among my people, and all the while he played the smooth peacemaker. He is a man with a troubled, miserly spirit, always keeping an account of who owes what to whom. The land I was born to lead began to rot from its head, like a fish."

"You could not fight him?"

"He knew my nature. This was entered into his book of accounts, to use when he needed. Men whose debts he held bore false witness against me, though the matter of their accusations was true. I stole away with the help of the one man in our court who bore me love. The fisherman's reed boat was not seaworthy, it was meant for the shallow marshes along our coast, but it was all that lay at hand."

"Will you ever return?"

"That is beyond my knowing today. I cast my fate with the *Black Phoenix* now, and consider myself lucky. And you, think you of home?"

"I left a long time ago. I caused great pain, and it pains me to think on it. But to lead my life as I wished it left me no choice that I could see. My city, too, bore no love for men like us, but is steeped in hypocrisy. I could not stomach it. Either I lived in pain, or I caused pain for others. I made the selfish choice for no one would make a selfless one on my account."

"Our histories are heavy with sorrow."

"Let us not sit upon the deck and tell sad tales of the lives of men. Let us look to ourselves."

"For no one else will, save those who love you."

"You speak of our captain."

"It is beautiful to behold. I never thought to see in flesh what lived only in dreams. And now my flesh is near your flesh and we call out to each other, do we not?"

"Oh, we do, we do, I fear."

"You fear it? But why? What danger is here?"

"The danger of knocking our handsome balance out of kilter. I fear losing again what once was taken from me, and was regained only after pain and travail."

"I wish not to take anything, nor to bring you pain. That is not my way. Long ago, my grandfather, a king of surpassing wisdom, taught me how to rule. Think, he said, of whether there is peace inside yourself. A man cannot rule wisely if there is a fearsome noise inside. My people believe that in each of us there lives a spirit. It lives in us in the form of a bird. He told me never to send that spirit bird to do harm, lest we lose our peace in such a fell venture. Without our spirit bird, we lose our entire self. I try never to send my spirit bird to another wishing harm or pain, but only good. Only good, Tonio, do I wish for you."

My spirit was a harshly squawking kite endlessly circling. I needed to act to stop its spirals. The African leaned on the rail, looking out to sea. I put my hand on his shoulder. Slowly he turned is face to mine. His eyes were gentle and smiling. He was silent.

"I wish to kiss you. To feel your power around me."

His arms reached round and held me fast. His smell was like the bitter rind of oranges from the east, mingled with smoke. He tasted of salt and earth. His lips were soft. Our mouths sought more and more from each other, and our embrace grew stronger.

"How do you, Tonio?"

"I know that I do no wrong, but still I feel I ought to think I do. My spirit bird seeks peace and I wish to quiet its fussing. Will you join me with my master? That is what I most desire, to have you join us both."

"Most heartily will I join you, for I can think of no finer men on such a night as this."

"Allow me to prepare, but find us in the cabin soon."

Rodrigo was below. He watched me as I washed myself, grinning widely.

"My boy moves with such dispatch I see a plan afoot. And I see his manhood standing to, a sign that always brings me joy. What, are we to have company?

"If so it please you. No, that is a lie. It pleases me to bring a third. I think that pleases you, does it not?"

"It lifts my spirit to hear you tell me what pleases you. I've hoped to enjoy Adjullo and it makes me glad to see you in action. You've shuffled off the heavy weight of duty to that phantom master within."

"I try to heave it from me. I chose to act because my thoughts had worn a track that deepened like winter's mud with much traffic."

"Out of the mud, then. Reach you for joy."

A knocking, then an opening, and Adjullo appeared.

"And high time you found your way to us, my lord," called out Rodrigo. Suddenly he was naked.

The warm light was softly golden across the furred bronze of my captain's chest. Adjullo stepped in, and the shirt he'd been wearing dropped away. Light from the candles on the table and the desk glinted in the sheen of the ebony smoothness of his body. The three of us stood still in the flickering light, looking from one to the other. Time slowed. We touched each other first with our eyes. Awareness of anything other than this moment faded. I heard my breath, and the breath of the other two men. Rodrigo let out a low, rumbling chuckle. My heart pounded. Each took a step, then another toward each other. Such fullness I had never felt as I reached for them both.

We fell laughing and holding each other onto the bed, mouths finding mouths, shoulders, arms, bellies smooth and ridged or covered with fine hair. Laughter faded into quieter sounds, inquisitive sounds, sighs of pleasure. Hands sought muscles, the broad ones of the thighs and haunches, the rounded ones of calves of shoulders and arms. No sense of rushing, of urgency, only the finding and feeling and tasting and enjoying. Finding an unknown arched manhood straining with excitement, holding firm to it, holding the strength and vulnerability of a man in one's hand. There was nothing but this moment, and each knew it.

Rodrigo and I found our places each under one of Adjullo's arms as he lay on his back. It was as if we knew how to work together, our mouths meeting at his for a moment, then one of us moving down the deep, fragrant flesh of his chest, his stomach, to find his cock, the largest I had ever beheld, as soft as velvet, as powerful as a god's. Rodrigo and I shifted up and down, finding all the ways to take him in, to know him. Suddenly Adjullo stopped me, held my face in his hands, and said,

"Tell me now, what do you want? I know what I want. Tell me what you want."

Rodrigo smiled, and nodded, but was silent.

"I can hardly recognize the wish that is forming. I want—I want—"

"My boy, do not fear," whispered Rodrigo.

"I want both of you in me at once. I want to hold each of you deep inside me."

Adjullo let out a gentle rumble of admiration and approval.

"Yes, I want to feel you hold me and your captain deep inside you.

I want to be there together with him. You know what to do?"

Rodrigo reached for a vial that held a subtly fragrant oil, poured a small amount in his palm, and began to massage my bumhole with it.

"My boy knows that he can take anything that his master can offer. He knows that his limits can be stretched."

I felt his first finger entering me. Lifting me this way, he guided me to straddle Adjullo's body. Another finger entered me, the oil easing the way.

Adjullo said, "You know just what to do, don't you, boy."

I was breathing deeply. "I want to open myself to both of you. I want both of you at once."

Rodrigo had poured some of the oil on Adjullo's magnificent cock and was pulling it firmly. Then another finger slid into me, and my breath released the muscles farther.

"Now, I want to feel the inside of you," Adjullo breathed.

I pressed back onto his cock, my breathing deepened, willing myself to open. Rodrigo's hand gently rubbed around my hole as I slowly sat, taking Adjullo into me bit by bit. Our eyes were locked. Slowly, slowly I sat back, his look penetrating as deeply as his manhood, I was entered more deeply than ever before. Finally I sat fully back on him and was still, feeling his presence filling me, feeling my opening grow wider, taking in more and more. A rivulet of sweat coursed down my brow and my chest.

Rodrigo licked at my sweat, rubbed my haunches, my belly, my cock, and whispered to me, "Lean forward, strong one, lean forward and breathe."

He had oiled himself and I felt the head of his cock pressed at my body's opening, next to the shaft of Adjullo. I felt the work of his hands releasing my muscles, as I breathed to open myself farther. I felt him start to enter me. Adjullo's eyes widened, then rolled back as he felt Rodrigo's warm manhood against his.

"That's my strong, remarkable boy. Breathe. Feel me coming into you, joining this fine prince inside you. Feel both of us, welcome both of us deep inside you. Feel how you can hold both of us inside you. Breathe."

He reached round and found my cock, holding it firmly in his hands. Adjullo had taken hold of my nipples, and pulled gently, then, very slowly and gradually, his tugs grew more and more insistent.

"Breathe," I heard Adjullo's low rumble.

"My remarkable boy, breathe." Rodrigo was at my ear.

I felt him pressing into me with each breath. The three of us were breathing together. The sound of the air passing into and out of our bodies grew. I felt more of Rodrigo inside me. My breaths had become moans, sounds that mounted. More of him was in me, I was opened more widely than I had ever known I could be. I held both of these men inside me. I reached round and urged Rodrigo all the way inside. I yelped with the deep fullness of it, as I took both men fully in me.

With a gentle slowness Rodrigo began to pull himself in and out, against Adjullo, inside of me. I began to move with his movement. I felt myself larger than I'd ever felt. I looked down at Adjullo, whose fathomless eyes never left mine. He began to move with Rodrigo, the two of them in tandem. I felt myself holding them and releasing them, I felt my body expand, I felt my spirit expand. I searched with one arm for Rodrigo, whose hands were round my haunches, and with my other arm I held Adjullo's chest. As my body relaxed, as I grew open, our movements grew larger, stronger, harder. Rodrigo grunted at my ear, Adjullo called out. I barked out deep breaths that mounted into a howl.

"Both of you inside me. My love is vast as an ocean. The more I give, the more I have. Give me all of you, inside me. I want the ocean of you poured inside me. Make us one vast ocean."

"Yes, my fine boy, yes."

Adjullo rumbled, "Mmmm, yes, here it is, I want to give it to you, all to you."

The rumbling became general, the three of us, surrendered to something larger than us, moving us, ravaging us from the inside, a blinding force that took us over.

Suddenly there was a peak, a height, and we were still, panting, I couldn't tell how much time passed. Pools of sweat formed in the hollows of Adjullo's chest. My brow was damp, I felt Rodrigo's thigh slick, and his hands gently guided me up as I felt him pull himself out of me. I rocked back against his chest and he pulled us up to lie with Adjullo, a mass of flesh warm, glowing, spent.

I drowsed against the bodies of my lovers while a silent rejoicing warmed me within. The silence marked not a void, but the achievement of peace. The kite within me serenely wheeled at a great height, turning on a warm wind. The quiet began in my breast and flowed outward. It was a thing not to be grasped after. It is allowed in after feeling, after one's limits are stretched beyond the customary compass that resides within and tells of what to fear. Custom bears a useless message, one that will misdirect the sailor and spoil the voyage.

⊕

As we plied the waters round the lands along the eastern rim, Adjullo shared our bed sometimes even as he shared himself with others. Drawn by his princely bearing and strength, the crew shook with the rustle of disturbance. A new force to be reckoned with on board required adjustments. Novelty threw sparks and some heat. But he was a skilled navigator in unfamiliar seas. In time he found a special place with Matteo and Pato. When work's requirements restored the quotidian rhythm of our lives few would guess that Adjullo had not long been part of the crew.

Otranto

My skills as a sailor grew. Matteo was a good tutor, and both Adjullo and I were eager apprentices. He taught us to set the ship's course by the stars, how to set the hempen sheets that rigged our sails, how many sails to fly when the wind was high, and which would find the wind when winds were paltry and scarce. The pleasure I found in this was keen. I thirsted for more. The greater scope I felt within invited greater accomplishment. Long since I had been restive working below as a cabin boy. Rodrigo saw my discontent and my ambition. He took to posting me by his side at the wheel. There I learned the currents, the treacherous parts of the sea that was our larger home, the stage for our adventures. Soon I could be trusted at the helm. I was a boy no longer, but a mate.

The wind was bright with the freshening of approaching autumn. Rodrigo bade me take the wheel so Matteo and Pato could mend the quarrel they had over Adjullo. The three of them huddled together aft. The patient Ethiopian waited until the old lovers traded bitter barbs, ready to pour his soothing voice like balm over feelings made raw with wounding words.

"My captain," I began.

"My love?"

"Again I wish to ask, but I wish not to nettle."

"I stand warned."

"I have learned so much at your side. I see how our life is made up of dangers but also of patterns. The patterns are consistent, aren't they? There is safety there, in the consistency, but danger also."

"And you wish for a remedy. You seek to change this."

"I question it. To live freely, danger is inescapable, this I know, but are we required to court all danger? Can there be freedom for those like us with danger not so close a companion?"

"Tonio, this is your torment and I fear you will make it mine if you do not leave it off. You want us to leave the life of the pirate, to become legitimate traders? Who do you think we place in danger but what you call the legitimate traders? We will be preyed upon if we are not the hunter. All dangers cannot be eliminated. Never."

"But some might. We need not live on land. What if we found a way to stay aboard our ship, with our men? With all our experience in trading and our knowledge of the sea, why should success be such an unreasonable prospect?"

"Do you not believe me when I tell you that the laws of men amount to slavery to the likes of us? I thought you had enough of that in Florence. But that was long ago, now, eh? What is it that would change, do you think?"

"Little would change but the likelihood of attack by a well armed navy."

"You know I am hunted. None of those I have disturbed would be moved if I changed my ways of doing business. Why do you test my patience thus?"

"I see that we tack near the edge of fatal risk. Nearer and nearer. I fear risk is a seduction that is too delicious to give up. I do not want to live without you, so this is my risk too. I'll not trouble you with my questions again."

"That will suit us better. We've chosen. Now we stand by our choices."

I felt chastened. To speak true, the constant danger was exhilarating and not only because of the pleasure Rodrigo took in it. This is what frightened me: that I could love that danger, too.

I left off my plans for making the *Black Phoenix* a merchant ship. In truth the fame of our ship was mixed with admiration. It rested on a particular detail, or so we were told, and so we heard when we visited those ports we could. That detail was this: Rodrigo had us use weapons as little as possible when we boarded the merchant vessels we plundered. And because of this, the stories of our adventures spread. Pirates we were, but pirates who lived by cunning of our wits, not by the cutting of others' throats. He was the corsair whose daring was matched by his care not to shed blood. His life was a graceful dance with danger and this was yet another reason his reputation was weighted with terrible liability. A beloved criminal is a far greater threat than a hated one.

The patterns of danger and consistency that made up our life were determined by the seasons, of course, and by the waters we sailed and the habits of men. We played with the patterns, as pirates must, to avoid capture by the navies of those kingdoms who sought our destruction. This was not at all unfamiliar to me, really. Fortune had woven a pattern like this one into the fabric of my days before: in my youth, when the freedom of those like me to love as we wished was policed and punished, we learned how to approach the limits of danger, and how to find our freedoms where we could. In my manhood at sea the life I led was free of disturbances of that kind, but fraught with baleful others.

So long as there were ships to plunder and ports to trade in, the crew was content. So long as there was danger to hazard, Rodrigo thrived. And I couldn't—didn't want to—imagine life anywhere but at his side.

⊕

And then one day I lost Rodrigo. Lost him forever, in a skirmish at Otranto with Venetian enforcers. Venice considered the Adriatic to be hers and demanded payment from all merchantmen that plied her waters. Corsairs roused a particular ire in the Duke, and his captains were encouraged to use all the force at their command. The *Black Phoenix* had become all too recognizable, and Rodrigo was so reckless that day. He had us stray close enough to the harbor to attract the attention of the Venetian fleet. He decided that the risk was worth taking, tempted by the leather and fur coming from the Slavs trading from the Black Sea route. That day, heavy clouds pressed down on us, and the winds were finicky. We were in the open waters between Bari and Durazzo, ready to intercept the Slavic merchantmen as they hugged the coast from Cattaro. But Venetian enforcers spotted us, and we had to make a run for the narrows at Otranto. There they choked us off. But rather than boarding and demanding tribute, the usual method of controlling trade in waters they considered their own, the Venetian galleons simply opened fire on us as they approached. Because Rodrigo sought to avoid the use of cannons we were caught starkly unprepared. Squeezed in the narrows, there yet was a channel for us to make a run for it. We managed to slip through, but not before taking a direct shot toward the stern. A hot ball of iron caught Rodrigo in the chest. Rodrigo died of his wound as we made our way to the open waters toward Malta. I held him and tried to stanch the bleeding, but it would not stop. His blood poured from him and I watched him slip away. I kissed him and there was blood in his mouth that I shared: the taste of his death.

Without thinking of it, as I was holding him, I shouted orders to the men. There was smoke and confusion, and we were all in mortal danger. Matteo held the wheel, the wind favored us once again, and the ship, even in our wounded condition, slipped away from the duke's galleons.

We set a meandering course through the Adriatic south to seek the seclusion of a lagoon where we might linger to make repairs and collect ourselves. During the hours after the Venetians fired on us men performed their duties in near silence. The ship might have been crewed by ghosts. I was cored, an empty husk.

The morning after the disaster, Adjullo and I wrapped Rodrigo's body in a shroud of linen. Matteo gathered the men together and spoke.

"Men, companions, my boys, we have lost him, the sun of our days, a glory of a man. Our sorrow can know no bounds, our spirits are dimmed, but our bodies remain strong and hungry. We honor our captain as we can. But now we give him to the sea that is his home."

Four of us, Matteo, Pato, Adjullo and I, bore his body to the rail and cast his body into the water. After the faint splash that was the water's embrace, there was no sound but the creaking of the ship's timbers and the luffing of the sails.

Matteo turned to the men. "Our ship can be made ready again, and our voyage will resume. But we face a decision. We are to serve a new captain."

There was a rumbling through the sorrowing groups gathered on the deck, some supporting each other, some sitting disconsolate with their faces in their hands.

"What were Rodrigo's wishes?" called out Lupo, the one man who tried to rally his brothers' spirits.

"I say Matteo is our captain. He was Rodrigo's second. I take orders from Matteo," someone called out.

Matteo raised his hands to quiet the men.

"Rodrigo told me his wishes, and they sail in the same direction as my own. His beloved Tonio, beloved of all of us, is to be captain. So Rodrigo commands, and so I obey. I serve Tonio."

He turned to me and stopped short. His eyes filled with tears and for a moment he could not speak. This huge man, stunned to silence, stood for a moment, drew his meaty hand across his face, smeared the tears away.

His voice rose again. "Those who wish to join me are welcome. Those who wish to find their fortunes on another ship, in other lands, prepare to seek them soon."

Pato called out immediately, "I serve Tonio. I serve as Rodrigo wished. Hail Tonio, our new captain!"

Rodrigo's blood still stained my linen. The scent of his blood lingered in my nostrils, the taste in my mouth. Sorrow and pride grappled like wrestlers within me. Yet I stood before the men as if a statue. No tears fell from my eyes, my hands were steady. Fortune's decision fell upon me like a blow. I opened my arms to the crew, men I'd lived with for many a day, men I loved; now men who asked me to command them. Whether I sought it or not, I was the captain of the *Black Phoenix*.

Part II

Illyria

You must allow time to move you as swiftly as a good strong wind takes sailing vessels, ever onward, as my story unfolds. Twelve years had passed since I first trod my ship's deck; six without Rodrigo as my guide and my partner; life as a pirate the only life I knew, the loving men of the *Black Phoenix* my only society. But the turning of time's wheel brings a man low as easily as it raises a man high.

After the disaster at Otranto, much was thrust upon me. Try as I might to reach for greatness, it ever eluded my grasp. Noting the paltry effect of my striving, my ambition began to wither and fade. I was like a perpetually waning moon only able to give ever less light. The first months I sought to rouse myself with what I knew I owed to the men. Responsibility weighed heavily on me, but in truth duty is a joyless master. I tried to measure up to the ideal of the captain and the lover I lost. His image might fire me for a while, but was easily doused by the floods of time. There was no denying that without Rodrigo I lacked the stomach for the sea; in truth I hardly had a stomach for life. If a half-hearted captain, I was practical. For six years I kept the men safe and goods passing through our hold. Toward the end the men could not but chafe under the dwindling power of my command. Even Matteo could not hide his chagrin from me, though he would not speak it. I relied on the pattern I'd learned; consistency kept us afloat. Our circuits took us through waters we knew, to coves that were safe, and to ports where we could trade. Then another disaster divided me forever from the ship and the life that formed me.

It was late summer, a time when storms erupt suddenly, and just as quickly subside. The coast of Illyria was short, the duchy being negligible, really, tucked between the Duchy of Savoy and the Kingdom of France, and sandy. The port there was not a busy one, but the duke's fleet, mostly flat-bottomed cogs and galleys, operated a steady trade. There were treacherous rocks protecting the duchy; they outlined a shallow lagoon, with an opening for the harbor entrance to the south-southeast. In a storm as black and sudden as that one was, there was no telling where the rocks could be.

The Duke Orsino's galleys were almost comically easy to board and plunder, if only they did not present so sad a state. They gimped along the coast, never making more than a comfortable half-day's voyage. We were recklessly familiar with the captains of his ships, and they'd grown accustomed to offering half the goods they were carrying, as if paying us tribute, before they pushed along to Illyria. There was no danger for us, and none for the galleys, for all had grown complacent.

The day had begun brilliantly, with the clear sharp air that promised the change of the seasons. Adjullo and I were at the helm. I spotted the little cog, laden with goods and passengers.

"What think you, prince? They look so meager that it seems a wasteful expenditure to board her," I said as we tacked landward.

"Our holds are not full as like to burst but not so empty as to demand feeding today." He grinned and his dark voice rumbled.

"We'll not board her then, since she is too small to be carrying anything of real interest to us. Besides, we make for Marseilles. We'll sell and trade well enough before the winter storms begin."

I never saw clouds gather so quickly. There was a swirl of darkness, obscuring the sun, and a sudden cool wind from the north rattled our sails.

"Ready to come about," I called, and leaned with all my weight on the wheel. "Adju, can we catch this new wind and will it take us beyond the danger of the rocky shallows?"

But before he could reply, a swell pushed us back toward shore, and another breached the rail, knocking some of the men on deck off their feet. Adjullo jumped down to the deck to make certain none were lost. The wind crossed the direction of the current obliquely, so the ship shuddered, shifted, and the wheel went suddenly soft in my hands.

The swells had grown so tall so quickly that we were in real danger of rolling if we could not turn the bow into them. But the shallow surf churned and the sails fluttered frantically; they could not catch the wind. Across our port bow I saw the little cog coming perilously close to the rocks that formed the cove's southern boundary. The wind was toying with the little boat like a particularly mean little boy with a toy he'd grown tired of, spinning it idly before deciding how to smash it to bits. Its shallow draft was no match for the storm and the current. The last I saw of it, a wave picked it up and hurled it on the rocks. Her passengers were spread out across the churning gray-green water, clinging onto broken bits of her hull.

This terrible sight distracted me. I didn't see the massive swell at my back that rolled the *Black Phoenix* over. She was tossed on her side. I watched as my men were swept into the gray chop and fought nobly against the angry brine. Lupo, dangling high in the rigging, was tossed into a rocky shallow like a doll thrown away in a fit of pique. With the wind roaring our doom in my ears, I hung on to the rail for a moment. I cast about in mounting frenzy but saw only one figure: a youth who found a timber to cling to, riding the crest of the surging surf. He gasped, fainted, and began to slide under. I dove into the angry churn after him. It wasn't safe to stay with the ship; we'd be ground to pulp on the rocks if we did. But if we could swim into the sandy cove, we'd have a chance. The boy was barely conscious. I swam as hard as I've ever swum, one arm across his chest, the other pulling the foaming gray water under me. Finally the swells carried us to the shore, and in two pounding tumbles, we were thrown onto the beach, sputtering and choking.

I pulled the boy up the shingle, and pressed the water from his belly. He gasped suddenly, opened his eyes and called, "Viola!" He choked, vomited seawater down his front, and, blinking, tried to look at me.

"What—who—" He couldn't speak. His eyes rolled heavenward as his head lolled back. I drew him toward the shelter of some trees, and pressed his chest, to make sure he kept breathing. I sat with his head against me, wrapping my arms around him for warmth, and waited for the storm to move down the coast.

I must have fallen asleep, sitting there with this boy in my arms, propped up under one of the scrub pines that lined the beach. Dawn checkered the eastern clouds with its pale greeting. The sea and sky were glassy calm. My mouth and throat were parched. My arms and back ached from holding this boy all through the night's storm. He snored quietly, peacefully. Heat from our bodies had nearly dried our clothes. I looked about us to see any familiar landmarks, but found nothing I knew. I decided to let this boy sleep as long as he could. I dared not leave him lest he awake and not know where he was and how he came to be there. I'd find some kind of provision once I knew his name.

But my shoulders ached so, I had to shift, and this movement roused him. His eyelids fluttered slightly and he squinted against the growing light.

"Viola—where is—who are you? Am I— Where am I?" He started up for a moment, then fell back into my arms and looked up into my face. I held him gently.

"You are safe now. Rest easy a moment. You are on a beach in a small duchy called Illyria. Your boat capsized and was broken to bits in the storm last night. I am Antonio. I pulled you from the sea." He smiled at me. Who was this boy, I wondered, who could smile into the face of a stranger at such a moment?

"I am grateful to you, sir. Can you tell me if you saw others from my boat? I traveled with my sister, my twin." He tried to sit up, as if to turn and face me, winced, changed his mind, and settled back against my chest as I spoke to him.

"And her name would be Viola. You called her name in the night, in your distress. No, I am sorry to say I did not see her, nor could I see any other travelers from your boat. But I was not in a position to scan the spoils of the storm, being in distress myself. I've lost my ship and all my comrades, I fear." My throat closed and I could not speak further.

His sobs shook us both. He left his arms at his sides, he hardly moved in fact, as he sobbed, only his chest and belly, heaving with sorrow. Finally, through his tears he spoke.

"My sister and I are the last of our line. If it is true that I've lost her, I am alone in the world. I wonder if I am truly grateful to you, a rescuer who puts me back in the world to face it alone. Your arms have warmed me; have kept the breath moving through my body. Can I hold onto you? I need to hold onto someone. Antonio. You are Antonio. These are your arms. That is the sun and the sea. I do see them, and feel you, and that is all I can manage."

I tried to slow my breathing and clear my mind. This boy's speech was obscure and his look was imploring.

"That is all you need to manage in this moment." I held him across his chest with one arm, and brushed his dark hair from his forehead with the other. "Take time now. Here is what we must do, but only when you are ready. I know this country a little, though it would be grievous peril to show my face within the city walls. First we must find sustenance, and possibly a change of clothes. Then we must try our fortune in finding others who survived this storm. Agreed?"

"Yes. Agreed. But first," he reached up and drew my head down toward his and found my mouth with his. I pulled away at first, so surprised at this. His kiss was insistent and warm and long when only moments ago he sobbed for the loss of his sister.

"I hope you don't think me impertinent, sir. You have my gratitude forever."

"Impertinent? No. It is just—you surprise me."

"It is not that I do not feel my grief, it is that I feel drawn to you, more." He turned and knelt as he looked into my eyes. "Your arms fished me from the sea, held me. Can I find my strength with you?"

His ardor was persuasive but the disorder of my thoughts claimed my attention. I tried to think.

"We'll find provisions first, and speak of other matters later. Just now I'm as homeless as you, handsome one. What say you to this: we'll cleave together and see what we can make of things. Can you walk?"

"I think I can. I feel no injury, no weakness, only hunger and terrible thirst."

"On, then, we'll find our way toward the city."

The youth still had a pouch on his belt, and some coins remained. Mine was still with me, too. The morning sun warmed the stiffness from my joints as we found our way through the low pines. We came upon two ruts in the sand, these turned into a path, and eventually a road. As we walked, he said little of himself, and he asked me about my ship. Occasionally he'd stop and look round at me. He pulled my arm, and as I stopped he put his hands on my chest, as if to assure confirm my corporeality. He looked up into my face and smiled a sweet, beguiling smile. He pressed his head against my shoulder, squeezed my arms, and then turned to resume our march. He was like a puppy declaring his lifelong fidelity. I felt myself awakening to a wonder I'd not known in the years since I'd lost Rodrigo.

Without ever needing to know that it was happening, I'd traded places. This beautiful boy's insistence forced me to see that a transformation had taken place. I had grown from Rodrigo's boy to his mate, sure, that I had felt and known and celebrated. That was possible because Rodrigo felt and knew and celebrated with me. But in the six years without him the strength of his absence granted me the license not to know myself. It granted me the license not to know much of anything. That is how my grief lived through me: I need not know anything.

This boy, his beauty and his need, worked to shock that complacence. For years I had no longer been the youth Antonio, then no longer Rodrigo's mate. What ever makes it possible to feel the changing of the roles one must play? What forces a man to know it? The lines around my eyes, the heaviness of my chest and arms, the flecks of gray in my beard, the hair that curled over the top of my soiled linen shirt, all these things drew this boy to me. As I began to understand this, to feel it, to feel anything, the boy in me protested, "Who will hold me now if I am to hold this youth? Who will protect me now if this youth looks to me for protection?"

Urgently in need of food, I pushed this yearning away. I could not make sense of this on an empty stomach. But whenever I looked to this boy, he'd throw his arm around my neck and press his cheek against mine.

"But you haven't told me your name, young one."

"My name—I am called—Rodrigo."

"No—what chance is there that your name could be that?" Scarlet rose steadily from his neck to his hairline. "Boy, your complexion is not a liar's ready accomplice. But no matter." I looked to the horizon. I felt no need to withhold my story from him. "I loved a Rodrigo once, who loved me well. And I lost him in a battle at sea. A long six years ago, now. You don't look like a Rodrigo to me, boy."

"That I cannot help. My father gave me that name, and I bear it proudly."

He spoke a bit too loudly and too fast to convince me he was telling me the truth. I cared little what his name could be, only that he felt the need to hide his real one from me. This boy was a puzzle.

"You said it was perilous for you to enter the city. Why, Antonio?"

"My Rodrigo was a corsair, and so am I—or so I was, I should say. Our ship was the *Black Phoenix*. For many years the Duke Orsino's merchant ships were easy prey for a swift vessel like ours, like an open bazaar for us. The duke's men were halfhearted in defense of their cargo. They cared little, and we never took all, only a portion. It was more like doing business than playing the pirate. Once, though, they put up a fight. It was a battle I'll regret forever, with a ship called the *Tiger*. It was said that a nephew to the duke lost a leg and that I was responsible. And so I am known to the duke, all too well, and to his men."

The track had turned into a road, and ahead appeared five guardsmen on horses and they cantered toward us. Their livery announced their status as Orsino's men. So soon was I to face the risk of my gamble. It was true that many of Illyria's seafaring men knew me, including captains of Orsino's galleys, but whether my likeness had been circulated among his guards was another matter. They'd certainly already seen us, so trying to hide was stupidly futile. We stood to the side of the road as they passed, but one of them, an officer, fixed his eyes on mine. I heard him call out to his men. He sent them on. He reined his horse up and wheeled back to where we stood.

As he drew nearer, I wanted to recognize this figure: this silhouette was known to me, but I could not think how. I began to make out his coloring: a red beard, run through with silver now, but red showing through, and red hair, and the eyes that seemed always to have a

Gil Cole

question in them. Tomasso pulled his horse up to a stop and addressed us.

"Strangers, I wager you've suffered some near distress. You are not known hereabouts, I think?"

"We are strangers here, it is true. The storm has done its worst to us. With no resources and in need of succor we are thrown on this land."

"You, sir, take a grave risk visiting this country, I think. Do you not?"

My fears were booted.

"You speak as if you know me."

"I am certain I know you, and you know me. You are the Captain of the *Black Phoenix*. Your vessel is known to the duke, but your face is known to me. If your ship has met the fate I think it has, the duke will be pleased. He'll be more than pleased to see the man responsible for so much trouble brought before him. I'm surprised you dare to show yourself here, Tonio"

"Tomasso. Our paths have crossed again, and again you wield the power."

He slid from his saddle and approached me. His look was appraising, as it had been so many years ago. I met his gaze coolly. The youth stood aside silently, his eyes all questions. Finally, Tomasso clasped my shoulders, tears filled his eyes, and he embraced me.

"I had long given up the hope that I'd be able to ask your forgiveness for the wrong I did you." I stood still, and he bowed his head as he wept. "I was poisoned, poisoned with my need. I mistook my need for love and I acted to protect what I thought I could keep and hold to myself. Instead I lost everything. I lost Rodrigo, my life on our ship, Matteo and Pato. Speak, Tonio, can you forgive me?"

"Long ago, Tomasso, I forgave you long ago. I was the lucky one, for I found Rodrigo again, and lived in his love for many years."

"The exploits of the *Black Phoenix* made their way to me, and with each tale, each bit of news, I felt the sharp bite of envy, knowing that your love held fast. You know you take the gravest risk, walking this sandy track in Illyria. You cannot stay here. And who is this handsome boy in your company?"

124

"Slowly now. We are in need of food and drink and dry clothes. I'll gladly tell you all, but first we must rest and eat and drink. I know that in Illyria there is safe haven for us at the Elephant."

"But the harbor keeps no secrets long and you'd not be as secure as I would wish you. My house is the place. It is modest but well and truly safe, and provided with all you need for the moment. The path to my cottage is at the bottom of this rise ahead of us. Come."

We made our way toward his turning. He walked his horse, carrying the reins in one hand and rested the other on my shoulder. I took my young Rodrigo's arm.

"This is another Rodrigo, a youth whose boat was destroyed in last night's storm. I pulled him from the churn, and we spent the night on the sandy margin of the sea. He seeks news of his sister, his traveling companion. Has knowledge of their fate reached your ears?"

"Alas no, but that tells us little of her actual fate."

"We shall have more of that anon, but what of you? I am amazed. That it should be you to meet us here. How long has Illyria been your home?"

"Oh, it must be the better part of twelve years," Tomasso answered. "I could not bear to serve on another's ship, so I turned to the army. I had no connections, but found protection from the old captain of the guard, a man who fancied me, and gave me respite when I had none. I could not love him, but I am grateful to him always. I am now an officer of the duke's guards. It is not a bad life. I keep this cottage away from the city and the barracks to find a little peace. But you, Tonio, you are notorious in this land. What am I to do with you? I'd be a made man if I took you before the duke this instant." He chuckled as he said this. "You have nothing to fear. Orsino is far too distracted with his bootless quest for the love of a great lady who shuns him. He's not a force to inspire any fear. And you have my protection. Just have a care. Not all of Orsino's men are so disposed. Come in."

He opened the low arched door of his cottage, and walked straight to the hearth where he set to stirring up a fire.

"Pull your boots off and set them to dry here. Water is there." He pointed to a barrel in a corner. "When you are ready for something more restorative, there is a flagon of Madeira on that table. Refresh yourselves. Not the finest, not such that we'd find on the Canary route, but good enough in this little duchy. And there is some cold meat there, too. Eat and rest."

The boy Rodrigo drank from the ladle he found hanging by the barrel. He handed it to me. Then I filled two goblets with the wine and found the covered dish that sheltered a haunch of mutton. We fell to it without hesitation, heaving ourselves into the chairs he'd drawn up to the fire. Tomasso smiled broadly, watching us eat as if we hadn't seen food in weeks. He had poured himself a small beaker, leaned back, and put his feet up on the hearth.

"So, what can you tell me, what of our Rodrigo?"

"You did not learn his fate? I thought the word would pass quickly along all our routes."

"I heard only that the Venetians fired on the *Black Phoenix* at Otranto, that you took heavy damage to the stern, and that Rodrigo was killed. I chose not to believe the last. I hoped that I'd live to see him, to feel his embrace once again. I prayed he made you captain to hide himself from the duke's more ambitious men. Tell me, does he live?"

"What you heard was true. He was lost in that foolish battle."

He covered his eyes a while. I looked over at the young Rodrigo. His eyes were cast down as he slowly chewed the meat before him.

After a moment Tomasso swiped his hand across his brow.

"But now, men, what needs can I provide for? You'll rest here. My house is yours for as long as you wish it. You must plan carefully your next move, Tonio. What of the ship?"

"Indeed, that I must learn of swiftly. I will make my return to the cove and see what remains. I must know the fate of any of my men, if any braved the storm as luckily as I. And you, Rodrigo, what think you?"

"I hardly know. I will make for the city, and appeal to the court of Orsino for word of my sister. But not now. Let us stay together here awhile." He clasped my hand.

Perhaps dreading the confirmation of a grievous loss led him to wish to tarry with me. I knew, though, what I had to do.

"Tomasso, will you walk with me to the cove to seek any remains of the ship?"

"Gladly my friend," Tomasso replied, "but you'll not dare the city walls, not while you've a roof here with me."

In the slanting afternoon light Tomasso and I walked back down the path toward the cove. We walked the length of the beach that had been my bed the night before and found little of value. Timbers had begun to wash ashore, but there was no sign of a living man, no trace of my crew. I tried to calm myself with imaginings: that they managed to reach the shore farther down the coast. But I knew how much more likely it was that they lay full fathom five beneath the waves. I'll never truly know what became of them.

We stood at the edge of the beach looking out to the horizon. Grief, no longer held back, fell like a blow across my chest. All my mates, all those fine strong men, all gone. Then came the terrible inward gnawing of guilt. If I had been a better captain, alert to the sea and wind, surely my crew would know another adventure. If only I had been the man I ought to have been.

Tomasso must have seen my clouded brow. "No sign. No trace. Can this be the end of the *Black Phoenix*? What a heavy blow, my friend."

"I was a reluctant captain and a poor leader for the men. My efforts at best were halfhearted in all the time since Rodrigo was killed. Now I have failed them all. Now all are lost, what, all? I fear to think on it. What blow can shake me so to the soul? I am like as dead as all my men. Oblivion is better than this. Oblivion is before me. My path is unmarked and obscure."

Tomasso rested his hand on my shoulder. Resisting the sway of sorrow I grasped at the sprig of life that I plucked from the sea.

"This boy.... What think you of this boy?

"A beauty, to be sure. But he's hardly uttered a word in my presence. There is no mistaking that he is taken with you."

"And something within me stirs when he is near, I will confess. But I fear to trust it. Old friend, my old enemy who is now a friend, can I be taken with him? Now? Is it not unseemly? I hardly know. His eyes, yes there is something in his eyes that quickens me. I'd nearly given up that—is it longing? Is it lust? I thought never to feel that stirring again."

"You may find that you can come to life, old friend. What a comedy, to suffer shipwreck at Illyria and come again to life."

"I wonder if that could really be true. To come to life again. Friend, how long can we rest with you?"

"My home is yours. I report to the garrison this night. Stay as long as you wish. There's work for you that would readily repay a longer stay, should you wish it."

"Work would suit me well, and I rejoice that I might repay this boon."

"I'll return in ten days. It is not the rudest shelter you could find here, nor is it the finest. But you honor me by staying."

He turned and embraced me. His arms were strong and warm and welcome. I wished for a moment to rest my head on his shoulder and give over to him, to find the home I'd found in my Rodrigo years before. But somehow the face of this new Rodrigo intruded. My heart was split. Could I feel this yearning, and could I provide a haven for another's yearning, both at once? What was it that the men found in my arms when I was a boy? Did they find rest, or was their restfulness provided by the knowledge of what they provided for me? This boy's eyes shook all that once was familiar to me about myself, all was altered. I spun in a maelstrom as if swept away once again by the storm.

Then I looked up at Tomasso and the gravity of events fell upon me again. "Share we more sorrow for our mates and for our Rodrigo?" I fell to my knees, the breath knocked out of me as I spoke. Hot tears fell to my chest. Tomasso knelt beside me. His voice was low and warm.

"It is boundless as the sea, and so defies the organs of speech or the power of the mind to compass it. It cannot be spoken. If we tried to speak it, the words would taste of ashes and turn false. It is a sorrow that will be with us always. But there is room for more than sorrow. There must be. You know it now. We honor him, we honor them all, with our friendship. And you feel something new kindling within for this boy. I wish it were for me, handsome one. You wear your years uncommonly well, you know."

He leaned in and kissed me. The wonder of a man's mouth on

mine. It was true: it was possible once again to come to life. I held him as our mouths combined, breathing in his smell of sweet pine and earth.

"Tomasso, you have me at a disadvantage. I am weak and yearning and confused. And you are fine and strong. Tell me, you must have your own lovers here in Illyria."

"There are the men I share my bed with, and there are those I love, but none with the steadfast love I knew on the *Black Phoenix*. That I could not find again. We feel this in each other now, and reach for it. Think of it, Tonio. I am here within your reach. I'll leave you now, with your boy. I must report to duty. Remember, what you knew is alive in me, still."

"Thank you, old friend."

He strode up the path toward his cottage, mounted his horse and rode into the city. I walked slowly, lost in amazement. Tomasso, this man who drugged me and cast me adrift to reclaim his place at Rodrigo's side, now willing to embrace me as a friend and lover. And sure it was that the talk of our past awakened my yearning. We shared the love of one we'd lost. Was it in his breast I might find the rest I longed for, his arms the strength I craved? I was falling and I needed to stop my fall. Tomasso? This boy? There was a stirring within me: a wish to claim something for my own, rather than to be claimed. Time, I needed time. In my distraction I shook my head and said aloud, "How could this boy have the best of me so fast?" Yet he did, and I could not account for it. Older, yes, I was older. Is that all I needed to understand? That my pleasure is found in providing now, where once I found it in seeking provision? This new stirring reached my cock as well, I was well and truly alive, and I exulted in that regained sensation. I opened the cottage door and peered into the shadows that shifted with firelight.

The youth was stretched out on the bed that occupied a corner, half obscured by a screen. He'd taken off his musky clothes, and lay under a thin coverlet. One arm covered his brow. His belly, with a tracing of fine, dark hair from his navel to his bush, rose gently with each breath. I stood watching him until he stirred slightly, opened his eyes, and spoke.

"Finally, you've come back. Was there any sign of your ship?"

"None but the leavings of an angry sea."

He said nothing. Exhaustion had drained his face. Still he held his hand out to me, and as he did, anticipation of my arrival made itself plain with the tenting of his coverlet. He pulled himself upright, knelt, and began to undress me.

I took his face between my hands. "Boy, you trouble me. Are your cares so lightly set aside?"

He said nothing as he loosed the laces at my collar.

"You set to work so readily. Do you know what you are doing? Do you know what you are playing with?"

"I know that I've wanted to do this since I saw you. That you are the man I've yearned for." He pulled my shirt over my head, unbuckled my belt, and pulled at the lacing of my breeches, which dropped to the floor.

"Youth, your cruelty is matched only by your beauty." I stepped out of my breeches and lifted his head in the crook of my arm as I kissed him. His tongue flickered in my mouth. He knew exactly what he was doing.

He laughed. "Antonio, I promise you I am not cruel. I want you badly. I owe you my life, and the only thing I can offer you is myself. You would be the cruel one to refuse me."

He dove for my cock with his eager mouth, and pulled me onto him. We wrestled and laughed. Long it had been since I laughed like this. I grabbed his middle and swung him around so our eyes met, and he nestled against my chest.

"Handsome boy, you take what you want so easily. But have a care. Once you claim me, you'll have me. I do not think you know enough to make this claim. And I'm a fool to let you have me so easily."

He stopped my mouth with a kiss. "No more. Just let me know you." He slid down in the bedclothes and found my cock again and took me in his bright hot mouth, rolling me onto my back. He reached up and found my nipples and pulled gently as he sucked. Finally I gave in to my wanting, and I reached down and rolled us over again, pushing his legs up to his shoulders, and buried my face in his round boy's backside. How I'd missed that musky fragrance of a man's inmost parts. I rooted hungrily as the boy moaned. His smell filled me with an urgent energy I'd missed, and the more I rooted into him the more I felt I wanted him. I opened him up with my tongue, then with my fingers as I looked into his eyes. Finally I pressed my cock into him. He gasped, then reached for my face and held me as I pushed into him and our eyes were locked together.

"Yes, you inside me. It is so perfect, you inside me. More. Yes."

Sweat poured off my brow and dripped onto his face. He lapped it up with his tongue and begged me to keep pounding him. Our eyes never left each other's yet I felt as if I was reaching for someone who slipped my grasp, even as we grappled together. It spurred me on, wishing to contact him more deeply, feeling him elude me, reaching for him again, until I felt my explosion coming.

"Oh God, here I come—"

He grabbed his cock and pulled on himself and shot jets of his juice as I poured myself into him. "Yes, give it to me, all of you, give it to me."

Finally I sank down and laid my head on his chest, licking the beads of liquid pearl from his body. Our breathing heavy, in unison, slowing, growing easier. The guttering fire gave the only light.

"Antonio, I have thought on it, and know now what I must do. Tomorrow I go to the court to seek my sister. I fear further delay, yet I hate the thought of leaving you."

"What? You can speak so to me now?" He toyed with me so easily, and I was such a willing plaything. I tempered my anger. "Soft now, you'll make your way to the court, but you'll return to me. You'll seek me here to tell me any news."

"Of that I cannot be sure. If I find her, I surely will stay with her."

The treachery of youth's blithe selfishness was fully revealed. I saw myself in this boy, the boy I was long ago, and I knew that he simply could not help it; he could not know how heavy the blow that fell on me with the simple words he uttered. But he knew enough to stop my mouth, and my ability to think. He leaned in to kiss me, and I was silenced. There was to be a night with this boy, the pleasures of this night I could accept, or I could mar with my objections. I struggled with my yearning and chose not to think what lay before me. I left unplanned any action beyond this night, though an absence of a plan cleared the space for one.

Our eyes were closed now, and we drifted into a soft sleep, nestled into each other. I held the boy who brought me back to life as if I held the most precious treasure I'd yet encountered. I drowsed with the sweet smell of his sweat in my nose, intoxicated. In my intoxicated state I could have no knowledge of the slough of danger I had just fallen into, a danger greater than any I'd faced since we washed ashore in Illyria.

⊕

I can hardly credit my memory as a reliable source to aid me as I tell the events that followed. With growing velocity, my bearings were loosed and I knew not where I stood. It was as if I was a character in a story told by another.

I know not why or how, but the boy's treachery seemed to grow in the night. He spoke but little when we rose. He dressed and ate quickly.

Finally he said, "I go to seek my sister at the court. This is our parting."

Only that. I was dumbfounded. I sputtered, "Will you leave me so unsatisfied? What, no other words for one you wanted with such heat? Nor will you not that I go with you?"

He begged my patience. He spoke to me as one speaks to an old man who must be soothed. He claimed it a kindness to shield me from the malignancy of his fate, as if mine could be distempered further than it would be with his parting.

And yet I protested, "Let me yet know of you whither you are bound."

And he refused. His every speech seemed calculated to make me despise him. In a tone of patronage, as if from some high noble station, he complimented my modesty. My modesty. This from the boy whose tongue reached deep inside me scant hours before, who begged me to pound him senseless in our fucking. But the course of this youth's innocent treachery did yield truth at last.

He offered, "You must know of me then, Antonio, my name is Sebastian, of Messaline, named for my father whom I know you have heard of."

I had indeed heard of his father, a wealthy trader. Thus began the imperious strain of revenge's dire music. The *Black Phoenix* had plundered some of his father's trade in years gone by. And now the youth plundered my heart; armed with what he'd learned as he listened so intently to Tomasso and me, armed with youth's cruel indifference and need.

He went on, "He left behind him myself and a sister, both born in an hour. If the heavens had been pleased, would we had so ended! But you, sir, altered that, for some hour before you took me from the breach of the sea was my sister drowned."

He spoke with a dignity that would move a post, and yet I could abase myself even further. I begged him to pardon me for his bad fortune.

"Fortune lost many times over, and more if I seek not any word of my sister."

"I shall help you. I have trod the path of one who sought to be reunited with one he loved. I know whereof you grieve."

"I shall go alone. I'll wager there is a bounty on the head of the captain of the *Black Phoenix*."

At this I stiffened and looked sharp. Could he be so willing to use what he knew of me freely, as if I was little more than a pawn whose sacrifice he'd hardly notice? And still the wily youth tried to melt me with a kiss.

"Nay, I jest. Fear not, I will not disclose your deliverance, for you have provided mine and set me on my course."

Perhaps the wiser course was to stay close to one who could be so treacherous.

"If you will not murder me for my love, let me be your servant." My desperation shocked both of us.

He spoke with a warmth that reached me, "If you will not undo what you have done, that is, kill him whom you have recovered, desire it not. Fare ye well at once. My bosom is full of kindness, and I am yet so near the manners of my mother that, upon the least occasion more, mine eyes will tell tales of me." He turned to hide his tears. Over his shoulder he called, "I am bound for the Duke Orsino's court. Farewell." He strode up the path to the city without a backward glance.

When I saw the tears spring to his eyes, my heart leaped, and my trap was baited as sure as death. Surely, I told myself, such tears were impossible in the eyes of a dissembler. In a flash my way was clear to me. I would detain him no longer, but I would follow him, and brave the certain danger that crouched within the city walls. To the tavern on the harbor, the Elephant, stealthily I made my way.

The Elephant was a haven for the rougher among us, and those that ran on the far side of the law found solace and safety there. I knew I'd find some protection and time to plan what next I might do. It was the kind of protection only those with no connection, no wherewithal, could afford. The tavern was on the water, and the salty air had weathered its timbers outside. The smoke of fires laid in a hearth with a balky chimney blackened the walls inside. The low ceiling was hung with lanterns that gave a clotted yellow light. It was a place of shadows, even in the brightest midday, shadows that seemed to promise protection.

The Elephant beckoned for another reason. It was haven to men who sought their pleasures with men and there they found each other. Illyria's laws did not pursue us with the vigilance of other cities, but the custom of the town was to render certain boundaries clearly. So long as these boundaries were understood and not breached, men and their boys could enjoy each other well. Even guards in Orsino's employ found entertainment at the Elephant, I'd wager. But part of the custom was to respect the fact that once out of uniform, they were no longer Orsino's men.

The mistress of the house had a thick beard of dirty gold entwined with silver. He was a big-bellied tar who had taken to skirts when he left the sea. He offered a special kind of mothering that deferred many a fight and soothed many a broken heart. And when all else failed, the strength of his arm could stop the most impassioned of the low-life who called his tavern home. His name once was Stephano, but in his skirts he was called Phoebe. To shun his embrace was to court a gale of complaint and the most withering of glances.

"Aha, a handsome stranger, come, embrace your mother." Though he reeked of ale already, so early in the day, I obeyed his command. He gave me a smacking buss and regarded me closely. "But I know you, don't I? I want to remember this face. Is it possible that you have never found your comfort in these walls?"

"Phoebe, I'll confess it gladly, I have enjoyed your company before, but not for these many years. Your keen eye is confounded by time. I was here last with my Rodrigo, of the *Black Phoenix*. But he and that fine ship are gone, and I throw myself on your good offices. I am Antonio, a youth when last you saw me, now a man brought low by love and ill fortune."

"Handsome one, sit and tell me everything. Will you eat and drink?"

"Neither for the nonce." I paused and he looked at me expectantly. I was to provide his entertainment on a lazy afternoon. "Oh, my story is common and tedious. You've heard a version of it a thousand times. I wait here to find a way to see my Sebastian. A beautiful youth I pulled from the stormy sea only hours hence."

"Is it tedium to pull a beautiful youth from an angry sea? I think not, my duck. This is your melancholy speaking. But you speak as if you were a miser dispensing precious specie, coin by measly coin. More, give me more, man; mother wants to know everything of importance. Is your Sebastian fair or dark?"

"Pale, perfect skin of alabaster, against which his dark curls invite a man to drown himself in a sweetness known only by the well favored. Clear eyes that do not flinch, but meet a loving, lusting gaze with ease. He may have a warm heart, but his head seems always cool. This youth knows exactly how to play with the passion he excites."

"You give your mother chills, and for that you deserve some sustenance. Here, this is newly brewed and has a chewy round goodness. Not every ruffian can taste this."

Phoebe poured me a tankard of dark ale and slid a plate of cheese in front of me. We were alone in the tavern, and as I spoke I found that to eat and drink was welcome.

"Now, what do you propose to do about this lovely?"

"My way is not clear. He seeks out his sister, fearing she was lost in the storm that brought us together. This is our business in the city. I'm a wanted man by the duke, and it is to the duke that Sebastian makes his way. I must find a way to keep close to the boy while avoiding the reach of his guard."

"You'll keep close here at the Elephant. There's a bed you can use in the second room above. We'll settle the bill when you've found your boy again, I won't hear talk of that now. No, save your thanks, just give us a kiss."

His beery embrace was impossible to resist and I sank into his expansive belly as he planted his lips on my mouth. He stood up to tend to three dark ruffians who claimed the table by the smoke-streaked window. I finished gnawing on a rind of cheese, drained my cup, and decided to test the narrow streets of the town.

⊕

My wary wandering was soon rewarded. I'd made my way windingly to the edge of the market square, staying in the shadows, where I spotted Sebastian as he lingered in front of a goldsmith's shop. He looked up, and I waved him to me. He carelessly strolled close and greeted me with delight, almost as if he'd expected me. His eyes darted, and I could not but wonder if his easy lightness was the sign of delight in a game of deception.

He spoke as if to soothe me, "I would not by my will have troubled you, but since you make your pleasure of your pains, I will no further chide you."

I was confounded, and my countenance showed it. It had been scant hours before that he'd been certain I must not follow him. I counted it a blessing that he would refuse me no longer.

I explained, "My willing love, the rather by these arguments of fear, set forth in your pursuit."

He thanked me and embraced me and spoke with an air of confession, "Were my worth as is my conscience firm, you should find better dealing."

At this I dared to hope again.

But then he asked, "What's to do? Shall we go see the relics of this town?"

My confusion mounted. How could it be that the former urgency of finding out his sister was so fleeting that it had given way to a wish to see the famous memorials of the city? Was what I took as sweet simplicity just another sign of the blithe selfishness of a youth? How easily he could forget the risk I took in showing my face in this street, as he prattled on about seeing the sights that brought fame to the town. He seemed to have forgotten all I told him of my misadventures at sea. And I, a fool, sunk hip deep in foolishness; I gave him my purse and told him how to find me at the Elephant, where we'd lodge together.

He agreed, too readily, and advised me, "Do not walk too open."

Can the young know how ridiculous they sound? Can the old know how ridiculous they appear when they listen to these young? He brushed my lips with a kiss, and turned into the blaze of the autumn afternoon. He had agreed to meet me, when hours before he'd resisted with all his might. In my foolishness I took this to be a measure of his love. And with a heart unburdened by the anxious care that had been gnawing at me all the day, I set out to return to Phoebe's sheltering, hairy belly to wait for Sebastian.

⊕

After a night at the Elephant I could bear no further delay. This was a cold-blooded youth indeed who could leave me with no word. In the morning I set out to find him once again. The events that followed sped in a blur; soon I felt as if I was spinning like a top, and the condition that guided these events was obscure beyond comprehension.

I picked my way with care in the shadows from the Elephant toward the center of the city. When I least expected to I saw Sebastian. I was sure it was he. He stood, as if amazed, before a whey-faced fellow who had drawn his sword in argument with him.

Without a hesitation, I pushed between them. "Put up your sword. If this young gentleman have done offense, I take the fault on me; if you offend him, I for him defy you."

Whereupon another fellow, fat and swollen with years of drink, drew on me as well, and as I went to make short work of this lunacy, easily keeping both of these bumblers at bay, two officers of the duke's arrived on the scene. I was recognized in an instant. The officers arrested me. The trap was sprung. I turned to my Sebastian, who had not called out to me in all the confusion.

"This comes with seeking you, but there's no remedy; I shall answer it. What will you do, now my necessity makes me to ask you for my purse? It grieves me much more for what I cannot do for you than what befalls myself. You stand amazed, but be of comfort."

He was silent, as if stunned, so I spoke again, "I must entreat of you some of that money."

He looked at me in wonder, as if I were a stranger. Finally he spoke, "What money, sir? For the fair kindness you have showed me here, and part being prompted by your present trouble, out of my lean and low ability I'll lend you something. My having is not much. I'll make division of my present with you. Hold, there's half my coffer."

The thoroughness of this youth's duplicity shocked me. "Will you deny me now? Is't possible that my deserts to you can lack persuasion? Do not tempt my misery, lest that it make me so unsound a man as to upbraid you with those kindnesses that I have done for you."

"I know of none." The moorings of sanity were slipping away. "Nor know I you by voice or any feature."

Though he went on speaking I could no longer take in his words. I begged those near to hear me.

"This youth that you see here I snatched one half out of the jaws of death; relieved him with such sanctity of love, and to his image, which methought did promise most venerable worth, did I devotion. But how vile an idol proves this god! Thou hast, Sebastian, done good feature shame."

At the mention of his name he looked stricken but said nothing. Despite my protests, the officers led me away. I feared my head would burst. Here was proof of what I'd kept myself from knowing: that the love of this youth was swift and changeable. But I struggled to cling to my delusion that his cruelty was innocent, that he had no knowledge of his power to hurt more deeply than a deliberate villain. That could be expected of a selfish youth. But this denial of all he'd sworn, of all we'd known together, this was beyond understanding. This brought me close to madness. Sebastian's beauty was inhabited by a devil. Could he have conspired to have me taken? Could he have lured me to my capture, trading on my good offices to insure his own good fortune? I could conclude but little else.

The duke's officers held me, scorned and manacled, until Orsino was ready to see the captured pirate in all his wretchedness. He retained a bitter fury for terrible events long past. He was implacable; I was to be imprisoned until the measure of his displeasure could be taken. I was led through Orsino's hall to my jail, and as I staggered under the weight of the chains I wore, I finally glimpsed the extent of the treachery of which that beguiling boy was capable. I saw duplicity made flesh. There were indeed two Sebastians, as like as two can be, though one walked with the crispness of a young girl, while my Sebastian had the heavier stride of the youth he was growing to be. So he had found his sister. In a brief glimpse I beheld enough to surmise the plot in which I was merely an expendable pawn. There in the court were the twin orphans, doted on and made much of by the duke and a beautiful lady of regal bearing. Capsized and lost at sea they might have been, but they certainly knew how to right themselves well enough. Beauty and smooth-tongued persuasion set them on a rising course, while I was led away into the dankness of a cell.

What a fool I was. A luckless, deluded fool. I was brushed aside like stray crumbs from a table. What I thought had been shared between this boy and me was as nothing. I saw him cooing with this lady like a bridegroom with his new wife and knew how utterly uncomprehending he was of what he meant to me. Had I for a moment meant something—anything— to him? What a performance he'd given. Perhaps he'd still claim that I did mean all the world to him. But it was no more than a momentary madness. More like the lightning that doth cease to be ere one can say, "it lightens." My usefulness to him was finished.

There was nothing to resist any longer. That was the last I ever saw of Sebastian, the boy I thought had brought me back to life. I had been brought to something, of that I was certain. I was alive, but worn and wracked with confusion. Not fit for the tidings of that day. Brother and sister reunited, fortunes made, marriages celebrated. I was excess, an inconvenience and a criminal to be disposed of. The duke's heavy guard led me to a cell more appropriate for a violent criminal than the crumpled poppet that stumbled mute before him.

$\oplus$

The disposition of prisoners seemed to have become a means whereby power proclaimed a message to the world. The lord exercised his will to lock men up and his manner of so doing displayed the quirks of his appetite. It was well known how in Mantua, for example, the Gonzaga palace sported iron cages on its outward walls, and thus did Francesco and Isabella display their enemies' failures to the world. Their heavy sentences expanded to include what insults the weather and the contemptuous rabble could levy. In Illyria, Orsino's prison cells offered a more modest detention in the underground level of the garrison, adjacent to his palace. More private, to be sure, but the isolation extracted a cost as dear as public ridicule. The guard's station was at the center, like the hub of a wheel, the prisoners' cells opened off the narrow hallways that formed its spokes. With this configuration, the fewest guards could keep watch over the highest number of prisoners. But prisoners were always to know they were watched. In my cell there was a small crescent-shaped opening at the edge of the vaulted ceiling that let in a sliver of light at midday. The light traced a shallow arc across the straw on the floor. The straw was there to soak up any stray fluids, water, blood, piss, and it was not changed very often so it retained a rank, sour smell. There was a narrow cot strung with rope that supported a canvas bag stuffed with more old sour straw. Prisoners were fed twice a day, gruel in the morning, and a thin kind of stew in the evening, with a mug of water. The guards had little cause to speak to me, and I found little reason to speak to them.

The first day I do believe I expected to see Sebastian. How readily our fancies conspire against our better natures. Every nerve strained to notice, nay, to effect his coming. I attended to the slightest variation in the sounds outside my cell's door. As if I could stretch the extent to which my ears could pick up a sound, I made myself see the stone steps that led to the dungeon, the masonry archway to the garrison, the walk paved with flagstones, between a stand of poplars, from Orsino's palace to the garrison, as if by seeing each of these places in my mind in as much detail as I could render them, I could also be able to hear any activity, any sounds that the footfall of a person would make. I strained to tell the difference between the heavy tread of a guard, his shin weighted by the grieve strapped around it, slowing his step, and the lighter tread of a leather boot worn by a youth. My listening was a way of willing him to come to me.

These thoughts wove a cocoon around me, a tight hold of hope against the growing certainty that he would not come. That his love, what he'd called his love for me, was a bright momentary efflorescence that was extinguished by the time he'd encountered his insistent lady and weighed his worldly progress against my fate. The webbed cocoon held me fast in torment. My Sebastian took a wife. More accurately, a wife took my Sebastian, and he, beautiful, susceptible boy, was in love with being taken. My torture mounted: I'd allowed him to know—how could I not allow him to know this—that he'd taken me. Perhaps that was my mistake. Perhaps he wished to know only that he was the one taken, claimed. Perhaps knowing that each takes, that each claims the other upset his delicious sense of being taken. Perhaps for Sebastian, this sense of being taken, of being plucked from the sea and claimed, had to remain untainted by knowing of his power to take, to claim.

I lay on the narrow cot, my thoughts wrapped in this tight cocoon of suspense, willing Sebastian to come to me and to prove me wrong. Willing myself to deny Sebastian's open betrayal. I could not hear the snorts and grumblings that punctuated the tedium of a prisoner's day, but I strained to hear any sound beyond these vaults, all my attention trained on the slightest sound that would tell me he was coming. My ears were so attuned to the distance that I hardly noticed the low voice calling my name just over my head, through the bars at the opening of my cell's door.

"Tonio, for God's sake, awake. Come on, man, bestir yourself!"

I looked up and saw Tomasso's face through the bars.

"You've been rash and foolish, and I'm not at all certain I can provide a remedy. Listen, I have no time. I hold command of the prison guard tomorrow night. Is there a place you can hide in the city until conveyance beyond our walls can be arranged?"

"Y-yes, I—yes. But—"

"Shhh—nothing more. If this can happen, it will happen in the darkest night, between two and three bells. Be ready, for I can make no noise to rouse you."

"Tomasso, I—"

"No more. Tomorrow night."

The clank of three men's armor echoed in the vaults at the changing of the guard. I heard them salute their superior and pass to the guard's station at the hub of the stone warren, where their voices blurred in raucous chatter.

⊕

There was only the flickering of a lantern at the guard's station, and the hoarse wheezing of snores. I heard two bells strike and waited. I stood next to the door to my cell, peering through the bars. The clank of the thick tumblers in the heavy door at the top of the stone stairs alerted me that Tomasso was as good as his word. His steps were light, measured. The guard's snoring changed, as if roused for a moment, then sank back into the lulled rhythm of oblivion. I heard quick shallow breathing next to my head as Tomasso fit the key into the lock on my door and pressed it open. Without a word he grasped my forearm and pulled me into the narrow hall, up the stairs, through the door he'd left half open. There was a pale crescent moon that cast its thin light over the poplars. He stood a moment, and I pulled him toward me to embrace him. He pressed his mouth against mine for a moment, holding me firmly at the back of my neck. Then, he pointed to a small door in the wall at the back of the garden. It was unlocked, and gave onto an alley. I looked back at him, but Tomasso had already locked the prison door and slipped back to his quarters. I saw only his shadow retreating down the path. I turned away from the duke's palace, and in the silent streets of the city, began to find my way to the quay, and to the Elephant.

The streets nearest the duke's palace were empty. I stuck to alleyways, dark in any light, but shut away from this meager moonlight by their crowding. The downward incline and the unmistakable salt smell of fishing nets drying along the quay told me I was nearing the harbor. The only light shone from the Elephant's greasy window, a shallow flicker. As I eased through the heavy door a glow from banked embers let me see that a couple of men had sunk into slumber over their cups of sack. Phoebe was nowhere to be seen, though his snores, magnificently loud, rang out over the others'. I climbed the narrow stairs to the loft where I'd taken a bed, found it to be occupied by only two others, made a place for myself by nudging them aside, and settled quickly into a black slumber of my own. Whether it was the strain of being locked up in Orsino's prison or the revelation of Sebastian's treachery that took the greater toll is useless to ponder. In a moment I was deeply asleep.

⊕

"My handsome pirate has returned to me and I bless the dawn that reveals such joy to me."

Phoebe had already roused the sots from the tavern floor and was at my side with a tankard of ale and some bread and cheese. My bedmates had apparently risen earlier, and from the look of the light streaking through the timbers of the loft, it was a blazing noon. Phoebe sat at my side and brushed the hair from my brow.

"More troubles strewn across your path, my duck?"

"More troubles indeed. The duke's men apprehended me and I spent the better part of the day and night in his fetid prison. My Sebastian, willing to make his way in the world with scant regard to the wreckage he might leave behind him, has betrayed me and I am forgotten entirely. I am undone. Can you hide me here until I can hatch a plan to make my way beyond the city walls? None of the duke's men take their ease here, do they?"

"By all the storms at sea they had better not. They tend to ignore my little establishment and those in my charge. Those few of the duke's men who have found comfort here have good reason not to make it known that they do. You are safe with me for the time. Here, eat a bit."

He set the plate of bread and cheese on my chest as if I were an invalid he was nursing back to health. I drank deeply of the ale, looking for ease in the mingled flavors of hops and grain.

"Have you any friend you can go to, my hearty?"

"All my friends these many years were my crew on the *Black Phoenix*, and I know not where they may be. It was a ferocious storm that smashed us to bits, and I fear their bones are mingled with the coral at the bottom of the sea. For lack of any other choice, I think I'll try my way across Lombardy toward Venice. I had a friend once, many years ago, as a youth in Florence. He left me there and made his way to Venice. Perchance my old friend still lives. But I have no money, no horse, no garments, even, to warm me from the chill."

"You'll not be moving until you are provided for, that is settled."

From the tavern door below a voice called out.

"Innkeeper! Anyone there? Hey ho!"

It was Tomasso's voice. Phoebe started to heave himself up with a look of annoyance on his face.

"That is a friend. He's a captain of the duke's men, but it was he who sprung me from Orsino's cage. Let him come up, will you, my ministering angel?"

Phoebe loved to be known as just such a celestial one, and he bent down and bestowed a beery, motherly kiss on my brow.

"Patience below, my good man, patience."

He made his way delicately down the steps.

"Now, my handsome captain, how can I help you?"

"Is he above? Surely he is. Let me pass, I have only a moment."

"He tells me you are his rescuer, and for that you have my thanks as well. He is above. Will you take some refreshment as long as you are my guest?"

"Nothing, I cannot tarry, but thanks to you, mother."

Tomasso took the stairs three at a time and was standing above me in a trice. He threw a pouch swollen with coins on my belly.

"You know the easternmost gate to the city? The road through it takes you to a path to my cottage, five miles from the city walls through a copse of poplars. There is a mare in the stable. Take her. She's not the spryest, but still able to walk steadily as long as you don't worry her too much, and water her regularly. She is yours. There is a cloak and a fresh doublet in the cabinet nearest the bed. They are yours."

He knelt beside me, set the plate on the floor, and embraced me.

"You bloody, incomprehensible fool. You might have been safe with me, but now I'm in danger too, because of the rashness of your love for that boy. You seem unwilling to take care of yourself. I cannot do any more to help you, but I give you my love to send you on your way. Tonight. The last patrol along the quay is at one bell. You'll have no trouble walking to the eastern gate."

I held fast to his arm. He leaned over and kissed me. I tried to speak.

"No, Tonio, no need, no time, for more."

He stood up and was gone.

⊕

All was provided as he'd promised, and as the sky began to brighten with the approaching dawn I was mounted on the chestnut mare ambling along the coastal path toward the frontier between Illyria and Lombardy. Alone, knitted up in a web of care, I bewailed my outcast state.

The Countess

The sun sank low behind me. My tired mare shambled into her shadow as she clomped along a rutted road. A scarred and pitted landscape exposed the ruins of vineyards and farmland ground under the boots of soldiers. Fields that bore scant traces of crops that once grew there were blasted barren, strewn with the telltale wreckage that man's insatiable appetite for killing things leaves behind. In place of vines heavy with grapes there were still remnants of bones scattered and picked clean by scavengers. No longer at war in myself but straying through fields of the wars of men, I sat my mount listlessly, lost in melancholy, nearly hoping to be roused from my stupor by some passing brigade or accosting brigand.

The sound of a coach, jouncing along at a brisk clip, came up behind me. The coachman shouted for me to pull my mount off the road to let the countess's coach pass. It took me a moment to come to myself, to understand the human language that stirred the air. I had heard no person's words for a day and a half. The blare of the man's voice shook me out of my trance, but it took some moments to comprehend just what had been demanded of me. I turned the horse about and stared at the coach a moment, then geed her up through the low gorse bushes at the side of the road. The coachman flicked his whip smartly and his team stepped quickly. They passed within a few feet of me. The coach was richly made, oxblood-colored leather with golden trim. A coat of arms I couldn't really make out, but I could have sworn there were the flaming wings of a phoenix encircled by a wreath of laurel. The coach was closed, its windows covered by curtains, though a slim hand held one aside, and a woman's profile, veiled, was clear to me. The coach raised a billow of dust. I waited a moment for it to blow aside, then brushed my mare's flanks with my heels and turned her head onto the road again.

The coach slowed to a stop. The driver stepped down from his bench and stood at the door, nodding. He gestured toward me, looked in my direction and shook his head. He walked up to his first team and held one of his horses by its bridle, apparently waiting for me to catch up to them. My heart quickened, less from apprehension of some danger than in happy anticipation of human contact. I urged my horse into a canter.

"Sir, my lady wishes a word with you," the coachman called out to me as I reached the back of his equipage.

"Gladly. So I may address your lady with the deference she clearly deserves, can you tell me who honors me with her summons?"

"Know you not her ensign?"

"Distinctive though it is, I am a stranger to these parts, and languish in ignorance."

The lady's voice called to me from behind her curtain.

"Enough, no more. Dismount and stand before me. I long to see that face again."

The sound was lower in timbre, weighted by the passing years, but the distinctive voice could belong to no one but my old friend and rescuer, Catarina.

"Look at me, handsome one. Do you not know me?"

"It took only a moment to realize it was you, but you must admit that the years have marked us both." I grasped the gloved hand that she held out to me from the open door of the coach and kissed it.

"Well, by all the gods, it is you, Antonio. Another miracle winds our paths into one braid. By the forlorn cast of your eyes I know you are once again thrown to the mercy of the wide world. And I again can provide you succor. But my time is precious. Tie your horse to the coach and climb in with me. I demand that you tell me everything, and in my turn, you will learn all of me."

⊕

"So you see, my long lost one, I am adrift in sorrow now, too. I took another husband, and another husband was taken from me." She looked out of the window of the carriage for several moments, seeming to forget that I sat near her, forgetting that she was a part of this world still. She shuddered. "But this time I'm better provisioned to withstand the vagaries this world visits upon us. You'll find yourself comfortably welcomed."

"Of that I had no doubt. But Paolo was not weighted with a county when we met in Genoa, all these years ago."

"He became a count upon the death of his elder brother. His beauty and skill had captivated me already, and I was hardly interested in entering into another marriage. What we offered to each other was straightforward then, and we had no need to make another arrangement. He'd told me his family was well appointed. Modesty rather than secrecy, I think, led him to leave out certain facts. So when Maximilliano was carried off by fever, and the responsibility for the family's domain fell upon him, Paolo was actually worried that I'd leave him. My dear one could never quite accept that his beauty had such an impact on the world. There is little that is so beguiling, I think, than a beautiful man who is blissfully unaware of the power of his beauty. Utterly unmarred by the impulse to exploit what has been granted by nature. The popinjays and posers at court who make these attempts curdle whatever appeal they might have had in an instant."

"But what of your fortunes now in this time of constant war?"

"Oh, there are pauses in the argument, and even the pitched conflict is not so difficult to navigate. Paolo's family has always been associated with the Sforzas, staunch allies so near and so powerful. And the Medicis are not so interested in nettling their neighbors as they are in calming the affairs of their own city. Supported as they were by the Spaniards, they've enjoyed their restoration. No, it is Ludovico's behavior toward Venice that is a mystery to me, and has proved to be my opportunity. Some time ago the Serene Republic boldly acquired Cremona, too close to Ludovico's playground not to have been the most brazen provocation. They had to be taught a lesson, and for a time the League of Cambrai aligned smaller powers in a larger bloc." Her eyes beamed with enthusiastic fervor. "The ideal

And that unctuous manner does not suit you or our situation." He bowed and disappeared through an archway. She led me to a smaller chamber where several chairs covered in embroidery gathered around a table. A richly carved sideboard presented a tray of goblets and a highly wrought silver pitcher for wine. She poured for us both.

"You are weary, I know. Refresh yourself, and I will take you to your room." She held my face in her hands and leveled her gaze into mine. Her gloves were beautiful sheathes that could not disguise the twists and thickening of her once slender fingers. Yet her face seemed hardly to be etched by that cruel tax collector, time. Her eyes, though, had a steely hardness I'd never known before.

"It pleases me very much that our paths have crossed. Our stars, it seems, are eccentric travelers, leading us to fortunes so wildly disparate and homes so far apart. Once I could offer you the paltry help of a comedian who'd ascended to the stage from the brothel. Hardly an auspicious transposition. Now I can help you in a far greater way, and you can help me, more perhaps than you'd ever imagined you could. But more of that after dinner. I'll show you up."

We walked through another vaulted doorway, into the vast entry hall, to the wide stone stairway leading to the floors above. Slices of late afternoon light drew diagonals through high narrow arches paned in yellow glass across the burnished marble floor.

As we climbed the stairs, she spoke over her shoulder. "I'll bring you some of Paolo's old linen. He was taller than you, but you've filled out quite beautifully in all these years. There are some of his things that will suit you well. When you are ready, join me below."

We stood in a long gallery, open on one side to the curved staircase she had just led me up. The other side was punctuated by torches mounted in wrought iron stanchions and large oaken doors that led to smaller private chambers. She pushed one of these doors open and turned to me.

"Take your ease. You are moored in a safe harbor now, dear one. When you are ready, follow the lit torches below to the dining hall." She kissed me and brushed my cheek with the back of her hand.

⊕

I'd done most of the talking through our evening meal, which was remarkable since I fell to it like a man who hadn't seen sustenance in days, which happened to have been true. I made short work of the roasted meats and vegetable stews that her cook had laid on for us. Whatever skill had been exercised in their preparation was lost on me, but it was the best meal I'd eaten in many days. Once I'd inhaled all I could, it seemed I couldn't talk fast enough for my teeming brain, retelling my adventures on the *Black Phoenix* as captain, the triumph of loving Rodrigo, and the losses any triumph it seems must usher onto the swelling scene. Catarina ate as she listened, with a slow, regal detachment that was her manner now. Time had not withered her, but her custom was altered by the accumulated changes in her station. She was not grand, but occupied her authority with ease; it was a thing earned well and hard. Her listening was keen but her eyes distant. My tale concluded, I drank another draught of wine.

"Alas, my Antonio, your love is sudden and deep at the same time, a combination that defies reason. This boy, this Sebastian, was not worthy of you, truly, but I trust you that he was wondrous fair, and that he may have meant every protestation that crossed his lips. I cannot help but hate him for the suffering he brought you, if for even a short time."

"Hate him not for my sake. I was susceptible and he was a deceiver. It was—is it putting too good a face on it to call it—an indiscretion? The only one who suffered was myself. I would be blessed indeed if it was the last suffering to visit me. But now I am keen to see what fortunes lie before me, for without knowing it he roused me back to life. But you spoke of a way I might help you. If there were a way I could repay even the smallest fraction of what you've given me, I would hurl myself into that service with all the celerity of thought."

She smiled with indulgence. "My Antonio. It was only my pleasure I felt when I offered you any help at all. I think you knew that. Whatever disappointment may have nettled me that you would not enjoy me as your bedmate yielded to the pleasure of our friendship. And you were really very good as a comedian. In fact, those skills you so expertly deployed on the stage may help in what I have to propose to you. You need more wine. Gianni." She gestured toward my cup and the handsome man standing ready in the shadow approached and poured. "I owe a favor to Ludovico Sforza, and I believe you are just the man to help me make things right. He has an ear in Venice, one Gerard de Norville, a physician of wide repute, from the court of Francis, and, Ludovico fears, a double-dealing rogue. He was sent to be a retaining mind and inquiring eye to record even the smallest bit of news of what the duke is planning for Ludovico. But my Milanese friend prefers never to be taken by surprise by the serene Republic again, and Ludovico fears de Norville is not to be trusted. I wish you to go to Venice, to deliver a gift to this Gerard de Norville. You may say that it comes from Sforza. That is all. Deliver the casket I will entrust to you, then wait for further instructions. You will stay in a small palace I have in Venice, and you will be comfortably provisioned."

She spoke with the insistent certainty of one used to command, as if a threat might be shrouded nearby.

"But Venice is a place where I've never set foot. And you know my ship was notorious and hunted by the duke's navy for years. If it were known that once I commanded the *Black Phoenix*, I'd be thrown into the dankest dungeon in some swampy fen to watch my flesh fall away from my bones in that foul and endless wet."

"But has your likeness been made known?" I shrugged. "I thought not," she continued. "You will merely be another man of business pursuing wealth in the teeming mercantile city."

"But how will I make my way in that city, where I know no one?"

"I will prepare the way. Whence these worries that ruffle you? Do you believe I would send you to distress and danger?" Honey was not smoother nor more golden.

I bowed my head. As I lifted my cup to drink, a face and a voice returned to me from distant years past. Even his smell came to me, despite the fragrance of the wine from Catarina's cellar. What if Franceschino were in Venice after all this time? What if he were alive? How might he look? Twelve years my senior, he would still be at the apogee of a man's life. How might he regard me, who looked so much older now than when we parted by the little church of Saint Cecilia? A faint dizziness buzzed through my brain and I could glimpse myself as a youth, nuzzling the lush beard of my lover, grasping at his thick chest, hungry for the cock I felt straining against his codpiece. The heat that rose from my chest to my brow was not the effect of that wine, but rather the spreading shame of recognition of my callow certainty in the face of Franceschino's true regard for me. His love required a painful sacrifice, and cut more deeply than a boy of eighteen could ever know. Suddenly the years swirled and grew disordered. My life at Rodrigo's side, a life that was supposed never to end, could be spanned in an instant. I felt in my arms his weight and his ebbing warmth, felt the heaving of his chest as he breathed his last, inhaling the cold, metallic smell of blood in his mouth. Then the fresher ache that Sebastian left behind, the heedless gesture of a boy who trusts that if a man says he loves him, then that man must want him to have whatever he wishes. Each of these moments another stripe of the whips and scorns of time that marks me as the man I've grown to be. Within that man, the boy still clinging to the cousin of the duke all those nights on the Old Bridge in Florence, giddy with that first love that ignited a sense of power too unreasoning and too impossible not to be the truest thing he'd ever known. Too true ever to be true again. If I did see Franceschino again, we each would encounter men who knew fatigue and sadness, one a deal older than the other, to be sure, but men who'd come to know that there is no such thing as that truth, and never was, even when it was the only thing.

"My darling boy, you have traveled many miles away from me," the countess said, her beauty and charm disguising a command to attend to her provisions and plans.

"If time were measured in miles, that would be entirely so."

"Who is it that summons you so? Is it still your wonderful pirate king?"

"It is he, and the cousin of the duke of the home of my youth, whom I told you about, and this youth I late have left in Illyria, and the youth I was, and the man I've become. All claim my thoughts yet I know not how to answer them. Or if an answer is required. Forgive my distraction. Tell me, how do you propose I make my way in Venice?"

"I have some business concerns there still. Paolo's family had an interest in a shipping firm, managed by a man who is competent enough, and serves me at my pleasure. You, I believe, can do a far better job than he. An ideal opening and vantage point, I think, from which you can make your way into Venice society. Once you deliver the casket to this man de Norville, I want you to cast your eye over the accounts of the shipping business. Turn your mind to commerce and see whether your skills can help us both. You'll do this for me, and for yourself, won't you?"

"As I have no other recourse, no ties to another, nothing to claim the restless working of my brain, what answer could I give to you but yes? I can think of no better way to make my way in the world but to turn my mind to business, even more fit as it benefits us both. And I give thanks, again thanks, forever thanks that our lives converge once more. But you will come to Venice yourself, will you not?"

"I care not for the climate. The damp makes my bones ache. Oh, it is a sad thing to grow old. But I'll give you no firm answer. It may hap that I will come to Venice, and it may be that my presence will not be necessary."

She rose from the table and walked to the huge oaken sideboard along the wall of the dining hall. She pulled open a drawer, disguised in the artfully carved vines, and drew out a plain bronze casket, fastened with a lock, and a small velvet pouch.

"Here is what I wish you to take to de Norville. The key is in this bag. You must see to it that no one open this casket but he. You are to tell him that it is a gift from Ludovico Sforza, a cordial that soothes even the most troubling aches and teeming brains. That is all. De Norville, I hear, is one of those doctors who cannot heal himself and is troubled by endless complaints. This physic that I have made for him is bound to interest him. You'll have his gratitude, I warrant you."

"But why must it be delivered by me? Why cannot one of your servants render this errand?"

"Truly, anyone might carry out this task. But I've asked you to do so. I'm surprised, Antonio. Do you balk at a request so slight? This is hardly the speed with which you promised your assent."

"I do not want to seem ungrateful or suspicious. It was a mystery to me, that is all. You need not explain. You have asked me a favor, and I will grant it. When do you wish me to go to Venice?"

"Stay with me another two days. Rest and enjoy all my house can provide you. I think you'll find Gianni is a willing bedfellow, if you like the looks of him."

"Oh, my thoughts stray not in that direction, but I thank you just the same."

"You tarry too long in your wintry gloom, my Antonio. Is this truly my friend? One who can foreswear the comforts of a beautiful young man's body? I trust a good night's rest will fill you with Zephyr's warmer spirits. I long to see the randy smile I came to know as we rambled from town to town, seeking out men's delight between our performances."

"Perhaps you are right. Perhaps finding my appetite for pleasure again is the best way to bind up the wound that deception has left in my breast."

I drained my cup and held it out for the man who had emerged at my side to fill again. He smothered a ready smile but his dark eyes flashed as they darted to mine.

"Your wine is excellent, my lady, and your supper unparalleled. But I flag, and yearn for the oblivion of sleep."

"Finish your cup and ascend. I have correspondence to finish, and I'll see you in the brightness of the morning. Linger abed as long as you wish, my darling, for my home is yours. Gianni, is our guest's chamber prepared?"

The man bowed slightly, saying, "As you've instructed, my lady."

"Very good. You are to attend the gentleman, a task I see you look forward to."

Her eyes dropped to his codpiece as she handed him the bronze casket. He retreated to the shadows that filled the dining hall and waited by the door. The wine and the change in my fortune conspired to fill my head with a giddy drowsiness. I pushed my chair back from the table and had to lean on its velvet arms to heave myself up.

"The exertions of the day, and the lavishness of your table conspire to send me instantly into the arms of Morpheus. I'll take my leave of you, my savior, my friend. I bid you good night."

"And I bid you sleep deeply, forgetting the trials you've endured. A new road lies before you. When your strength returns, so will the brightness of your eye, and the eagerness of your cock." She reached down and gave my codpiece a brisk squeeze.

"Is this the comportment of a countess?" I laughed.

"As I am a countess, and as I comport myself thus, why so it must be. I see through your censoriousness, my sweet, and will not rest content until your antic nature is restored. But now, good night. Enjoy what comes your way. That is what I charge you with. The task to enjoy."

Gianni held a taper and led me up the stairs. His powerful haunches and backside would inspire admiration from a stone. I was not calcified entirely. He lit the candles on the cabinet in my chamber. Their warm light allowed me to admire the arras behind my bed. Iolaus, peerless charioteer, victorious, held in one powerful arm by his lover Hercules who crowned him with laurel with the other. Their naked embrace so skillfully rendered in silk that the contrasting bodies, one graceful and pale with the rosy fullness of youth, the other massive, dark and hairy, heavy with the heroic accomplishments of more than two score years, seemed to burst out of the plane of the woven cloth into the room with us. The passion of the lovers was intoxicating, and clearly meant to incite a similar passion in any passing admirer. Catarina's planning was pertinent.

"May I assist you, sir?"

Gianni stood behind me, reached around, unbuckled my belt, and held it in his teeth as he drew the linen shirt over my head. He tossed it onto the bed. His hands began to knead the muscles of my neck and shoulders. They slid down my back and around my chest, grazing my nipples, then sliding down over my stomach. I smelled the warm dark scent of his breath, felt the gentle rasp of his beard, as he pressed his mouth into the top of my shoulder. I leaned back and grasped his hair, then turned to face him.

"Gianni. You must not think me ungrateful for your attentions. I am weighed down with care, and will prove paltry company for a man as fine as you this night."

He knelt to pull my boots off, looking up at me.

"Sir, I am here only because I desire to be here, to do what I can to lighten the burden that weighs so heavily upon you. It would please me beyond measure to share your bed and do nothing but sleep by your side. If you wish a bedfellow, then I am he."

I was seated on the bed and he pulled off my boots as he spoke. I leaned forward and found the comfort of his fathomless eyes.

"How could I turn such a one as you from my bed? Serve me not as a master, but ready yourself for slumber, and then let me wrap myself in your arms. But where's the chamber pot? I must piss a flagon's worth."

"We'll piss together, then. We have none of the accessories you name, but a small chamber between the inner and outer walls of the castle for such of our needs as can be accommodated there. Come, and we'll prepare ourselves."

After pissing and washing we settled into the softness of the downy mattress, throwing aside any coverlet. The warmth of our bodies sustained us through the night. I fell to sleep holding this gentle, simple man, a man I knew nought of, but that he was handsome and kind and wished to sleep at my side.

$\oplus$

The urgency of my hard cock nestled in the warmth between Gianni's thighs woke me. Rosy light of dawn sprayed the walls at the edges of the heavy draperies at the window, and, just as Catarina said, the gentle plashing of a fountain beyond the window soothed the senses. Gianni's breathing was slow and measured. His head rested in the crook of my right arm, and my left held his swarthy torso. I shifted as I looked down at his body, wrapped up in mine, and he stirred. He pushed his hips against me and smiled.

"Your cock is a fine greeting for the day, my lord."

"Not nearly as fine as finding you in my arms as I wake. No, stir not. Stay just as we are for now." Bending my face to his thick neck, I inhaled his smell. "How long have you served your lady?"

"I was a child in this castle. My lady's husband's family took my family in when they left Naples at the time the despot Ferrante first assumed power there. My family was a target for his wrath, and they had little choice but to flee. The count was very good to us, and this has been my home since I was a boy. The countess treats us well, as if we are family, not as servants. I have been content."

"Stay here." I rolled out of bed and padded to the cabinet on which the casket she gave me the night before rested, and brought it back. "What can you tell me of this? Of the countess's cordials?

"Ah. This is an interest she cultivated in her grief. She consulted with an apothecary whose craft was famed too much for his safety, and he retired to a solitary life in the forest outside of Cremona. It was as if she were his apprentice. This was in the first year after the death of the count. My lady found no other consolation. She spent her solitary hours searching out the herbs and oils her apothecary described to her. She learned all she could, and began to refine her master's creations. I should say that now she is peerless in her art."

I opened the velvet bag that held the key, drew it forth and opened the casket. Nestled in black velvet was a small crystal vial filled with an emerald liquid. Gianni started when he saw it, his eyes darted toward me, then he turned his face away.

"Do you recognize this, Gianni?"

"I do not like to say, my lord."

"I'm not your lord, Gianni, I'm only Antonio. Why did you start so when I opened the casket?" He was silent. "What is this, Gianni, that stops your mouth? Is this the product of an art so dark that men dare not speak of it? You have my word, the countess will not know of what you tell me."

"Antonio, if I betray my lady by telling you what I know, I belie the word I gave to the kindest benefactress I've ever known. Yet you put your trust in me, a man whose bed and company I enjoy, a man whose beauty gives me rich pleasure. I know not how to speak."

"Say, Gianni, do I enter a web of deceit or danger by discharging this favor for the countess?"

"It pains me to say so, but you do. The cordial is poison of the swiftest power. No remedy can save one who has drunk of it, so fast it does its work. It is a recipe my lady created after she surpassed her teacher. He despaired that his guidance led her to such pastimes as this, and begged her to forswear such creations. She would not obey."

"But the reason, Gianni, what led her thoughts to such creations?"

"What other reason than vengeance? She has told you to present this as a gift to Gerard de Norville, has she not?" I nodded. "De Norville attended Paolo in his last days. His suffering was relentless, and the countess swung from fury to despair as de Norville could do nothing to save him. When the count was gone, she told me she'd have her revenge. I heard this as the wildness of grief when it is new. I see that she has nursed her revenge like a child, and it is now of an age to be sent into the world on its own. You are the means of its conveyance.

"An unwilling one, if no longer unknowing. You have my thanks for telling me all. I will not be the means of another man's death, not willingly. What do you know of this de Norville?"

"He has friends in Milan and in Venice. You would have been hard pressed to escape blameless, even when the gift had been sent in the name of the Sforzas. Mischief in his name would court greater danger, to be sure. My lady snares you in treachery; it is the passion of her grief that drives her so. But her love for you has been sacrificed. Such are the offerings demanded by these treacherous times, my friend." He looked up at me, grabbed my hair, and drew my face to his. "You must avoid this intrigue." His tongue insistently found all the contours of mine, and mine of his.

I pulled my face away. "And so I will. Can you guide me to this apothecary who taught my lady what she knows?"

"Our thoughts run together in a swift torrent. He counts out his solitary days not far from the road toward Venice. I will guide you there. You have two days until your departure. There is time enough to plan. This morning, though, is ours." He rolled me onto my back and pressed his mouth against mine again, wrapping his legs around me, covering all of me with his fine warmth. I wanted nothing more than to enjoy him, and so I did.

⊕

"You've found the fairest spot in my garden, as I hoped you would," Catarina said when she found us later.

Gianni and I were sprawled under a chestnut tree, at the edge of the beds where the last of the late-blooming flowers and herbs nodded, his head in my lap, mine lolling against the trunk, dreaming in the waning light of an unusually warm October afternoon.

"Do not bestir yourselves; I'm pleased to find you so disposed. Gianni, you've done well. I do believe our guest has found his way to pleasure once again."

"Madam, he has, and so have I. And so, on an afternoon like this, has all the world, it seems. Is there a service you require?"

"Anon, Gianni, anon. All the world, sweet boy? If only that were true."

I squinted into the late bending sun. "Is there news from one court or other?"

"When is there not? Nothing to trouble yourselves about."

"It is your troubled heart that finds no pleasure, is that not so?"

"My Antonio, I learned long ago that expecting to find such a thing as pleasure or contentment was the surest way to kill it. My pleasure is found in what little work I can perform for those whose lives overlap with mine." She turned away.

"You've not told me what became of Paolo."

"Nor shall you hear me tell of it, for it is nothing but the same tale of woe. The same as every other. Now I turn my sights to the world beyond my little castle, though I care little to leave this place. What little I can do, to that I turn my hand."

"You speak of the great as friends."

"Ludovico you mean. He became a friend, of sorts. It served my husband's family to hold him so, though his affections are as changeable as the March wind. It serves my safety to hold him gently, as it were, in amity. There were times when soldier's savagery spilled over my walls into this very garden. Times when young Gianni here proved himself valiant indeed. Nay, you'll not deny it, I was here too, remember? No, pleasure is not what I seek in my long twilight. Quiet is all I hope for."

"The quiet here has restorative powers, that is sure. I hate to think of leaving, though I yearn to find my way again in the bustling world."

"When the world has impressed its woes on you, and asylum

is what you seek, to me you can return, and here you'll find respite always."

Her words struck my ears less like a benediction and more like a taunting prophecy, one lacking in good offices. It may have been quiet in the garden, but a tension crackled in the air between us. A rook called raucously, and swooped over to light on the garden wall. He shifted balefully from foot to foot, watching us.

Catarina stiffened. "Tomorrow morning, then, hie you to Venice."

"As you wish, my lady. A favor—?"

"Speak."

"Gianni, to accompany me—say only halfway there. I care not for the open road alone, and his company will brighten my travel."

"You've asked him, of course, and he's already packed and at your side."

"We could not lay our plans without consulting you."

"I require your presence, Gianni, but will release you for five days. Have a care that you turn toward home as soon as you see the lagoon of Venice. I will direct Antonio with care to his Venice digs, and the good doctor, and all who he must consult for me."

"Thanks, my lady."

With a start, Catarina turned toward a bed of herbs at her feet and quickly stooped and gathered a handful. She strode with purpose to a bed at the foot of the garden and did so twice more.

"Gianni, know you the herbs she picks with such dispatch? It is as if she were under sudden, quick command."

"There are herbs of several varieties in each of these beds, so I cannot, with any confidence, tell you. Why, what troubles you?"

I was troubled, Gianni saw true. Catarina was distracted, haunted, I could only guess, by the errand she had set me on, and the double-dealing this required of her. In the brevity of my visit I could see that the grandeur of her maturity hid an icy reserve, something even her actress's wiles could not disguise. The tension between us she seemed determined to ignore, and my confusion held me in a kind of thrall. How could I tell her I knew of the true intent of the errand she set me on, and that I'd already planned to disobey her? Perhaps she cared little if her gift reached its intended destination, performed its terrible work, and the messenger was apprehended because the message was so dire. Perhaps the gesture was all, and she could finally turn her mourning, so private that it ate her from the inside out, to greater purpose. Or perhaps she was implacable in wrath, and there was more peril ahead than I could know. But I was not willing to be sacrificed in her ill-fated plot. To preserve my honor, I must engage in double-dealing of my own.

"Antonio, your brow is furrowed with care."

"You know your mistress better than I. Can you read what occupies her mind with such urgency?"

"Who can read the occupations of another? She mourns, and she is proud, and she approaches the end of her years. What other occupations would you have her troubled by?"

"You know well what other occupations trouble me. And I fear for your safety, too. Promise me that if trouble stirs here, you'll find me again in Venice."

"I'm certain your fears are bootless, but yes, I'll find you again, if for no other reason than to tell you the latest news. That Violanta has had another crying fit, and needed to be calmed down, and that the grape harvest was excellent, and all is well in Lombardy."

"See that you do, my friend. See that you do."

⊕

Catarina rose early to see us off the following dawn, and pressed a purse well stuffed with gold into my hands. As her groom brought our horses round, she held my face tightly.

"You look at me as if you looked for the last time."

"I am a good deal older than you are, as you know very well, and as you've always had the good manners never to speak of. It may well be that you behold me now for the last time. That is only a reasonable expectation. Sweet boy, now a handsome man, do not fail me."

"What cause could lead to failure with a boon so small?"

I shifted in her grasp and she dropped her hands. I turned to mount the horse, proud and shining with good care. I bent down from the saddle and took her hand.

"All that is possible for me to do with honor I will perform. I will live with the hope of enjoying your hospitality here again, even as I enjoy the fruits of your generosity in my new home."

"Enjoy, my sweet, all that you can while there is time. I'll expect news."

"And you shall have it, of that I'm certain. Ready?"

Gianni had mounted and wheeled his dappled gray around.

"Let us depart, Antonio."

I raised my hand to Catarina as we urged our mounts to a canter out of the yard, onto the road to Cremona. It was the last I was to see of this uncommon lady.

⊕

"Apothecary, what ho, apothecary!"

The path to the door was as overgrown as this woe-begotten cottage. Weeds and grass sprouted from the thatch, between those stones that remained in place to present the semblance of shelter, and those that had fallen away were strewn in the brambles that choked off what light fell through the branches of the ancient oaks and elms that made this forest. Yet a curl of smoke leeching through the rocks that once were a chimney beckoned the curious closer. I called again. "Brother Anselmo, ho! Apothecary!"

A shadow emerged in the doorway, hooded in the Franciscan manner.

"Stop this infernal caterwauling. I'm here, you ruffian, though why my peace should be disturbed for the likes of you is beyond my imagination. I seek no company, and company no longer seeks me. Who are you? What brings you? What noise, what news, what words have you to break across my pate?"

"Old man, you ought to make up your mind as to whether you want company and conversation or not. You pepper us with questions as if hungry for diversion from your solitude."

"Impertinence will gain you nothing, sir. State your business or go."

"In brief, then, I seek a cordial whose effects are benign, but would provoke a sleep so profound that one innocent to its use might think they beheld not a sleeper who will waken refreshed but one passed forever into eternal sleep. I'm told that you are the man who can provide such a mixture."

"You have heard aright. For what purpose do you seek such a thing? I do not dispense the potent products of my arts freely."

"You had an avid student once, the Countess Catarina di Tramonte."

"A student who quickly surpassed me in skill, but whose sorrow warped her intent. What have you to do with this lady?"

"Many years ago she rescued me when I sorely needed it. And many years later our paths have crossed again, and again she provided succor when I knew not where I should find it. But she has assigned me a task that I cannot on my conscience carry out without some emendation."

"Enough, no more. I fear to think what favor she has asked of you. You seek a way to seem to carry out her request, but without any fatal effect."

"Old man, you see with the clarity of the freshest brook in spring."

"If you are being impertinent, you will gain none of my aid. You, there, I know you, don't I?" He was speaking to Gianni.

"Brother Anselmo, many a time I accompanied my lady here when she sought to learn all you could teach her."

"Yes, your face is familiar to me. Wait."

The old monk ducked inside his ramshackle cottage. The light fell in a green shimmer through the drying leaves, kept rattling by a freshening breeze. There was a crash of something falling inside, a cry of consternation, the yowl of a cat who suddenly streaked through the doorway and between us into the woods. The squeal of rusty hinges complained of their disturbance.

"Yes, I was certain. Here it is," we heard the monk cry in excitement.

He emerged at the door holding a crystal vial containing a deep red liquid.

"This is the cordial you require. It will cost you dear. How much money do you have?"

"How dear is the price you demand? I believe in paying for the skill you wield."

"Thirty ducats."

His eyes darted nervously about as if he was guessing wildly, knowing that I could not pay this price. But I could, and his eyes popped when I opened the pouch at my side and began to count out the gold. Gianni put his hand out and spoke softly to me.

"Antonio, that is far too high a price for this, I am sure. He will be told what he is to be paid for his skill, and will be happy."

"I am content to pay what he asks. It is less likely that he will speak of this if he is paid what he feels he is worth." I made three towers of ten gold coins on the sill of the window next to the door where the old monk stood. His eyes glittered with excitement as he watched the towers grow.

"You, sir, are a gentleman and I am pleased to make the acquaintance of one so honorable. Your name, sir?"

"Is Antonio. A man without a place in the world, but one who is grateful to you for your silence in this matter."

"To whom would I speak? Look about you, sir, and you see the only company I keep."

"We both know that the countess could find you out again, and demand to know if any treachery prevented her own from bearing fruit."

"Understood, sir, understood. And quite right you are, sir, to cut off the young pip before its maturity. Your trust in me will be well placed."

"I knew it would be, Brother. This is your recompense, and you have my thanks. We have a day's journey ahead, and so we bid you good day."

"Yes, yes, good day," he muttered as he gathered the gold coins and held them in the worn canvas apron he wore over his moth-eaten habit. He didn't raise his eyes as Gianni and I retook our mounts and turned down the overgrown path back to the road toward Cremona.

⊕

"But Antonio, what is your plan?" Gianni asked. "The countess will surely hear that de Norville is not dead, and she will not doubt the power of her cordial. She will doubt the surety of the performance of the favor she asked of you."

"She can hardly bruit it about that I have failed to kill the man she wished me to. But I would surely be arrested if I did as she bade me. There seems little question what I must do. I only hope this cordial Brother Anselmo has sold me is truly the benign draught he said it was. What do you know of de Norville? How will he greet an emissary from the countess he failed so?"

"With care, to be sure, but with curiosity. He seeks a cure for what he thinks ails him, too, and that will get the better of him. When he ministered to the count, many a time and oft it seemed it was he who was the patient, rather than the doctor, so pressing on his mind is his condition."

"And what was his condition?"

"That I could hardly say. He appeared as well as any man, as vigorous. He fell to his food, slept through the night. But the main entertainment and occupation of his days was the careful tracking of the signs of his affliction."

"He suffered from the general affliction—that of being alive."

"Now you have hit it. Caught and measured and stored in his sputum and fluttering heart and queasy breath, he did not live. Rather it was a performance of living in the relentless and tedious care of his mortal flesh. He was not a man I'd care to know for long, so gripped he was by this fascination."

"Your description hardly recommends making his greater acquaintance."

We'd turned onto the road leading east, toward our destination. I gazed at my companion, a man who cared little for how his flesh performed its tasks, but reveled in the fleshly doing. He looked back at me and grinned: the sun emerging from a momentary cloud. We urged our horses into a run. Thoughts of treachery, thoughts of mortal flesh, thoughts of the accumulation of event that dizzy the mind, all dissolved in the cool air of the forest, the pounding of the horses' hooves, the beauty of Gianni's fine broad back ahead of me on the road. Ah, how that beauty urged my thoughts to argument again. For all his beauty, the love of a man was an encumbrance I sought not, not if my attachment could not be other than the fetters in a weighted chain. Could I love a man, or could a man love me, and could we both be free in our love? What attachment could be as light and as strong as that? I had known such a love, and it nearly killed me. When such a love is too much to be trusted, it disrupts too much, and fear makes a man cast it away. Too much like the constancy of the sun as it follows the night, and the night the day, it fades from our awareness and we see it not. I was held without being held, until that love was killed by a cannon's ball at Otranto. A boy's beguiling need hinted that a love might be mine again, but I was fortune's fool to think it could be so. I felt the prick and perversity of yearning so to think these things as I looked at the body of a man I'd enjoyed these past few days. No. No more attachments for me. I rode toward another precipice, distant and different, a free man and alone.

⊕

By the dawning of the third day, we had descended to the flat marshy lands near to the tidal basin, and the towers and domes of the city shimmered in the distant mist. The air was heavy with moisture and the faint breezes that approached us on the cold still morning were laden with the salt air of the sea. It was time to send Gianni back to his mistress.

"My friend, our time is up, and the countess requires your presence."

"This is a parting no amount of anticipation can ease. I regret this moment more than I can say."

"Gianni, your friendship has soothed the storms that shook me. Your face will always be before me."

"Until another eclipses mine."

"No, think not so. Our lives were knit together for a time, there is no gainsaying that, however brief it was. Our paths separate now, and there may be pain, but no regret. Joy, rather, that we shared what we could share. Pain comes when we grasp after what cannot be held."

I'd dismounted and stood at his stirrup. He looked down at me, loosed his broad smile on me, then threw one leg up and over and slid off his horse. He wrapped his arms around me and our mouths joined in a hungry kiss. In that moment I could not be certain that what held me fast on my way was the favor owed to the countess, the hope of a life altogether different in this new city, or my wish to flee what was promised in Gianni's dark eyes. Probably I was a fool, but I had to be my own fool that day. I handed him the reins to my mount. We were near the crossing where I could take a ferry to the serene island in the lagoon.

"You know how to find me."

"And you me. And should you ever need my help, know it will be there."

"Fare you well, sir."

"Farewell, friend."

Part III

Venice

November is a poor time to enter Venice. Shrouds of gray mist hang low about the city, like mystery or pestilence. The cold seeps in with little remedy. I found the countess's house with no difficulty. Though she called it a palace, it was small, comfortably furnished; reached by turning two spiraling twists off the Grand Canal. There was a housekeeper, Marina, a sturdy woman whose years of work showed in her countenance, who lived in rooms at the back of the house. Her welcome was phlegmatic, but with evident excitement at the idea that now she'd have some company that belied her manner. The fire roaring in the wide grate in the main hall offered comfort. Sitting before it, warming myself, I had to admit that it was good to have the salt in my nose again; the rhythm that the sea that imposed on the city made my entry nearly a strange homecoming, one I did not expect.

The errand I was contracted to perform was a burden that rested uneasily on me. The potion I substituted for Catarina's would have no malign effect. But it was sure she would learn that de Norville had not suffered from it, and would hold it hard against me that I betrayed her. And I was equally certain that the first act of a life in this new city would never be one of vengeance. If de Norville were, as Catarina told me, a man whose intelligence reached far in many directions, he would be a valuable man to know. A hard-hearted calculation, trading old loyalty for new advantage, but one I had to make. Here was the spur that pricked me quickly to carry out my double-dealing errand: the sooner enacted, the less time there was to squander in uneasy speculation about its cascading effects. The day after my arrival, then, I found my way to the house of the doctor Gerard de Norville.

It was a handsome building, with a broad façade on a wide canal.

Like others that had been standing for a long time, it was faced with white marble from Istria set off by figures of inlaid porphyry and serpentine. I had sent ahead a request for an audience, and it was granted. The servant at the door regarded me coolly, taking in all of my appearance with a slow, calculating gaze. There was no time to consider the boldness of his regard. He showed me into a gallery where the cool late-morning light glinted off the polished floors inlaid with deep red and green marble in an intricate lattice pattern. The furnishings were sparse but fine. Antique statues of the ancient gods and goddesses lined the walls: the collection of a connoisseur. At the back of the long, narrow room was a couch covered in Turkish carpets and furs. A fire danced in the grate behind. After several moments, a voice called out to me from the bundle of fabric.

"You are the man from Ludovico Sforza."

The voice was like the wheeze of an organ whose bellows are torn and flapping. He dissolved into coughs with the effort of calling out to me. I walked to the foot of the couch and made my bow.

"Sir, I am he. Antonio is my name. I bear a gift from the house of Sforza by way of the Countess di Tramonte."

"You are a striking figure of a man, to be sure, but then Catarina always surrounded herself with masculine pulchritude of the highest order." When not making the effort to call across a room, his reedy voice, hardly requiring air to produce the sounds, burbled unimpeded by his rheumy cough. His eyes were clear, but heavy with the bags of one who rarely sleeps. So different was he from the way Gianni described him during his stay at the Castle di Tramonte that it was clear something terrible and strange had happened to this man.

"I do not wish to disturb you, sir, in your convalescence."

"Ha! Convalescence implies improvement. But I decline and decline and decline. Soon this declension will be the ultimate one, and my researches will draw to a close. Oswaldo!"

From a shadow behind the couch a liveried servant appeared with a bronze basin. He held it under the doctor's chin as he coughed and spluttered into it. De Norville carefully regarded what he'd just produced as if the key to a mystery lay there, then he waved the man away. Oswaldo's eyes were never lifted from the floor.

"Knowing the esteem in which the countess holds me, I feel quite certain that I ought to fear for my life were I to accept a gift she had a hand in devising." His eyes were as alert as a hawk's, though his voice quavered in a performance of pathos. "What do you think, sir? Ought I to accept this gift with an easy heart?"

"My office is only to deliver, not to advise. But I am confident of the gift's good intent."

"Your handsome brow could be that of a ministering angel. It would be a great pity if that face hid deception. I know of the countess's skill in devising medicaments. Perhaps she's sent me that which finally will give me peace at last. Is that what she's sent me? The ultimate peace? Her friend Ludovico would not be pleased if that were so, however much I may long for it. Oh, sir, you are still blessed with the vigor of a man at his zenith. You cannot possibly know what life can hold for those who are not so strongly made."

His wheedling voice had a slow, insistent power: the implacable tyranny of the weak. He'd outlive us all, no doubt.

"My lord, I am certain that this gift is a benign one, and you are right that it is a cordial of the countess's creation. She hopes it brings you ease."

"Of course she does. Oswaldo!"

The servant stepped into the light, and the doctor produced more fluid for his own enraptured inspection.

"Give me the casket, then."

His hands were small, pink and oddly porcine. He looked like a greedy little boy as he eagerly untied the cord the held the pouch closed and brought forth the casket. He pried open the gold clasp, lifted the lid, and held the small crystal vial up to the light.

"Oh, this is a lovely color. Very enticing indeed. Oswaldo!"

This time de Norville waved away the basin. He opened the vial and held it up to the servant's mouth. He obediently dropped his chin open. The doctor poured a small amount of the crimson liquid onto his tongue. He replaced the stopper and sat back to watch the cordial's effect. In a few moments, Oswaldo shook his head, as if to clear away a feeling of lightheadedness.

"Words, Oswaldo, use your words!"

"My lord, a creeping numbness rises from my belly to my head. My lips grow cold, and I fear I shall—"

He fell into a heap. The doctor sat back and watched, then reached out and placed two fingers on his servant's neck.

"His heart beats steadily, if a bit slower. His breathing is shallow, and his skin is cool to the touch. And he yet lives." He looked at his servant as if he regarded a mildly interesting specimen. "It appears that he will continue to do so. Most interesting. I will interview him when he rouses himself to see if the sleep this cordial brings is a pleasant one. Now, what ought I to do with you, sir? Surely this gift is not one sent with warm regards for my well-being.

"As I have told you, sir, my office was only to deliver. The debts I've accrued to the countess are profound, and out of respect of the care she has given me, I undertook to perform the favor she asked. She reported no intent to me beyond honoring a friend among friends."

"It is tempting to believe you. But I don't. Do you take me for a fool? Catarina has wanted to end my days since I failed to cure her husband. That is hardly a secret. She is a treacherous hell-kite. It is only because I am a useful tool of her ally Ludovico that she's not made an attempt on my life until now. She well knows that if Sforza knew she harmed me their uneasy peace would be at an end. A friend among friends? We're all playing a short game and there are no lasting alliances. Surely you've reached your maturity having learned this."

"To be sure I have, sir. And I'll no longer try to dissemble, a talent I know I lack. I did learn of the countess's wish to provide your quietus, but I would not deliver its means. It was, perhaps, a clumsy attempt both to please the countess to whom I owed my life, and to escape the peril of bearing the murderous cordial. No doubt I will suffer the sting of her scorn. But I preserved my honor and brought you a substitute. A foolish plan, and one that could not succeed in fooling any of the interested parties. I am unskilled in these ways, you see. I am accustomed to simpler dealing."

De Norville chuckled. "You are so earnest. That is endearing. And so refreshingly original in these cynical times, when everyone is so utterly knowing. That is such a bore, for it quite smothers the capacity for surprise, for true enjoyment. We all already know everything, and that is so stiflingly tedious. But you, you bring something new to Venice. The new earnestness. It will sweep the city, mark my words. Soon everyone will seek you out for this new sensation."

"My purpose here is to oversee the countess's shipping concerns, not to become a source of amusement for the weary and the jaded."

"I'm afraid that the uses the world sees fit to put you to are none of your business. The world will have its way with you without seeking your consent."

Oswaldo began to stir on the floor. De Norville clapped his hands, and a small boy appeared from behind the tapestry that hung along the wall near his couch.

"Raffi, bring Oswaldo some water, will you?" He turned his attention to the servant sprawled on the floor. "Oswaldo, wake. You must tell me everything. Was it a pleasant sleep? Or marred by dreadful visions? Raffi," he shrieked, his excitement building, "just some water, for heaven's sake. Oh, there you are. That's right, carefully"

The boy held Oswaldo's head and helped him drink. I understood my superfluity, and began to edge my way toward the door.

"Don't think I don't see you, Antonio. Your earnestness has impressed me, and I'm inclined to let you go, provided you return to visit me and revive me with your candor. You may have brought me a cordial I'll enjoy very much. I have trouble sleeping, you see, and your substitution may be just the thing. I'll render my thanks to Catarina in the most fulsome manner, which will drive her to distraction, and make her doubt her skills. Oh, it thrills me to think of disturbing the dream of vengeance she is enjoying. So, come back to see me, sir. I can be of use to you, if I care to. I know everyone, and everyone thinks I am a strange old thing, and so they tell me far too much. Discretion seems to wither away in the face of extreme eccentricity. Don't you find that funny? Go on, then, I must interview my servant. But return to me. I'm always here. Go—go."

He dismissed me with a wave and as I turned to the door I heard him question Oswaldo urgently.

"Tell me, was it cold and drowsy numbness, or a heat that thrilled your veins. Speak, man. I must know. Does your head ache?"

He was so enthralled with his interview that he took no notice when I opened the heavy door to his chamber and left him. The light was a cold violet on the canal, and I made my way back to my new home, dizzy with wonder and relief. And so alone. Achingly alone.

⊕

Dank solitude drained me of energy. My thoughts were haunted by those I'd lost. I carried on lengthy conversations in my mind, correcting the mistakes that ordinary human days are made of, a bootless attempt to remedy the calamity of this, my too long life. In my mad way I kept myself company with an endless rehearsal of things past, things cast in the bronze of time lost. Like an ambassador negotiating a treaty that could never be ratified, I sought peace within myself through bargaining. But all I had to offer my melancholy were scenes of long ago.

The clamor rose to such a pitch that, sometimes, I'd seek surcease in the busy life outside. Old ways seemed to be stored in my sinews, in my very bones, and with certainty I noted which sheds at the building sites of new cathedrals were aptly suited to shelter the couplings of men who sought each other there. I guessed which alleys were most apt to turn toward pleasure beneath a balcony, and which quays more likely to be frequented by the randiest sailors. I toyed with myself, summoning up the vision of an encounter that promised engrossing diversion. Perhaps even Franceschino would miraculously appear in the shadow at the next turning. But alas, my stratagems and my wanderings yielded nothing. There was simply no desire left to move me, as if all had been extinguished.

The only respite I found was work. The accounts of the shipping business had fallen into disarray, and when I could summon energy to rooting out the solution to one problem, pulling out one strand of the tangle at a time, peace soothed my brow and new stores of energy fueled me. I turned to another problem, and solved another mystery. I had a purpose. I knew not if my efforts could restore the countess's esteem. I could not plan so far. I could not see beyond the morrow. I knew only that work was balm for a troubled man. If the business could be restored to a functioning proposition, if I could perform the role of the man of business, perhaps the life of such a man would be palpable to me, within my grasp. I would have a chief occupation of time beyond sleeping and feeding. I would know life again.

And then, suddenly, news. It was some three weeks since my visit to de Norville. I was drowsing over a book that described the ways of the courtier: I sought every means to make my way in this strange new world. Marina had just lit the candles in my chamber when there was a pounding on the outer door.

"Jesu, what a noise and bother," Marina muttered as she waddled to the hall, puffing out the taper and shaking her head. "Yes, yes, I'm here. But what urgency is this that cannot be reasoned with not to pound so loud?"

She pulled open the door and Gianni nearly fell through the opening, panting, his eyes wild, battling the cloak about him that, once unwrapped, disclosed his shirt streaming with sweat.

"Where is your master, where is Antonio?"

I had followed her into the entry hall. "I'm here, Gianni, rest a moment, compose yourself. What trouble can there be to bring you in this state? Marina, some wine for Gianni."

Her grumbling diminished as she was swallowed by the shadows on her way to the kitchen.

Gianni fell on my neck and held me, his eyes brimming with tears.

"I hardly know how to tell you the news I bear. The countess is dead. She is dead, oh, Antonio, my countess, my protector, my other, better mother, she is dead, she is dead, she is dead."

His knees gave way and he would have crumpled to the floor had I not held him up. I carried him to a soft couch in the small library off the main hall.

"Marina, we're here, bring me the wine. And a damp cloth. Tonight, if you please. Gianni, breathe a moment, let me open your shirt."

Marina's complaints announced her presence. I took the damp cloth and pressed it to his brow, wiping the tears and sweat from his face. He looked up at me with terror in his eyes. "Can you rouse the embers to warmth, Marina?"

Gianni burst. "She's dead. And I know not what I shall do. She gave me this. She bade me give it to you."

He held out a letter, sealed with the crest I had first seen on her carriage: a phoenix.

"Here, Gianni, slowly now, drink some of this and rest. And breathe. You are here now, with me, and safe."

He leaned back against the cushions. I bent down and kissed him. He held me tightly by the neck and pressed his head against my chest. He took the goblet I held for him and began to sip. I brushed the hair from his brow, then bending my eyes to the letter, I broke the wax and unfolded the thick paper.

My dear boy Antonio, now a fine man, if you are reading this, then Gianni is in your care, at least for the moment. Know, then, that I am dead, at my own hand. I have left the house you are living in and my business interests in Venice to you. Letters to that effect have followed Gianni to the lawyers who know my affairs there. Your future ought to be secured, if you are half the man I take you to be. You have the wherewithal, now use it. It is my final gift to you, my treacherous darling.

Of course I learned of your duplicity easily. I never thought for a moment that you imagined your scheme could possibly escape my notice. I believe you intended that I know it. Your betrayal hurt me deeply. But I also know that your betrayal was the only way you could build your own life. This is the way of things. The old finally are tilled under so that heedless life goes on. You were my last, my only ally in a world far too busy to care for an old, grieving widow. My erstwhile friends used me as they wished, when I could further their march toward power. But I outlived my utility. Obsolescence is a sentence of limitless boredom. You know me well, my dear. I have survived much, but I will not tolerate being insignificant and bored. So bored. I have bored myself to death. I drank the cordial you were to have delivered to that ineffectual impostor de Norville. Gianni will report that my skills were undiminished.

I understand why you betrayed me. And I am sensible

enough, in my prison of boredom, to forgive you. De Norville suffers in a hell of his own devising, as I do, as you do, as we all, poor pathetic human beings, do. No punishment that I could visit on him would be half so effective. And so I find I am grateful to you, in spite of myself. Your betrayal led me to see the extent and the borders of my hell, and that I am the author of it. That no one can devise more delicious suffering for de Norville than he can himself. I hope that one day you can know this, too: that your torture is so perfectly voluptuous because only you know the precise dimensions of the void it must fill.

I have sent you Gianni to bear these tidings. He is faithful and loving, and he adores you. That is no small thing.

You have all you need to prosper. I charge you to enjoy it while you can. It is wrong not to.

Your Catarina

I slowly sank to the edge of the couch next to Gianni. He held my hand, his breathing slowed now, and he looked at me with expectation. Now it was certain: I was to be a man of substance in this new city. My work was ready to hand, the hours of my days to be filled with matter. Yet any joy over my good fortune was tempered by the mystery of it. That I should be the only one left to the countess on whom to bestow this fortune seemed the workings of capricious chance. The countess chose me because our paths crossed in an accident of passion, a comedy with an unforeseeable resolution, one that might well evoke tears and laughter and wonder.

"Antonio, what does she tell you?"

"That she has died by her own hand, and that she has left me this house and her business interests here in Venice. Did she leave a letter for you?"

"Yes. She made me master of the castle. I can hardly believe it. The home I've known these years is now truly my own. I never thought of a life without the countess to serve. I hardly know what I must do."

"What do you want to do?"

"What I want has always been simple, and framed by duty. Without duty, I swim in a sea I know not of."

He quietly began to weep. I slowly stroked his head.

"You needn't know right now what you want. You will rest here. The two of us are reborn with Catarina's generosity, and with her loss. But your world is familiar to you, it holds the comforts it always had, and maintaining your life there carries the same round of duty. And what of your family?"

"They will live there as always, to be sure. But there is much talk of my taking a wife, now that there is land and fortune. Antonio, I do not know if I want to take a wife."

"Oh my young friend, there was a time when I was in such a spot, and I fled rather than bend to my father's wishes. And my life has tumbled on, full of event and noise and silence and emptiness. What concerns you about taking a wife?"

"That I'd lose the love of men like you."

"Well, that is preposterous. It has never stopped most of the men I've known who were married. My boy, you needn't decide today, but you'll always have a home here in this city with me. Now, perhaps you'd like to bathe. I'll have Marina bring you fresh linen, and you'll eat with me tonight."

His mouth was hungry for my kiss and he held me tightly by the neck. His breath quickened as he choked a sob back, then I felt him measure out his breaths to calm himself.

"That's right, my boy. Softly now, there is nothing to fear. We will mourn our beneficent countess together for a while, and after our tears are shed we'll turn our attention to our freshly minted fortunes."

Gianni shared my bed that night and for the following six nights before he returned to his newly acquired home. His sweet disposition and all his experience were far better suited to a rural setting, and soon he knew it. Our parting was fond and tearful and for the best, but it left behind a keener emptiness, no longer void but ready, a plot of ground stirred and tilled and awaiting new seed.

⊕

I paid a visit to de Norville. Now that my position in the city had become established with some formality I wished to know how I was regarded. Upon my arrival, he was overseeing the unpacking of a crate newly delivered. Raffi showed me into the gallery, where the light sliced through narrow windows paned in orange and ochre and white, shining on the polished pattern of marble in the floor. Oswaldo held a crowbar and was prying one board after another off the top.

"Oh, hurry up, man, I'm overcome with anticipation." De Norville's voice had more force and body today, and he was standing, his hands opening and closing as if he was unable to contain himself. He bounced a bit, on the balls of his feet, like a child who was about to be given a very special treat.

"Ah, Antonio, welcome. You are just in time to join in the pleasure of the latest addition to my collection, if Oswaldo can ever get this crate open."

"De Norville, I am happy to see you looking so hearty. When first we met, you were indisposed to a degree that was worrisome."

"And you are partly to thank for my improvement, my boy. Don't look so shocked. That cordial you delivered was, in a very small dose, the best sleeping potion I have ever encountered. However fell and dark your lady's intention, your substitution has given me new reserves of life. You have my gratitude. Ah, good, man. That's enough, now, lift it out, carefully. The coast of Ischia, who could have imagined it, is a treasure trove of antiquities. And my eyes there are cunning. Very good."

Oswaldo struggled as he drew a bundle of wadding from the crate, and as he pulled away the rags that wrapped it a mottled deep green statue emerged. Eventually he revealed a young boy, an athlete, perhaps, seated, adjusting his sandal. The boy was perfect in form, intent in his task, transporting in effect.

"Ah, yes. A touch of heaven here in my gallery, don't you think?"

As De Norville walked round his new acquisition rubbing his hands with pleasure, drops of moisture formed on his lips.

"Have you ever seen something so arresting, sir?"

"He is fine indeed. How has this come to you?"

"Oh, my agents are everywhere, and know everything. They know, for example, that you have taken over the Countess di Tramonte's business interests here in Venice, and seem poised to resurrect a once derelict business. Oh yes, news travels very quickly along the Rialto. And they know how to learn where the evidence of the first great flowering of art is to be found, and they know what will please me. Raffi, some wine for my guest. Come, sit and let us admire my new young boy."

"Not a move is made here that you know not of."

"Once that was so. I fear that now my powers are waning. But news of important events does reach me still. Congratulations can be offered to you for the improvement in your fortunes, is it not so?"

"Is it an improvement? The more I learn of this city, the less certain I am that it is a place I can truly flourish."

"It is a city with its distinctive customs, to be sure. I have lived in many places, and I will assert that, once you learn the steps, there are few places where the dance can be so rewarding."

"There is much that mystifies me about what you call the dance. For example, what is rewarding about this wearing of masks, for no apparent reason."

"Oh, there you betray your woeful lack of sophistication. Masks may be necessary and useful for many reasons, and reasons multiply. Remember this: there is never no reason, only those that are not apparent to you."

"Players wear masks in the comedy that announce their character."

"Ah, yes, the earnest observation fits your character, ever unmasked. That is what you believe of yourself, and what you'd have us all believe. But consider the mask that is put to use with cunning and economy to suggest more at one hazard. Masks may boldly shout, 'you may be certain of what you see' even as they whisper a confounding riddle."

"You lose me, sir, in the twists of your logic."

"Arise, sir, to the new occasion. Open your mind to the mysteries you encounter. Your way will become smoother if you do."

"Can I ask you, how am I spoken of, if I am spoken of at all, among the other men of business?"

"The countess's affairs have not, of late, been so closely followed as once they were. Neglect, you see, withers the general interest. But now that you have cleared away the detritus neglect allowed to accumulate around it and there are signs of health in the ailing creature, you have kindled the world's curiosity. Curiosity tinged with malice, I can tell you, for competition seems to breed it, whether we like it or not."

"Can you advise me, how am I to find allies?"

"Oh, sir, your natural talents give you an advantage."

"I'm not sure I—"

"You do amuse me. You really do not know the effect of your open face, do you? No help from me, should I be able to supply any, will help half so much as the honest gaze of your eyes."

I knew not how to reply, but it seemed clear that he declined to provide a direct entry to the world I sought. A shadow of a hope occurred to me.

"I wonder if in your experience of this city you have heard of someone, may I ask?"

"To ask is a harmless thing. Of whom would you inquire?"

"A man I knew once, long ago in the city of my birth. Franceschino de' Medici."

"Oh ho, another of the smitten? He leaves such a long trail behind him. Not only have I heard of him, but I have had occasion to meet him more than once. A man who keeps his councils close, but whose remarkable form has always caused a stir. But why do you seek him? You knew him, you say? You were conquered by him? No, no, I see now, as the clouds part for the morning sun. It was quite the reverse. It was he who was conquered by you, isn't that it?"

"Once, in another city, another life. And when we parted, he spoke of coming to Venice."

"You are a Florentine?"

"I've not been home for many years now, and have no place I call a home. Perhaps you can tell me how to find this man?"

De Norville turned to a writing desk, dipped a pen in a bronze inkwell in the form of Perseus, and wrote on a small piece of vellum.

"The last I knew, the handsome Franceschino kept a fine house on this small canal. But if you frequent the Rialto, there is no doubt you will encounter him. He cuts a commanding figure, though he will not easily be found at night. The more prudent men of his kind shun evening adventures along the quays in favor of more private gatherings. Now that you know he is here, perhaps you will find the life of a merchant congenial and Venice will be your home. You are young yet, and you have wasted no time in establishing yourself admirably."

"Thank you for this. Not so young as once I was. To truly establish myself in business here requires some means of entry."

"The countess's concerns are not entry enough?"

"The neglect of those concerns long ago drove her business to others more attentive, and that is only sensible. Perhaps you can help me, sir, knowing all, seeing all. Perhaps a door, an introduction."

"The irony of my being asked for help by the agent of the woman who was to have been my murderer is not lost on you, I hope."

"Not lost at all, but the chief impediment."

"Well, you seem to have dispatched that impediment with ease. That ease of manner must help you in the world. Tell me, are your inner recesses as easeful as the surface?"

"I do not feel so easy, yet I do not feel that I dissemble, if that is what you ask."

"It is not that I do not trust you. It is that I am curious. Infinitely curious. A rewarding trait, I have found. Most people like nothing more than to be asked about themselves. Do not you find that to be so?"

"I find that it depends on whom is doing the asking, and what it is they ask. You, my good doctor, reveal only a little, yet seek to know so much more. You have told me that this has made your fortunes what they have been. I cannot dissemble, nor can I feign interest in those I care not to know."

"That is a mistake. If you wish to prosper, I advise you to school yourself in taking an interest. You ask how to make your way into the world of business. Present yourself as one who is interested in every detail of what a man might be inclined to tell you, and the business will follow. Follow his lead, avoid taking the first step, but learn to make him feel that you hang on his every word. Mark me, sir, success will follow as the noontime thaw follows the chill of the morning. More wine?"

"Thank you, but I must decline, and take my leave. I will consider your advice well."

"There is little to consider. Put it to action, and you'll find your way. And do not hesitate to come to me again. You refresh one whose palate has become so jaded."

"I will not hesitate."

My heart was cold and sinking as I took my leave. I'd lived so long in my own private world where dissembling was not required that the idea that I must learn to do it chilled me to my core. Could I learn to smile and smile and still be honest? Could I turn my face into a mask, and play a part? Not as I had learned long ago with Catarina. That was play, not dissembling. If every man expected dissembling, then what could be the gain but an endless play of reflections, as in two facing mirrors, where appreciation of the artfulness of the deception bred ever more appreciation, and ever more deception? That was the key, and I recognized it in an instant, for I had practiced it before, long ago. That was the taste to be developed, the appreciation of the artfulness of the deception. That was the sophisticated art of cities, an art I was praised for as a youth, and from which I thought I had found escape. There was to be no escape for me, then, from the ways of society. My escape died in my arms, at Otranto. Now I was where fortune took me, and perforce required me to learn the ways to navigate that life. And perchance to find my way to the pleasures of the city, too.

Franceschino

After Gianni returned home the gloom of solitude was more emphatic. My hours were filled with turning my mind to de Norville's tutelage, as dreary a prospect as the lowering iron skies of Venice in the winter. I had put the vellum he gave me in a box in my chambers, wondering at my hesitance in seeking Franceschino out. Perhaps it was a determination to make my way myself, or perhaps it was the apprehension that an attachment from long ago could not withstand the intervening years. To leave it intact in memory was safer, after all, than finding it sundered by time's resentments.

I turned my energy to restoring the enterprise that the countess entrusted to me. Documents I found in the study had gathered dust, but yielded promise. There were three ships, leased to others, that remained the property of the business. I bought out these leases with her legacy, and I set to work making sure they were seaworthy and their holds ready for filling.

For that I needed to establish relationships with enough suppliers to fill them up in Venice, sufficient to allow the purchase abroad of goods to fill them for a profitable return. Those contracts she once was signatory to had long since lapsed. It was necessary to meet the makers of what Venice produced: woolens and kersey and silk fabrics wrought in precious metals, items fashioned in copper, caps made by those who would dress the people of fashion, and the paper from makers whose product permitted the wide world to record its doings.

Three former customers of the old business were persuaded to resume an old relationship with a new merchant. It is commonly said that men of business fare poorly when fancies weigh more than facts in their calculations. So was my business mettle tested. Venice was known for its masters of the loom. I did not know whether to smile or sigh when it was clear I would traffic in fabric—the finest of the highly wrought gold and silver fabrics that were famous throughout our world, to be sure, but, fabric, alas, all the same. How the spinning whirligig turned. A business shunned became a business pursued. In truth there was no need any longer to avoid what linked me with my father. Long ago I learned that the inward bite of memory would never fade altogether. Sorrow and shame grew tamer in time, though both would snarl when kicked awake by a passing thought or vision that too closely resembled what lay in the past. But the past aroused could not render me incapable of doing what I must do. If I knew anything, I knew that. Peace was to be found in conviction: to build my own business was the best way to honor us both.

I walked one day along the Rialto, where any intelligence worth knowing about anything passed from group to group among the men always to be found conferring there, like the series of signal fires that bore battlefield news from camp to camp. I set out determined to greet the men of commerce with ease and confidence and an interest in their concerns, no matter how feigned. I would smile my way into new contracts. De Norville's advice was sound: the owner of a workshop that produced fine fabric already had agreed to talk terms with me, and to his workshop I was headed. And if I encountered a man with another sort of business on his mind, I would be heartily pleased. This hope was a spark that warmed me still, I will confess it. Work and solitude did not render me so melancholy that I could not be roused to lustful life by beauty and what bodies can do together.

About twenty paces ahead of me I saw a man approach. His hair and beard were silvered, his face deeply lined, his shoulders broad and his carriage upright and vigorous. It was a silhouette I recognized, though I had dismissed the notion that I would see it once again. He was richly dressed, a brocade doublet snug about his torso, fine linen shirt, the thick hair on his chest still curled over the collar, his legs still strong in dark stock hose, and a wine-red cloak hung off one shoulder. His eyes met mine and we stopped, facing each other with only a few feet between us. Neither of us was sure that the man we beheld could possibly be the man we swore we recognized once again. How long had it been? Twenty years? More? He studied me from top to toe. We were still standing in the middle of the passage, we blocked the way of others as they hurried to their business. He reached out and took my elbow and guided me to the railing of the bridge.

"Antonio. My beautiful boy, it is you, isn't it? I'd long ago stopped hoping you would fill my eyes again, and here you are, striding along the Rialto as if you were a man of business in Venice." He held me in his arms a moment, then took my face in his hands and looked into my eyes. "I want to kiss you."

"Then what detains you?"

"The restraint that the custom of this city imposes. But let me hold you."

What powers prevailed that brought Franceschino to me again? His eyes melted the years that had passed, and yet the difference those years exacted on each of us remained between us, too. Our bodies fit together in the way that I remembered, but mine was a different body now, a man's body. His was an older man's body, sinewy where once it had been plush with flesh. His beauty was burnished by the years, not diminished in my eyes.

"You have become a very handsome man, my boy. You know that, don't you?"

"No longer a boy, either."

"In my arms you still fit, and the ache for you has remained. I will always know the boy inside, and want to hold him close to me." He moved his head in gesture. "Come, step we aside so the bustling world can pass, and I can look at you. What strange fortune has brought you to Venice?"

"My story is improbable in the extreme. I've been a wanderer, buffeted by fate in many adventures. To be brief I can say that I've taken over the affairs of a friend, a countess who no longer wished to attend to the shipping business her late husband left behind."

"So it is you who has resurrected the di Tramonte fleet. Ah, you are surprised to find your reputation already bruited about? On the Rialto, where nothing is created but everything is sold, rumors of business sound loudly and swiftly. Even the news of her death. It is you are the mysterious heir. Everyone here knows who is on the ascendant and who dangles precariously on the precipice of ruin." He heaved a sigh. "My boy. This is not an easy city in which to make a beginning."

"I am finding my way. There were relationships that could be restored."

"Of course. I ought to have known that with your enterprising determination little would constrain you. Contracts already?"

"A few. I seek more to fill out the first venture."

"I may be able to provide an introduction to merchants whose goods will fill that ship. Will you permit it?"

"Do you remember me as one who refused you anything?"

His chuckling smile implied much more play to come. "But where do you lodge?"

"My countess had a house she willed to me. A small palace is how she described it to me, though 'palace' would be an exaggeration. It is well furnished and comfortable, though."

"And lonely?"

"I've been here only a matter of...." I could not belie myself to him. "Yes, it is too large for one."

"Where are you headed this morning?"

"A workshop that produces cloths of gold and silver is my destination. The owner has agreed to meet with me, but we have no appointed time. I will not rest content with so brief a meeting with you."

I reached for his face to draw him near.

"As impetuous as the boy you once were. Business first. Or is it possible you forgot so instantly the errand you embarked upon this day?"

Abashed, I felt myself go red with confusion.

"Antonio, I am more glad to see you than you can know. But let us take a bit of time, now. A great many years make a gulf between us. We'll not bridge it in an instant."

He grasped my hand and stooped slightly to catch my downcast gaze.

"Walk with me now. I have business too, you know. This morning I hie to meet a certain dealer in paper who owes me a favor. He is someone you should know. Conducting my own business wearies me, and change I think will rouse me."

He looked into my face and relented.

"My boy, the vision of you soothes my brow, like a fresh napkin dipped in cool water." He held me once again, glanced quickly round, and kissed me. "Let us see what this serendipitous reunion leads to. What do you say, Antonio?"

"I say that what I hadn't dared to hope suddenly brightens the way." He guided me by my elbow and we made our way toward the crowd that had gathered while the bridge was drawn up for the passage of some larger vessels on their way out to the lagoon. "But tell me everything. For how long has Venice been your home?"

"Soft, now, in time I'll tell you all. First you tell me about the man you go to meet. Then we'll return to my house and you will tell me all of your adventures. A maker of precious fabrics; do I know the man?"

"Do you know Silvio Gattinara?"

"But of course I do, but not because we do business together. At least not the business of trade in cloths of silver and gold. His workshop is hard upon us, just across there." He pointed over the canal to a building with three arches. Men crossed through the openings, wheeling barrows laden with bundles.

The bridge dropped and the men of business carried on their crossings. As we walked my chest seemed to overflow. How easily the sight of him filled the dank within. Delight rose upward and spread across my face and it felt as if I'd stepped into sunlight after being locked up for days and I could not stop grinning. Franceschino saw my translated state and smiled indulgently. At the foot of the bridge a street opened in front of us, with a narrow alley tucked away at an angle to the right, and another, broader way to the left along the canal. I drew us toward the dark opening of the alleyway where I could snatch at opportunity.

"No, this is the way, my friend," he protested.

"Just a moment, I want to attend to something." I took hold of his arm and pulled him into toward me, pinned him to the wall and hungrily kissed him as I reached for the laces at his codpiece.

He forcefully pressed my hands above my head against the stucco wall.

"What the devil do you think you are at? We are not in Florence all those years ago. We are in a city with very different customs, which you'll have to learn if you are to survive."

"But we've hardly—"

"Enough, no more." He looked about him, satisfying himself that we had not been observed. The alley was dark; I was not so very great a fool as not to take any caution at all. He grasped me by the shoulder and steered me back into the street.

"Franceschino, I cry you mercy, for the sight of you has set off a galloping in my heart and through my body. You are a surprise I dreamt of, yet it was a dream I dared not nurture. I remember a time when we'd agree about a proper greeting."

"I know, I know, my headstrong friend. Assure yourself, it is not that I do not share your excitement. You must possess your soul with patience, for our affections must live constrained here. Not by as fanatic a man who hounded me away from Florence, to be sure, but by the rules of the men who govern this city. I'll tell you all in time."

He cast his eyes about and reached round to squeeze my bum.

I grinned at him. "Why then, so I must possess myself."

"Good. To the business, then, to make the acquaintance of a man who can bring some money into the coffers of the di Tramonte shipping company."

"This man, what do you know of him?"

"Silvio is a good and honest man. Fair to look upon, and good company. He moves through the world with the confidence success confers. Once I did him a favor that brought him more than he thought he was bargaining for. If need be, I can add my voice and urge that he use your ships."

"Let us see if your voice is needed."

He stopped and turned to me again. "A man, now, not the impatient, heedless boy, but a man who knows his mind. I've missed you sorely, more than I can ever say." His eyes were full. He squared his shoulders and regained his stride. I trotted to keep up.

We drew near the awnings that shaded the arches of the house before us. Men wheeled crates back into the damp recesses of a warehouse where they awaited their final destination. Just inside of the first archway, seated at a small table, was a compact man, strongly made, his shiny pate ringed with unruly curls. His eyes were lively and suggested that they missed nothing. He jumped up.

"Franceschino, my friend. Your timing is perfect. A lull in my morning allows me a moment's leisure."

"Silvio, your countenance never seems to betray your dissipations."

The cloth merchant laughed and clapped my friend on the back.

"What fantasies you entertain, you infernal tale-teller. You're nothing but a corrupter of youth, and such a fallen one you trail along with you, I see. Sit, sit," He waved us to chairs round the table.

Both men chuckled.

I held my hand out to him. "I am Antonio, the ship owner you agreed to meet."

He grasped it. "Ahhh. This is the man who has taken over the di Tramonte concern. I am honored, sir, to make your acquaintance. Please." We sat.

I said, "Since I trust my old friend Franceschino, I know that the honor is mine."

"Luca, two more cups for my friends," he called out to one of the boys who bustled about as he took his seat. He drew our eyes to the items laid before him. They were so small, as if to make a table setting for a poppet: a tiny cup, no bigger than a thimble, and a larger beaked vessel of shiny copper. "You, sirs, are about to taste something rich and strange. It is newly brought here from the Levant, though I understand that before that it came all the way from Ethiope. Smell."

He lifted the vessel to us and held back its lid with his thumb. If the color black were a perfume, that would be the liquid.

"What do men call this?"

"Coffee. It is a relaxing drink, though without the befogging that a draught of wine can bring." Luca set down two more cups and a plate with strips of lemon rind on it. Silvio poured, then took a strip of the rind and twisted it over his cup, then nudged the plate toward us. We did the same, and then watched as he drank. Exchanging a shrug, we lifted our cups. The drink was bitter, but not bad. The lemon added a ray of light to the dark. "You'll see. This is a taste we Venetians will acquire, and soon all will demand coffee." He smiled as we put down our cups. "Now, what can you tell me, what news this fine day?"

"Oh, it is from you that one learns the choicest bits of news. I haven't any for you," Franceschino leaned back in his small chair.

I took my cue. "Sir, you know that I have a fleet, newly refurbished and seaworthy. I will provide conveyance for your goods at a very agreeable rate."

Silvio glanced at Franceschino. "I admire this direct line of attack." He looked back at me. "No foolishness, no compliments and no currying of favor."

"Those are talents I lack. I wish to waste no man's time, but I know we can come to mutually agreeable terms."

"We shall come to terms in good time." He regarded me as if appraising merchandise. "You are new to this world?"

I glanced at Franceschino who sat back with a broad smile. Warmth glowed from his eyes. I fancied that he enjoyed watching to see if I'd acquit myself well.

"New to the city, it is true, and untutored in many things. But as to the business at hand—"

"Rest you easy, gentle sir. You will have my contract, for how could I refuse a friend of Franceschino's? Especially one who is so pleasing. Pause we awhile, and let us take our ease."

He had few questions for me. I told him how I learned about trade in my home at Florence and in Genoa and he was content.

"But have you no family, no ties that bound you to those places?"

"What family I had I sadly lost. The world finds me as you see me, a solitary man ready to deal. And grateful to those with whom I can do business." He dipped his head with a smile.

"Your hand, sir." Franceschino rose. "You are not leaving so suddenly?"

"Alas, Silvio, we must. Business presses upon us. But you have our thanks for this Levantine innovation. You are always in the vanguard." A grin played at the edges of Franceschino's mouth. "Come, embrace me."

"Until the next time, then."

"Of course."

"Antonio, I hope to see more of you anon."

"Undoubtedly you will. You have my thanks."

A good morning's meeting, a contract agreed upon, I could brook no further delay until the moment my recovered lover and I were to be alone.

⊕

Franceschino's house was small and finely furnished, on a narrow crescent of water that spun off the Grand Canal near the field of Saint Margaret. We sat in his study, a chamber made of finely carved wood inlaid with mother-of-pearl and precious stones. A cabinet with what appeared to be hundreds of drawers, some tiny, some commodious, dominated one wall; in each was stored some precious keepsake from days past. There was a soft couch covered with carpets from Turkey where we sat together. Leaning against the cushions along the back, we sipped a ruby Tuscan wine.

It was not as easy as I'd hoped it would be to find out whether and how we might fit together once again. We talked, and our talk was different from long ago. We talked to test the distance, to test ourselves. Could a love so long suspended span so much time without any strain at all? Only those unbruised by fate would assert it. Mine had been so callow and so selfish. His tailored by the undermining compromises required by our world. Yet we were so insistent that we only saw the same lover of old in each other. We both wished so strongly to overlook how each was different in the other's eyes. Our talk edged us nearer, then farther from each other.

Franceschino warned me about the rules men like us played by.

"You hoped it would be different here, and now, didn't you? You hoped that this city would be free of the kind of regulation that we both fled all those years ago."

"I did. I do. But I also know just how zealously sodomy must be policed, and the infinite pleasures such zeal yields. The skill, the invention of the rules, the methods, and the punishments to be meted out, it is all quite marvelous."

Franceschino smiled with rue. "It has been a bit easier for me here.

Here I am not the cousin of a prince but only a businessman. And my tastes are such that it is unlikely that a complaint would be made to the Ten."

"The Ten are not so different from all those who would rule over others, I think."

"Indeed. Just another group of those who know so much better than the rest, and who are good enough to take upon themselves the onerous duty of protecting us all from the fate of Sodom and Gomorrah. The justification is very like that of the mad Dominican in Florence. The punishments have been severe. But the lists include names from all the grandest families. Some were executed in the most terrible way. The direst punishment has always been burning. Something about how the execution of the sodomite by burning protects the city from heaven's fire raining down upon us. The Ten amended the punishment slightly, some years ago, when a nobleman's son was condemned. Now the guilty are beheaded first, between the pillars of Saint Mark's, then the body is burnt. Sorry now that you've come to Venice?"

"I've lived so long beyond the laws that govern whom we love and how that it is difficult to imagine how men have survived."

"The hypocrisy of the world swirls ever more vividly."

"I heard the most remarkable story. I was in a tavern one day. I sought relief from solitude there, but the only relief I found was in overhearing the raucous talk of others. You must have heard it too—about the grief of Pope Julius over the murder of his lover?"

"I begrudge no man his grief."

In spite of myself I bridled. "Nor do I, do not misunderstand me. It is the remarkable capacity for duplicity in all men that so astounds me."

Franceschino nodded, "Yes, all knew that the late Pope took as his lover a Cardinal, the beguiling Francesco Aldosi."

"Beguiling but prone to impiety, so they say. Wise, then, to have a powerful lover. Who better to intercede but a Pope when one is accused of peculations? It is a sad story, if it were not for the corruption it exposes. The fellow who recounted it said that the Cardinal was murdered by the Duke of Urbino."

197

"Ah, yes, a monster himself, fit for the pits of Tartarus." Franceschino fidgeted. I kept on with my jabbering.

"The man said the crime left the old Pope quite mad with grief. He said his sobs sounded so through the draperies of his closed litter that all the way from Bologna to Rimini birds ceased their singing."

"Does it surprise you that the Pope can feel a loss as keenly as you can?" Franceschino seemed to reproach me. All was going awry.

"No. I think not about the old man's feelings. I am amazed that his passion can be known so openly while yet the church condemns us. That they round us up and execute us. This I cannot think of for too long without seething. That the cloth is the best protection for men who love men—"

"Then think not on it." Franceschino's quiet dismissal deflated me utterly.

I looked away and murmured, "Yes, so a man of sense would reply. But there are moments when the sensible is almost beyond imagining."

"Ah, now, I've hurt you, Antonio. I am not your enemy. Forgive me if I seemed to chide you. That is the last thing I wanted to do. I must welcome you with warnings, though. We face dangers in this serene city that are treacherous and subtle."

"I know, I know," I heaved myself from the couch with impatience.

"What do you know?"

"I know that the Night Officers sweep the usual places where the young are meeting each other and their elders, to gather up the accused and so justify their poxy existence. Invariably the arched colonnades of the smaller churches." I turned back to him. "It is almost amusing, isn't it? And nearly comforting that some things seem never to change."

"Yes, it is a comfort." He opened his hand to me. "A comfort that men like us will find each other. And what better spot than a church for a trysting place?"

"We find communion in our own way." I knelt beside him.

"So you most surely did, with the fervor of deepest commitment."

"You were the inspiration of my fervor." I leaned into him and kissed him.

There were tears that I held back. Tears of confusion and longing. He pulled his head away from me.

"You are going to have to be very careful, my boy. We have another way here. There are groups of us who meet privately for our pleasure, and you will be very popular at my next gathering. It is not foolproof. Some groups, meeting in the home of a prosperous businessman, have had complaints lodged against them by those who had to go to great lengths to find a way to see what was going on behind closed doors, so to be offended."

He fought me off. He kept his distance. Perhaps it was meet that it should be so.

I could not wish the years away, nor he the habits that time accumulated. He had another story to tell me. I gave way and listened.

"Some years ago there was the most unfortunate case of Benedicto, who was called Capello, and a youth who shared your name. The young Antonio was being trained by Capello to be a herald, and they had been carrying on for weeks, even though they were in the Ducal Palace. Reckless, to be sure. But the hapless Capello apparently thought they'd secured some privacy on the fateful occasion, in a chamber with a locked door. Regrettably, any privacy could not be counted on, for two neighbors, nosy women—oh yes, by heaven I even recall their odious names, Dymota the wife of Giovanni di Spagna, and Blanca, wife of Menegi. These fine ladies spied on them through a chink in a wall. Yes, a chink. In a wall."

"What effort these women exerted to spy on the luckless lovers. It might be funny if it did not make one run mad."

"Do not go mad, handsome one. But take heed. Dymota and Blanca raised such a hue and cry that Capello and his young herald had to be arrested, else the officials suffer the embarrassment of a hypocritical inattention to the dreadful sin of sodomy under the duke's very nose. I forget what their punishment was. Since there could be no proof of actual penetration, I believe they were merely fined and banned from the city."

He shook his head with care-worn amusement. "But enough of these troubles." His voice caught. His eyes were dark pools, and sad. "It is a soothing balm just to look at you. I can just look at you, can't I?" He paused and measured the length of my body as I lay stretched out next to him. "Can it really be you by my side? Do I dream?"

"I am no dream, no phantom. But a man."

"Age suits you, you know. How old are you now?"

I laughed quietly. "I'm forty, forty-one, I can't truly say. I have never paid much attention to my age. And I wish just to look at you, too. You must have had many lovers here."

"Oh, a few. I had enough of danger in my early years in Florence. Here I buried myself in work, and the young men who I knew I could trust came to me quietly and we found ways to be happy. And then I discovered comrades who wished to devise ever more ingenious ways to be happy. Pleasure in private, with a selection of men some new and some familiar to us. You'll come to one of my gatherings and you'll see. You'll be mightily entertained, I'm sure of it. And you'll be treasured."

"I wouldn't miss such an event for the world, so long as I can find some entertainment with you." I reached over, untied his codpiece, released him, and slid down to take him in my mouth once again. For a moment I felt his hand against my forehead as if to stop me. Then I heard him sigh, and his hand fell away. He could not hide his eagerness. Clumsiness was banished, and I fell to it with a vengeance. The smell and the taste of him vaulted me backward, reeling through time. What though our reunion was faltering and strained? It was a reunion all the same. He arched back and allowed me to take him deep into my throat. Time, absence, the laws of men, all dissolved. When his warm salty jet burst forth I held him in my mouth as our breathing slowed. The chamber was dark and warm, and we eased into a sleep together.

⊕

The work was well and truly begun. A new crew, a captain I could trust, and a reasonable first route, all was found and readied in a fortnight. My first ship sailed out of Venice's harbor laden with fabric of gold and silver, trinkets in amber and coral fashioned in Venice workshops and woolens from Venice looms, to trade for the wines that kept Venice veins warm through the last of the cold. Such trade risked little, so long as the ships hugged the Italian coast to Sicily where the fine woolens were to be delivered, then turning east along the rocky coast of Greece to find the resin-flavored wine prized by a dealer who favored me with a contract. The voyage was a success: calm seas and no disturbances too great in the course of the trip left me with a slim profit.

I sought my first customer in his workshop, close to the Rialto, to confirm the safe delivery of his wares.

"Silvio," I called out, as he emerged from the dark, "How do you this gloomy day?"

"Ah, Antonio. All is well, and I am satisfied. Franceschino was correct in asserting that I need not worry with you as my shipper. Join me in a beaker? Of wine, today, if you have not the taste for coffee."

He reached to the bottle on the table behind him. I smiled in relief.

"A toast. To our continued profits?"

"With pleasure." He handed me the cup of fragrant wine and we drank.

"Tell me again, how was it that you come to Venice?"

"Ah, the hunger to make my way in the world. Who would not wish to be in this great city, where men of business can build their fortunes with greater ease than in cities ruled by tyrants or overrun by invaders? Knowing that my friend could help me led me here, after learning all I could in my youth at Florence and at Genoa." I paused a moment, and set my cup down. "But, Silvio, a question for a question. Allow me to ask you. Knew you once of an annoyance to the shipping trade, a pirate, one Rodrigo, I think, whose ship, the *Black Phoenix*, once sailed Mediterranean waters?"

He rubbed his chin and stretched. "A pirate? I don't trouble myself with the names of their ships, let alone the rogue's proper names. Only when my money is lost at hazard do I think of them at all. It is the duke who sets his fleet on the vermin, and good riddance to them.

But why do you seek to know about this man?"

"Oh, I was told about him once, by one who wished to warn me. It is no matter. As you say, good riddance to such pests." I drained my cup. "The day wanes, and I must haste. I'll see you in the next week, and we'll determine what service more I can render to you. Goodbye to you, Silvio."

Walking along the canal toward my lodging, I could not tell the difference between the shiver set off by the chill of the winter afternoon and the shudder of recognition. As well known as the *Black Phoenix* had once been in many ports, here I found no memory of the ship or of its captains. So swiftly did fortunes rise and fall that a man's reputation lingered only for a moment. A larger shadow with a longer reach required a steady fire to make the light to cast it: a long-burning blaze of glory or regret or resentment or grief. But an annoyance swatted away left nary a trace.

To understand how little a mark we'd left, and how faint a memory there was for Rodrigo was an insult and a blessing. A mixture of relief and pique held me a moment as I realized that worries I nursed about making my way as a man of business here were blown by inflated hopes of fame. My fears were wishes in disguise. I saw with a clarity withheld from me before that whatever marks I left behind were private and so perished with their bearers. That is, so long as the private remains private, so long as one is not entered into the lists of the Night Officers, whose records transform private pleasures into a public archive, to be put to uses undreamt of by the original actors.

⊕

I made my first visit to a gathering of Franceschino's after some weeks of assiduous attention to work. I felt no hardship in the delay, no deprivation. Establishing myself fueled my resolve and whetted my appetite for pleasure. Once my affairs and my spirit were robust, there was little cause not to seek out what he promised I'd find there. The evening attracted perhaps twenty men, some young, some whose beards were silver, but all of the men's dress showed clearly that they were prosperous. The men arrived cloaked and masked, the torches they carried cast long shimmering reflections on the canal as their boats nosed to the landing at his door. Most greeted each other fondly but quietly and stepped into the door a servant held open. A room of moderate size off the main hall was where we left our clothes, neatly stacked and watched over by another servant. A tray of sweets sat on a sideboard near the door. The house was dimly lit by two torches in the hall, and by tapers held in bronze candelabrum in the smaller chambers. Musicians played, a lute and viol de gamba, from behind a screen, and their music spread gently though the house. At the back of the first floor was a large room hung with tapestries and furnished with several couches arranged in groups of twos and threes. Velvet cushions were spread about, and several low stools lined the walls. There were basins of water, linens for drying oneself, and two tables laden with wine and fruit at either end of the wide room. A fire burnt in the broad hearth in the middle of the back wall facing the main door.

As I entered there were but a few of us present. In the flickering light I saw a man stretched out on one couch blindfolded. Dark whorls of hair covered his chest, and traced a path down his belly. Another man stood above him, gently twisting his nipples as the first nuzzled and licked his ballsack. Another bent over the reclining man and took his hard cock into his mouth slowly, easily. The reclining man chuckled his encouragement and glee. As more men arrived, other groupings formed and dissolved. A young man, his beard the softest red silk, knelt in front of a man whose chest was covered with thick dark hair, swallowing his manhood as he held those of two other men in his hands as the three standing men hungrily nibbled at each other's mouths. Franceschino saw me from across the room and ambled toward me, greeting his guests with a kiss and an embrace. He wrapped me in his arms and slid his hand down my back and rested his fingers against my nether hole.

"Welcome, sweet Antonio, to my gathering. Here there is play with no censure, no fear, only pleasure."

"Wondrous beauty, to be sure." I kissed him.

"Explore, enjoy, and take your time." He turned toward a group that was forming on a couch, stood with his legs apart as a man hungrily snuffled in the forest of hair at the top of the arch formed by his well-muscled thighs. He threw his head back and sighed at a youth that caught his eye, "Ah, fickle Lorenzo, the breaker of hearts. A dalliance here, then away to your dark-eyed Jewess?"

Pairs of men grew into trios into quintets and dissolved again as men shifted and pleasure moved them to explore other bodies, other sensations. Arms entwined round thighs, and legs stretched into the air. Throughout the night one heard gradual crescendi of sighs, then yelps and moans of pleasure, first from one corner of the room, then from another: an antiphony of joyful lust fulfilled. I dove into a group and lost track of whose body began where and where my body left off. It was a blissful oblivion of flesh, and the tension that precedes release mounted, then receded, mounting again, receding again in waves. Time was not stopped exactly, only meaningless. The wonder of flesh, of skin and cock and nether hole, of musky smells and the salt bitterness of piss all available to knowing, to losing of oneself. Midway in the evening, stretched out on a couch, I enjoyed a big man's strength as he entered me, with a smaller man down my throat as he straddled my chest.

Moments after we'd untangled ourselves, a youth with a soft dark brown beard, lush curls like a smoky nimbus round his head implored me to take him. I'd seen him earlier in the night, and noted his beauty and the warning thrill of my susceptibility. I decided then not to seek him out, but to enjoy what was in my path. But once we'd found each other, he wouldn't leave my side. His body was muscled with the symmetry of a statue of antiquity, with a soft cloud of hair across his broad chest. As he gave me his warm sweet hole, his legs wrapped round my waist as I heartily plunged into him, his blazing eyes spurred me on to greater exertion than I thought I could manage. We came together, his eyes locked with mine as he begged me to give him my seed. I grunted and heaved and felt the muscles of his hole grip me tightly as I emptied myself deep inside him. Jets of his stuff spurted from his stout cock across his belly. I leaned down and lapped them up. He clamped his hands round my haunch to hold me inside him and I dropped down onto him in a swoon of spent joy.

I emerged from a brief doze, held in the arms of this handsome youth who slept the sleep of the contented. I gazed about the room at the slow movements of men as they gently roused themselves to gather their clothes and depart. It had been perhaps three hours, and all were spent and happy.

I looked down at the sleeping man in my arms, and as I was looking closely at his face his eyelids fluttered open. He spoke.

"I am Bassanio. I have never seen you here before, I think. Is this the first time you've come to Franceschino's?"

"Yes. I am come only recently to Venice, though I knew Franceschino long ago in another lifetime. I am Antonio."

"I believe you are the most beautiful man in Venice."

I did not stop my chuckle. "It does my sore heart good to hear you say it, though I think you may be a bit of a fool. A sweet fool, and an expert lover."

He reached up and drew my head down to kiss me.

"I wish to see you, to be alone with you. Tell me that is possible."

"It is possible, young man, but is it likely? Have a care. I have borne many wounds. I know not how many more I can survive, and your beauty is a certain snare I am but poorly guarded against."

"I would not have you guard yourself from me. I would have you capture me, and keep me fast."

"Oh, slowly now, slowly, boy. This is a story I know, and it never comes out well. The night's pleasures have intoxicated you beyond reason. Let a day pass before you think to see me again."

"That would be a day of misery. But if that will convince you, then I will endure it. How will I find you?"

"If after a day passes, no, two, if after two days pass you find that you still wish to see me, ask of Franceschino where I can be found, and he will tell you."

"I want to wake next to you, so that I can feel you inside me as the day begins, and to return to your bed in the evening, to feel you inside me as the night falls."

"That is something you can't possibly know after a night such as we have passed. I think you are trouble, young man. Your honeyed words and favored form have always gotten you everything you wished, I think. Is that not so?"

"You seemed to take your pleasure heartily in me this night. What harm can there be in claiming more?"

"Silken speech like these silken curls. I am not adamantine. You come and find me out after the passage of two days, and we'll see how much you still wish for me."

$\oplus$

Whether I doubted that Bassanio would seek me out I cannot tell. Perhaps I hoped he would not. My hoping so did not alter my course once I greeted him, and so hopes once again proved worthless. It is action that is all, and my actions were all too predictable.

He came to me on the third day following our meeting. I heard Marina's labored breathing, like a complaint, as she approached my study.

"A youth, sir, waits for you below."

"Thank you, Marina. You can tell him to come up. I see by your hardened brow that you do not approve."

"It is hardly my place to approve or not to approve. An idle, handsome youth seems an unusual visitor to your study, that is all."

"That is not all, and you and I both know it. Though how you can tell that he is idle I cannot say. Bring us some of that new wine from Chianti, bread and olives, please. Marina, you have never given me cause to doubt your loyalty, but if something chafes you, and if you would be happier elsewhere, all you need do is make the request. I will do all I can to help you to a household you will find more to your liking."

"It is not my disliking that matters sir, only what others conclude when they observe men like you consorting with youths like him."

"Men like me? Can you tell me what exactly do you mean?"

"Oh, sir. You know what I mean. I mean bachelors. Beyond a certain age. We all know."

"Yes. We all know. And this paltry knowing is worth little except to those who seek to sow misery. And youths like him? Of what sort is this youth?"

"Of the idle sort."

"And what of that? Surely there is little risk of venomous words coming from my own household. Is that not so?"

"If it is not so, my lord, may I be stricken with an ague."

"Oh, gently, Marina, gently. I rest assured. Send the youth to me."

Her mutters followed her down the stairs. The next moment I heard the bounding strides of a youth taking three steps at a time. I rose from my desk and turned. My breath was a bit faster. I'd been eager for this moment, in spite of myself. My racing heart gave the lie to those reasoning thoughts that counseled caution. He appeared in the doorway, dropped his bronze-colored cloak on the chair, and strode toward me. His keen eyes shone with knowingness as he dropped to his knees and grabbed the laces of my codpiece. I reached down and pulled him to his feet, grasped the back of his neck as our mouths met for a moment. I held his head firmly as I pulled away.

"Franceschino did not tell me you would be coming."

"I asked him to allow me the pleasure of taking you unawares. You do not regret the sight of me, I think."

"Few would, but then you know that, don't you?" His smile did not waver. "I will tell you something about myself, Bassanio. I do not dissemble, except when I do not know myself that I am doing so, and that amounts to something quite different. The few times I have tried were failures, and so you'll find that I say only precisely what I mean. This is not the custom here, I have observed."

"You will not find that I dissemble. I have no wish to play falsely with you. I have thought of little but of you these many hours."

"A youth should have many diversions to occupy himself with, and not an old merchant."

"You are hardly old, and if a merchant, the handsomest merchant in all the city. Of that I am certain." He reached for me again, as Marina's heavy sighs announced her approach.

"I've sent for some refreshment. Sit. I wish to learn who this youth is that accosts me so. Ah, Marina, thank you. Set the tray down there, and that will be all we require."

She heaved a sigh of acknowledgement and like a ship coming to, shifted her bulk toward the door and down the stairs. I poured two beakers of wine and turned to my young guest. We sat together on a couch strewn with charts, papers and pillows.

"So. Who is this wondrous youth before me? What occupies the busy hours of your life?"

He set his beaker on a table and leaned toward me, his hands on each of my thighs. Urgency scored his brow.

"That which distracts any of us here, the general pursuit. A pursuit of business, of fame, and pleasure. Distraction, I should say, anything so as not to fade away in boredom."

"Is there really so little for you here?"

"There is too much, and the muchness cloys with familiarity. The appetite wanes though the profusion of delights is ever increasing. You see through all of this, don't you? Your eyes tell of something else."

"Have a care. What you might see in my eyes may be nothing more than what you put there."

"I don't believe that. I see sadness. Tell me that is not so."

"One doesn't attain my span of years without knowing sadness, handsome boy. And your family, do they know nothing but joy and harmony?"

"My family is of the unremarkable nobility. I am a gentleman, but that says so little. I have been provided for, and the usual expectations hover. A more distracted man than my father would be hard to find at this moment. No tragedy, simply a distracted disposition. There are some ships it is up to me to manage, but the consequences are few if my management is lax. Ease, a life of ease, boring, easeful ease, and I fear I shall fade away. Am I not contemptible?"

"Only in your own eyes, perhaps. You have not been tested, and you yearn to know your limits. That is what you seek in me, isn't it?"

"I can't know that. I only know that when I was with you, when I felt you in me, I no longer feared fading away."

"What do you seek with me?"

"I want to be with you."

"And what of me? Why should I want to be with you? You've never had to bother yourself with such a question, have you? Your beauty and your position have rendered you deaf to such disquieting thoughts."

While it was true that I saw this in Bassanio, it was clear this left him so unsatisfied. That is what caught me, this bit of grit, this disturbance—it was a flint that sparked a sense that there might be another's sensibility that mattered. Or was I reading in him what I wished to find there—just as I warned that he would read what he wished to in me? What satisfaction could he have with me? And what satisfaction might I have, beyond gazing at his beauty and finding new distraction from my solitude? A queasy fluttering filled my gut. I knew this story, I knew it so well and yet I could not help myself. I stood up.

"Kneel here, handsome one. Unlace your shirt."

His breathing quickened. Without taking his eyes from mine he shrugged off his linen and it hung round his waist. I took his nipples between thumb and forefingers. He moaned softly and dropped his head back. I pulled.

"Lift me up. Hurt me. You can't hurt me. Lift me up. Tear them off. You can't hurt me."

I pulled him up. He lapped at my beard, my neck, my ears.

"Please, please, let me see you."

I released him and he sank back to his knees. He reached for my leg and traced the muscles as he stared at me, his chest heaving.

"Oh, please let me see you."

I drew my shirt over my head and stood over him.

"Just to look at you. Just to look at you." Tears spilled from his eyes. This youth surprised me beyond measure. I was choked with rising tears of my own. I reached down and drew him toward the couch. I punched the swelling muscle of his breast.

"Harder. Yes. More. You can't hurt me. Hurt me."

With each blow he threw his head back and let forth a yelp. He reached for my head and pressed his mouth against mine, whimpering, shivering. I shuddered with the recognition that something rare had been uncovered. This boy knew what he wanted from me after all, and knew that I could give it. And it appeared that he wanted to receive it.

"Softly, now. This is enough, no more."

"Oh, yes, more, please, more, sir."

"Later. Quietly now. Lie here a moment. I must attend to some business soon." I stood back and reached for my linen. "So, it seems you do know what you seek in me, don't you?"

"Oh, yes, that is certain. But I could not have told you before this moment what it was. Thank you. Thank you. Thank you."

"Quiet, now.... It is for me to thank you, beautiful boy. There is much for us to discover, I think. Dress, and walk with me to the Rialto. And you shall tell me exactly how you fill your days."

I popped two olives in my mouth, one in his. He sank back into the cushion and smiled at me.

"And you shall tell me your history, too, yes? There has been much speculation about you. The city buzzes with tales."

"Buzzing with inconsequentiality."

He drank off his beaker of wine, pulled his shirt up, slid his arms through the sleeves, walked over and picked up his cloak and wrapped it about him.

"Help me with this."

As he laced my doublet for me I could smell the scent of his hair, his sweat, the sweetness of a youth's body.

⊕

He came the following day, and the next, and soon, in some parts of the city it was expected that we appear together. I enjoyed his sweetness, and he enjoyed my—what? My weight, my grounding I should say. To the mercantile world of Venice I was a young man's benefactor and a tutor of sorts, a serious man of business and so ballast to a youth's lightness. So long as my role as merchant was successfully performed, the world was content to go on with its buzzing but show us no sting. But I was not content, not at first. I had known so much more. I had known what it was to show the joy I found with a man, to freely share our love. I wanted that again. To return to the domesticated duplicity of city life was a slow strangulation. All who counseled me swore such duplicity was essential. Franceschino angrily warned me to curb my oppositional nature or I would suffer a terrible punishment. De Norville sharply predicted the direst of fates for my reckless defiance of the city's ways. Even Silvio, sympathetic and susceptible to Bassanio's charm, was certain that my love for Bassanio would be fatal to me. To each I demanded a reason for a man's love to be so condemned. And each only repeated the reasons I knew so well. This fair companion of my days lightened my heavy spirits, sharpened my resolve. What though Bassanio and his pack gambled and idled, such were the occupations of many a young man. Protest I might, but well I knew the truth of my friends' warnings. And so I trained myself to comply. I adopted the dissembling ways of the city and found that my sober mien worked to silence tongues that were wont to wag. Months did pass in this way, my happiness vouchsafed by the mask I learned to wear in spite of myself.

Warmer weather allowed my ships longer voyages, and I shipped Venice silks round all the way to England and brought Flemish lace back. In time I had a fleet of five stout ships and contracts with dealers throughout the city. Nine months of assiduous work and I was made. Fortune shone warmly on my affairs.

⊕

It was a season to enjoy. Fortune, Bassanio, Franceschino, even the eyes of Venice seemed to smile upon me. But much was in that "seemed." Of all men I knew how easily some storm could blast this happiness away. It could be the Republic's laws or the bruised feelings of men—I'd been harmed by both in my time—yet still I survived. I looked not for the assurance of long life. I looked only for what I could reliably set my hand to.

One night a soft breeze's caresses soothed me as I looked across the lagoon, idly waiting for ships that were expected to return this day or the next. There was pleasure in an evening's respite. But not for Bassanio, who stood next to me, worrying the fingers of one hand with the other.

"What troubles you?" I asked him.

"I do not like to tell you. Yet you see clear and I will be quick to tell you all. I am indebted and I fear turning to my father."

"What debts are these? You've told me of no misfortune in your affairs."

"These debts that plague me are from the gaming table."

I looked away because my disgust was plain. When I was a youth, my reckless gamble was the pursuit of my desire, not the chase after luck and specious profit.

"I do not know what pleasure such an occupation can afford you. It is the sheerest foolishness."

"The pleasures are the camaraderie of the table, and there are benefits to the practice, though I know you hold such in contempt. But there are friendships to be cultivated there that lead to business."

"What friendship can grow from attempting to take another man's money with no effort but the throw of the dice?"

"It is mutual."

"Mutual contempt. Little that is good grows from such a conception."

"My friend, my love, my luck has left me of late. Do not chastise me with your frowning disappointment. Leave off your censure, and I'll swear to leave off those habits that bring you displeasure."

"Truly? You'll leave the gaming to others who can better afford to lose? What surety have I if I believe you?"

"The surety of my love."

I fixed my eyes on his. "Do not trifle with me. If you know anything about me it is that my love is constant and sure. What amount will relieve you?"

"Five hundred ducats. I'll repay you when my ships are returned."

"It is a manageable amount. Let this be the last time, Bassanio. The last time."

"Take me home, will you? I am weary of these games, and you are the one sure port where I can find my peace."

It suited me to believe him. I sighed and clasped his hand. As a velvet evening drew about us we found a boatman to row us home. Night's mantle shielded us and I did not shrink when Bassanio leaned his head against my shoulder. The gentle rocking of the boatman's stroke lulled us to such sweet closeness that the moment etched itself in my bosom.

⊕

And then one early morning there was a pounding at my door. It was Bassanio—frantic with news. Marina was still abed, and I shuddered awake from a dream that chilled my bones. I wrapped a cloak about myself and descended. The gray light of another November dawn smeared the marble floor. I pulled open the door and he fell across the threshold, into my arms.

"It is Franceschino—he's been denounced to the Night Officers, and arrested. He is to be tried by the Council of Ten. Rounded up last night, several of us, five, six. If we'd been with him, we'd be there too." He stopped and gasped for air.

"Come, sit a moment. Breathe." I paced to the back of the house, poured a flagon of wine, drank off half of it as I stalked back. It was as if we were pursued by harpies. Lunatic, inexorable harpies. For years, now, Franceschino had counted himself safe in Venice. His gatherings were thought to be secure. Men arrived masked, servants were trusted, and the guests always included many from the leading houses in the city. It was the mad hypocrisy of our age that flared up when an answer was required, an expiation demanded for the random event that cannot be explained. This was the universal explanation: round up the sodomites and their Lord God would be satisfied.

"Is there any word as to when he is to be tried?"

"That I know not." He looked wildly about him as he spoke, nearly shouting with indignation. "I know not if there is to be a trial at all, or merely the denunciation and the sentence. But to be called before the Council, this is no small event. Antonio, I don't think anything can be done."

"No. They mean to make of him an example. They felt the need for the grand gesture, and since he is not a son of Venice, but a significant figure, he is the obvious choice. An unmarried man of his age, of his prominence: this is their warning to us all. Do you know where he is held?"

"I'm to meet Gratiano on the Rialto. He was to learn what he could."

"Wait while I dress. You need some food? Back in the kitchen, find what you need, I'll be down in a moment."

The fleetest way was on foot. That early there were few stirring, and the dank chill of night clung to the stones we trod on. As we approached the bridge we saw Gratiano pacing, and Lorenzo leaned on the railing with his head in his hands.

"What news?"

"Little to lift your spirits, Antonio. He is held in the new palace of prisoners. It is so new the scaffolding still o'ershadows lover's wanton meetings. Have you seen it? Directly behind the Palace, it has its own covered bridge. So those who would force confessions need not be troubled by rough weather. It is impossible to enter any other way. He is permitted no visitors, nor is he granted an advocate. He is to appear before the Council tomorrow. Apparently this action is to be swift and fell. It is certain they mean to execute him in the traditional way, at Saint Mark's."

"Oh God, a flaying?" cried Lorenzo. "Then the public burning of the carcass? That barbarous practice hasn't been demonstrated in years."

"Precisely. All the more reason for dispatch" Gratiano snapped.

"But who betrayed him?" I nearly shook him. "Who denounced him to the Night Office?"

"That I could not learn. It might have been any number of men. A political favor, a chance to gain a toehold in the upward clamber. Or even a jealous courtesan, whose charms are fading and who needed to spark a new excitement. Who can say? We, none of us who frequented Franceschino's evenings, are safe now. It is the time for the public gesture, the posture that will impart a measure of safety."

I was glad that it was Gratiano who urged this.

Lorenzo retorted, "Oh, come now, you know most of the men condemned by the Night Office were married."

I spoke, "Marriage may be no surety that a man loves not a youth, but I do recommend such an action for all of you. And besides, you are of an age when this has been expected for some time now."

Bassanio, who'd been silent, holding my arm, staring off across the canal, spoke urgently into my ear.

"And what of you, Antonio? You know you are one of the bachelors they most suspect. Your age, your alien state, your association with Franceschino. What of you?" There were anxious tears in his eyes.

"I am known as a sober man of business who conducts his affairs quietly, not as a ribald. Besides, it is far too late for the public gesture to avail me any safety. I've lived my life in the way I choose for far too long for the insincere atonement. Now Franceschino has been taken, we're probably safer than we've been for some time: they have their scapegoat. All my thoughts are on him and how to see him. Who will come with me to the prison?"

"To appear as an interested party is to confess to the same crime. It is obviously unwise to go." Gratiano merely expressed what all three knew to be the truth.

"He was my first lover, and is my oldest friend." Bassanio gasped and gripped my arm. "Love strong enough to reach through the years does not willingly release its grip. Such is his hold on me and I will not consent easily to his absence again. A protest must be lodged. When I was a good deal younger than you, and he was near to the age I am today, we were hounded from Florence by this same fiery madness that means to extinguish another of us. There could be no doubt that I will go. Besides, he is a business partner of mine. That is beard enough."

I looked at the three young men. They trembled in the chill, but they could not meet my eyes. Bassanio writhed with shame. I took his hand.

"My boy, do not suffer so. Come to me later, if you wish, but there is no need for you to punish yourself."

There was more misery in his look than I'd ever seen darken his open, handsome face. And fear. He squeezed my hand before he turned away. Gratiano and Lorenzo followed across the bridge.

With a gnawing in my belly I turned toward the canal to seek a boatman to carry me to where my old lover was held.

⊕

The warden was implacable. I gained no entry, and no message was conveyed to Franceschino. I was told only that the meeting of the Council was to take place at two in the afternoon, and that it was to be a public hearing.

De Norville was the man. To his house I made my way.

⊕

"Yes, yes, yes. It was only a matter of time, you see. It generally is. What men like Franceschino do for the wheels of power is so important. It is not the sodomy so much as it is the importance of the office. The upward progress of the career. And men like Franceschino are simply too—"

"Yes, yes, yes, I know. I've always known. It has been ever thus. What, what, what can be done? That is the question I put to you."

"I believe that is the first time my earnest friend has ever interrupted me. I forgive you. I quite understand your heat." His wattles quivered, and he blinked back a tear—of surprise? Of shock? "If there were something to be done, it were best that it were done quickly, and that none may know of it. Will you grant me that? That none, not even you, can know of it?"

"And I am to live—"

"If you *are* to live, it must be as if you forgot Franceschino. Let his name not cross your lips. Let your business fill your life. The iron bars bear down, Antonio, and if you wish to live, you must give up much."

"To feign forgetting is the price for life. What can feigning be but folly? Can the world be so credulous?"

"Ah, you feign yourself if you tell me you do not already know the answer."

"You mystify me, de Norville. You do not play with me, that I know, and yet you spoke of that which must be done, and done so no one knows it. Do you mean that I might live with hopes deferred?"

"Can you possibly not understand that if I were to answer, I put us both in peril? There simply is no answer. You've come to the limit. Feel it. You must know it, succumb to it, or not, as you please. But if you choose not to, you must know that you are marked for another spectacular sacrifice to their ravenous Christian god. You would be beheaded, flayed, and burnt at the stake as sure as we stand here. Mark me."

I turned away from the only man I thought I could turn to. I could no longer look at the rosy jowls, at the jewels on his fat, tiny hands, at the folds of his emerald gown. I could no longer countenance any human society. Yet he was right. This was the limit. The edict that brooks no negotiation. The edge that borders no territory beyond, into which one might stray but for a moment's respite, to find restoration enough to stand a life so bounded and so hounded by the wickedness and venality of men.

De Norville spoke again, with a warmth I'd never heard. "You know, of course, what it is that must be done quickly. Your young friends must take wives. I believe they all can do it easily, and it will benefit them all beyond the immediate crisis, for if my ears on the Rialto are right, they are all encumbered by estates that are tattered and fading. Dowries are what they need. Dowries and respectability. I do not dare suggest the same to you, but if you consort with the ostentatiously married, you will have done yourself a favor. I do not speak of love. Love is more than possible—it even may be easy when it is mandatory. But then what we call 'love' in Venice is...well...the Serene Republic offers and it demands. At this moment its demands are urgent. You need not forget about me, my friend. You may come to me when and if you will. You will always be welcome. Now go. My boatman will take you to your door."

⊕

The announcement was posted and the news spread with the speed given to all news of others' misfortune. Franceschino was to be executed for the foul crime of sodomy and the corruption of the youth of the city on the eighteenth day of November. The sentence was to be carried out in the small terrace at the side of the Palace. He was to be held in chains as his head was cut off, his body flayed, then burnt. It was the custom that such an announcement attract a crowd of eager observers. Those tradesmen who sell food to be eaten at public festivities rejoiced. Business would be brisk.

⊕

Days passed and I did not rouse myself from my study. Bassanio came
to my door every day, begging to see me. I turned him away. He sent
me this message:

> I know not why you will not see me. I love you. I know
> you love me. I will not fail you, though you seem to press me
> beyond my patience. There is news about Franceschino that
> I hoped to pour into your ear myself, but I must be content
> to set it down here for your eyes to devour. And yet I know
> not what it may mean. Few know this, but I have it on good
> authority. It is denied by those who are well served by its denial,
> but when the guards went to his cell on the day his sentence
> was to be carried out, he was not there. And yet no one had
> gained admittance to his cell at all. As you well know, all were
> barred, not even a message could be delivered. It is a mystery.
> The Ten think that they can deny what is known by so few, and
> it has been announced that his execution for crimes against the
> laws of god and man was carried out in the little square, and
> there are those who have sworn they witnessed it. But it could
> not have happened. It did not happen. It is said they burnt a
> goat to produce the charred remains. And yet he is lost to us.
> Vanished. He is no more. But I am. I am here. When you care
> to see me, I am here.

What was I to make of this? Vanished is vanished. I could make
nothing of this, and so I worked. Days became weeks, then months. I
worked. I profited. I risked more and more. I set more ships to hazard,
and they always returned, full bellied and fine. The thrill of the risk
became the only sensation I sought. But as my fortunes rose a chill
spread through my heart. I became a true citizen, a man of business, a
Venetian. My dissembling knew no bound, no edge. The performance
allowed no intermission, no respite. Soon I could smile and smile and
be a villain. An upright, prosperous villain. A villain who is generous
to his young friends. Who indulged his favorite, and drank and jested
with his favorite's friends. A villain who could lend—nay give—money
to those overextended young men. A villain who could support their

folly. A villain whose success announced to the world that he was no villain, but a pillar of the community.

My chilled heart allowed me to despise. Aha! I quickened to a new sensation, one that had never seemed to be needed before. But now, ah, the chilly pleasure of finding another more contemptible than myself and all the other curs that fouled the rough walkways, the fetid canals, the ancient stones of this corrupt low city. A city that seems to be sinking as it gathers into itself all men's desires to buy and sell, and to make of others nothing but poppets that will buy and sell and buy and sell. A man is worthless if he cannot be bought, and if he cannot sell. I was now a true citizen of a city whose soul so resembles the canal that is coiled like a snake, the canal it depends on—nay lives and breathes by—coiled round in merchandise and business, in deceit and petty vengeances. Coiled in hate. I could hate. I found that I could hate. I could hate the wanton youths. I could hate the comely ladies and their dowries. I could hate the lackeys and their scraping. I could hate the clerics and the monks. I could hate the councilors and the notaries and the scheming politicians. I could hate the lawyers and the scriveners and the moneylenders. I could hate the grasping Jews and the passionate Moors. The lisping Spaniards and the wild-eyed Ethiopes. I could hate with an appetite that would never be sated. Oh God, I was gone. Consumed. The once fair and loving Antonio was truly gone. I was not Antonio. There was no Antonio there. Antonio was lost. Antonio became a glutton of hatred. Oh, you terrible, implacable, absent gods, you ground me to a powder, under your mortar in this pestilent pestle, you ground me into nothing. Nothing but hatred and dissembling.

The Moneylender

Spring light glancing off the stones of my terrace did not pierce the cloud of melancholy that I wore about me as I stepped into the day. So accoutered, I felt scant difference twixt dawn and dusk. My spirits lifted when Bassanio was near, though our time together was brief. What was once a prudent necessity—finding a wife—had become a pastime that sparked his enthusiasm, a new respite from the creeping boredom he complained of when first we met. Once I was an object of novelty. Now he spent his time in another pursuit. Such had been my counsel, so I could stand no ground to complain. This was my season of renunciation, and I bent to its harsh necessity. What love of his I could retain was comfort, though, and charged me with a vigor that reminded me of what once I was.

This morning two men who said they counted me a friend paid me a visit, though I cannot with any confidence say whether they came to lift my spirits or to collect what news they might to make sport withal. These were not objectionable men, not with any outward signs thereof, though it was a measure of the enfeeblement of melancholy that I could no longer really tell. Salarino and Solanio were men of business who I often saw as I walked from appointment to appointment. Their frequent greetings assumed an air of quotidian responsibility, as if they sought to mark some progress, though what or whose I knew not. They jested, they wheedled, they drank the wine I offered them, but always with a purpose that remained obscure. They knew of my fondness for Franceschino and now Bassanio, and tales of dalliances of their own reached my ears as well. But could I count them friends? No, surely not. But neither did I show them out. I had learned that keeping such men as these near was far wiser than shunning any of those who frequented the Rialto. It was far better that I play the game.

"In sooth I know not why I am so sad," I began, and already I was weary, though the day had just begun. I spoke a falsehood. I knew quite well what pressed upon my spirit, day after day. The countenance of the one who was lost to me was embossed on my mind and on my body, and the warm presence of the other reminded me perforce of that which must remain beyond my reach. I behaved like one who believes that by feigning ignorance he would finally find the lie that would most convince himself.

Salarino, as free of distinction as a stone rubbed smooth, observed, "Your mind is tossing on the ocean," as if to explain myself to me. What moves a man to try to explain another's mood to him? It cannot be in good earnest, can it? Is it not a ploy to flush out some confession?

As if in sympathy his anodyne companion Solanio mewed, "Every object that would make me fear misfortune to my ventures, out of doubt would make me sad."

They both fell to work. Salarino speaking at length about the losses he most feared, concluding with a visible satisfaction, "I know Antonio is sad to think about his merchandise."

Merchandise. I felt my soul shrivel with each incantation of the word. I parried his assurance, avowing that my ventures were so various and wisely chosen as never to hazard all at one throw. Mark you all: my dissembling here was key. All my fortunes were at sea, and little that passed my lips in conference with these men was true. Money was now what I lied about. This was part of doing business. Like a spreading spill of wine on a damask cloth, the parts of my life that demanded dissembling grew. A man's love for other men of necessity had to be hid, and then necessity swelled, and it was tales of money I must tell. I was utterly a creature of this city.

Then the teasing dart was shot.

"Why then you are in love," Solanio said with an insinuating intimacy so mistakenly assumed that a stronger man than I would find it comic.

I could only scold, "Fie, fie!"

He had hit the mark, it is true, but only partly. He knew full well of my attachment to Bassanio, and of the younger man's to me. Yet still he tried with an antic spin to bait me. No one mentioned Franceschino in my presence, and only hints that could not be confirmed glinted in jibes crafted to deliver both a knowing compassion and a taunting needle. It was so easy to forget that once there was a time I dissembled not. Now, I did not even feel myself reach for the lie, so easily did it fall from honeyed lips. Such was the art of conversation among the merchant class.

This morning's jousting was interrupted when my band of young men arrived for our daily reconnoiter. We were held together still by what we could speak not of.

Salarino, when he saw Lorenzo, Gratiano, and Bassanio approach us on the terrace, pouted, "I would have stayed till I had made you merry, if worthier friends had not prevented me."

It was hardly the handsome worthiness of the men that prevented him and I could guess that what drew them away was a galling awareness of their awkward superfluity. With my young friends present they were simply outnumbered and their game could yield no advantage to them. I ushered the moment to completion.

"Your worth is very dear in my regard. I take it your own business calls on you, and you embrace the occasion to depart." Bland smiles obscured opaque faces.

Bassanio noted the change in the weather, "Good signiors both, when shall we laugh? Say, when? You grow exceeding strange. Must it be so?"

Knowing that their disguise as friends fooled no one in this company, Salarino weakly tossed, "We'll make our leisures to attend on yours."

Their exit did not merit comment. Instead, Lorenzo and Gratiano made it clear that they had conveyed Bassanio to a meeting only with me. Gratiano, though, told me at length that I did not look well. Such is the kindness of the young that they grasp the thorns of difficulty and press them back into one's own palms.

"You have too much respect upon the world," he reminded me, "they lose it that do buy it with much care. Believe me, you are marvelously changed."

At last I could say exactly what I meant. "I hold the world but as the world, Gratiano: a stage where every man must play a part. And mine a sad one."

I had handed him an opportunity to make much of: that is to speak at length and to say very little, as he was known to do. He explained that he was happy to play the fool, as if informing any of us present of something we did not know. Still, his was a loving disposition, fuddled with these young men's waywardness and too much drink.

He and Lorenzo agreed to meet us at dinnertime. Alone, I pressed Bassanio to tell me of his pressing need.

"Tell me now what lady is the same to whom you swore a secret pilgrimage, that you today promised to tell me of."

But first it was of money that he had to speak.

"'Tis not unknown to you, Antonio, that I have much disabled my estate." This was the world we found, and so we became those who deserved such a world. Before speaking of the lady, there was money to consider, or rather the lack of it. Then he could tell of the object of his ambitions.

"In Belmont is a lady richly left; and she is fair, and fairer than that word, of wondrous virtues. Sometimes from her eyes I did receive fair speechless messages. Her name is Portia."

But to court this richly furnished lady, he must have the means to complete. And so, of course, he turned to the man he loved and who loved him. How could he doubt me?

"All my fortunes are at sea; neither have I money, nor commodity to raise a present sum. Therefore go forth," I told him, "try what my credit can in Venice do; that shall be racked even to the uttermost to furnish thee to Belmont to fair Portia. Go presently and inquire, and so will I, where money is; and I no question make to have it of my trust or for my sake."

This is what a loving friend does for another, is it not? I could not lie to Bassanio, as I could deny him nothing, so to him all I spoke was truth. Here was the telltale trace of an Antonio of old, that one day, perhaps, I could recognize again as myself. That for the man who fired my love I could not, would not dissemble. And if there was one for whom I could not dissemble, then my balance was skewed. Bassanio upset a balance that was so precarious. He touched off a fire that had been banked long enough that I'd hoped its heat could remain a faint memory. I ought to be grateful, now, I think, though he brought me new suffering. For without his presence there would have been little need for an Antonio I knew. Though I was on the cusp of an age that I thought would render me some safety, if not satiety, I was willing, nay yearning, to lose all in forgetfulness. But Bassanio turned to me, desired me, loved me, and I beheld a part of myself that was not lost, but found in a well-worn path.

⊕

Bassanio located a ready lender, one Shylock, a man known to me enough to have inspired a caustic contempt that festered robustly between us. Then, too, he was father of the dark-haired Jessica who had captured the heart of Lorenzo, whose mordant sobriety distinguished him among Bassanio's circle, and so I favored him. Shylock led me to his quarters in the Ghetto, across the Grand Canal to the northwestern reaches of the city. I hoped this interview would last not a moment longer than possible, though if my errand allowed a glimpse of the lady who could snare Lorenzo, I would be pleased.

"Shylock, albeit I neither lend nor borrow by taking nor by giving of excess, yet to supply the ripe wants of my friend I'll break a custom."

His face betrayed no malice or heat. "Ay, ay, three thousand ducats."

"And for three months," I uselessly reminded him.

"I had forgot—three months, you told me so." I am certain he had not forgot. "Well then, your bond. And let me see—but hear you, methought you said you neither lend nor borrow upon advantage."

I sought to convey only the truth, not my feelings about it, "I do never use it."

And he was off: "When Jacob grazed his uncle Laban's sheep—" He spun out lengthy scripture to demonstrate the importance of lending at interest. His memory was prodigious, and he relished his temporizing torture. This was just the use of religious writings that maddened me, and he stirred me, I admit it, he did. Scripture meant little to me, but the hypocritical use of religion in business of this sort raised my ire.

Foolishly, I disputed him, "This was not a venture, sir, that Jacob served for, a thing not in his power to bring to pass, but swayed and fashioned by the hand of heaven, was this inserted to make interest good? Or is your gold and silver ewes and rams?"

"I cannot tell," he simpered before making his vulgar boast, "I make it breed as fast. But note me, signior—"

I could not help myself. I turned to my young friend. "Mark you this, Bassanio, the devil can cite scripture for his purpose. An evil soul producing holy witness is like a villain with a smiling cheek, a goodly apple rotten at the heart. O, what a goodly outside falsehood hath!"

Shylock was impervious to my insults. "Three thousand ducats— 'tis a good round sum. Three months from twelve, then let me see, the rate—"

I boiled over, "Well, Shylock, shall we be beholding to you?"

He was icy with resolve to maintain his smooth demeanor. "Signior Antonio, many a time and oft in the Rialto you have rated me about my moneys and my usances. Still I have borne it with a patient shrug, for sufferance is the badge of all our tribe. You call me misbeliever, cut-throat dog, and spit upon my Jewish gaberdine, and all for use of that which is mine own. Well then, it now appears you need my help. Go to, then. You come to me and you say, 'Shylock we would have moneys'—you say so, you that did void your rheum upon my beard and foot me as you spurn a stranger cur over your threshold: money is your suit. What should I say to you? Should I not say, 'Hath a dog money? Is it possible a cur can lend three thousand ducats?' Or shall I bend low and in a bondman's key, with bated breath and whispering humbleness say this: 'Fair sir, you spit on me on Wednesday last, you spurned me such a day, another time you called me dog; and for these courtesies I'll lend you thus much moneys'?"

That would have been precisely how I would have it. "I am as like to call thee so again, to spit on thee again, to spurn thee too. If thou wilt lend this money, lend it not as to thy friends, for when did friendship take a breed for barren metal of his friend? But lend it rather to thine enemy, who if he break, thou mayst with better face exact the penalty."

He had the best of me, he knew it, and he used his advantage, "I would be friends with you and have your love, forget the shames that you have stained me with, supply your present wants, and take no doit of usance for my moneys, yet you'll not hear me. This is kind I offer."

Bassanio, whose discomfort at my passion was clear, weakly urged, "This were kindness."

But instead of interest, Shylock proposed a bond of his devising. I wonder still if I heard him speak the words, or if the vent of hearing was stopped by my hatred for this man.

With no trace of feeling he calmly reasoned, "If you repay me not on such a day, in such a place, such sum or sums as are expressed in the condition, let the forfeit be nominated for an equal pound of your fair flesh, to be cut off and taken from what part of your body pleaseth me."

He tossed this off with such ease that another man might have taken it for some ghastly jest. He'd done his work well.

Without hesitation, and condescending to demonstrate my superiority I snapped, "Content, in faith. I'll seal to such a bond, and say there is much kindness in the Jew."

Both Bassanio and the moneylender urged my caution, but I heard it not. So inflamed was my pride that there was no reasonable Antonio present to save myself. No further disaster could befall me. The greatest disasters were all behind me already.

The notary affixed his seal to the bond and the Jew delivered us the ducats. I had no doubt that my ships would return a month before the bond came due. This loathsome day would hardly warrant its memory save as evidence of what I'd become: a man to be held contemptible.

Money. It was impossible to feel the poison fatal to friendship start its work when money conveyed the dose and contempt held us together. The poison's effect was obscure because we were aligned against Shylock, someone we so easily could hold in contempt. Our contempt helped us maintain a balance. So long as we could hate, we could ignore the corruption eating away at what was between us. But with a menace as soft as one of Catarina's stealthiest recipes our lives were surely poisoned.

Because Bassanio had agreed, finally, that finding a wife was the wisest course, we were balanced. Because I staked my credit to raise him the money, we were balanced. Because the Jew would not forfeit his bond, letting us despise him the more, we were balanced. But the balance demanded that a lie beget lies without comment, without notice. Balance begot lies, and lies maintained balance. Would mere survival allow a person to admire such handiwork? Most heartily. But oh, the cost, the cost that had to be paid.

⊕

The public quality of my ill fortune galled me. It seemed that others knew even before I did that one by one my ships were lost. One, a ship of rich lading wrecked on the narrows at Goodwin Sands, a dangerous shoal my captain had good knowledge of, but foundered on all the same. Even the Jew knew of this, and of each of my losses somehow, at the moment I learned of them. For his part, the Jew himself had been traduced and mocked—the elopement of his daughter Jessica with Lorenzo relieved him not only of his child but of some trinkets precious to him. Vengeance in all of his dealings was his only wish. I was numb, hollowed out by loss, first Franceschino now Bassanio. That I knew it was coming, indeed had urged him toward it, availed me nothing. My young companion was successful in his suit and won the hand of wealthy, worldly Portia. And so, when the term of the loan was expired and the debt due, it surprised me little that Shylock himself brought the jailer. No pain could reach me more. That collector of any and all of the news on the Rialto, Solanio, was with me when they came.

"But hear me speak, Shylock—" How wearily I knew the futility of any speech.

He oozed contemptuous satisfaction. "I will have my bond. Go to, Jailer."

Solanio looked at me as if eloquence might change this course. I answered him.

"I have no wish to follow him more with bootless prayers. He seeks my life. His reason well I know: I oft delivered from his forfeitures many that have at times made moan to me. Therefore he hates me."

Solanio sought to soothe me. "I am sure the duke will never grant this forfeiture to hold."

His naïveté surprised me. Surely a man of business well knows the importance of the smooth functioning of the machinery that moves our world. I felt little, though. Tired. I felt tired.

"The duke cannot deny the course of law; for the commodity that strangers have with us in Venice, if it be denied, will much impeach the justice of the state, since that the trade and profit of the city consisteth of all nations. Therefore go. These griefs and losses have so bated me that I shall hardly spare a pound of flesh tomorrow to my bloody creditor. Well, Jailer, on. Pray God, Bassanio come to see me pay his debt, and then I care not."

On we were conducted, to my end.

⊕

In the court I could barely see, breathe, know what was happening, so dully thrumming were my senses. I do know that Shylock refused twice, even thrice his three thousand ducats, a sum I learned much later that remarkable Portia, Bassanio's bride, so willingly provided. And I do remember that the duke introduced a young doctor of law from Padua, whose countenance could hardly inspire my confidence. He was a youth with a cheek of smoothest ivory, whose eyes were clear and untroubled by care. Only much later did those of us in the courtroom discover that this youth was a creation of Portia's fancy, and her performance a masterpiece of deception and skillful argument. She did draw things out a bit, I don't mind saying, whether by art or happenstance, I'm not in a position to say.

Out of the thrumming of my senses came a chaos of reminiscence. With my fate sealed, I gave myself up to a procession of visions from time past. Florence, Franceschino, the *Black Phoenix*, Rodrigo, Adjullo, my Countess Catarina, young Bassanio. Franceschino's lips again claimed mine, filling my mouth with the taste of his skin. There again were Catarina's eyes, mocking and loving at the same time. Then the surety of Rodrigo's face and strong rough hands, his broad chest and steadfast arms. There was the burnished glow of Adjullo's fathomless complexion and magnificent muscles. Though all were lost to me, all returned, impervious to time's impartial degradation, as if taunting me again as Fortune's bastard.

There was stillness in the courtroom. The inward masque of memory vanished. I opened my eyes and saw all attention directed to me, so with all my strength I called out, "Most heartily I do beseech the court to give the judgment."

The young lawyer from Padua, with a coldness only the young can attain, replied, "Why then thus it is: you must prepare your bosom for his knife."

Shylock fairly drooled with enthusiasm. "O noble judge! Oh excellent young man!"

And they further specified each detail of the bond. That the pound of flesh was to be removed from my breast, from that part nearest the heart. Those were the very words.

The young lawyer went on, like a pedant listing the most incidental of items, "Are there balance here to weigh the flesh?"

Indeed the Jew had it ready.

"Have by some surgeon, Shylock, on your charge to stop his wounds, lest he do bleed to death."

The Jew argued. A surgeon to stop my bleeding was not so stipulated in the bond.

Finally, all terms recognized, his knife was ready. Finally I found I could speak.

"Give me your hand, Bassanio; fare you well. Grieve not that I am fallen to this for you, for herein Fortune shows herself more kind than is her custom: it is still her use to let the wretched man outlive his wealth to view with hollow eye and wrinkled brow an age of poverty; from which lingering penance of such misery doth she cut me off. Commend me to your honorable wife. Tell her the process of Antonio's end, say how I loved you, speak me fair in death, and when the tale is told, bid her be judge whether Bassanio had not once a love. Repent but you that you shall lose your friend, and he repents not that he pays your debt; for if the Jew do cut but deep enough, I'll pay it instantly with all my heart."

Bassanio's anguish was clear. He called out so all could hear, "Antonio, I am married to a wife which is as dear to me as life itself: but life itself, my wife, and all the world are not with me esteemed above thy life. I would lose all, ay, sacrifice them all here to this devil, to deliver you."

He said it. All present could hear. None and nothing he esteemed above me.

She heard it, too, for in her guise as the lawyer she observed, "Your wife would give you little thanks for that if she were by to hear you make the offer."

And yet this lawyer, this counterfeit who had just heard her husband so declare his love for me, found the strategy that would rescue me. There was the wonder of it.

The young lawyer plodded on, "A pound of that same merchant's flesh is thine. The court awards it, and the law doth give it and you must cut this flesh from off his breast. The law allows it and the court awards it. Tarry a little, there is something else. This bond doth give thee here no jot of blood: the words expressly are 'a pound of flesh.' Take then thy bond, take thou thy pound of flesh; but in the cutting it if thou dost shed one drop of Christian blood, thy lands and goods are by the laws of Venice confiscate unto the state of Venice."

On and on this lawyer pressed.

"Prepare thee to cut off the flesh, shed thou no blood, nor cut thou less nor more but just a pound of flesh. If thou takest more or less than a just pound, be it but so much as makes it light or heavy in the substance or the division of the twentieth part of one poor scruple—nay, if the scale do turn but in the estimation of a hair—thou diest, and all thy goods are confiscate."

Shylock stood over me, his knife gripped tightly. A rivulet of sweat coursed down his brow. He tarried.

To say that I had prepared myself would overstate the case. I was strapped to a chair, my linen rent from my naked chest. There was a leather belt in my mouth to bite down upon to bear the stroke of the knife and to muffle my howls. What I remember most is that this belt tasted of a man's salty sweat. In what was to be my last conscious moment there was that tang of a man in my mouth. My breathing was uncontrollable and the pounding of my heart in my temples, through my whole head, made it difficult to hear, to see, to know. Here was as certain a limit as I had ever known. I did feel it. And taste it. I saw Shylock's blade raised to my chest, I shut my eyes, and felt—nothing.

There was a silence. A shuffling, a whimper that was not mine. There was a murmur through the crowded courtroom. I was exhausted. My jaw was clenched tight—I had nearly bitten through the salty leather. The muscles in my jaw ached as I dared to open my mouth, to breathe more gently. I felt hands upon me, soothing my clenched shoulders. When I dared to look, I saw Shylock crumpled in a heap on the floor. Bassanio tended me, and Gratiano, wiping my brow, kissed and held me. I was faint, so weak I couldn't hold my head upright. Those boys cradled me. My vision cleared, I could begin to hear what was going on around me.

I understood that this young doctor of law from Padua had prevailed, had confounded Shylock's inexorable vengeance. I was to be free. I was to receive half of Shylock's wealth. My life was not to be ended.

I fear there was little I could do to sweeten the bitterness I felt, once I knew that I lived to tell the story. It is true that Portia saved my life. Portia was a remarkable young woman, to be sure. She saved my life and then she claimed her reward: Bassanio. Did he even remember that she heard him swear that he loved no one as he loved me? In open court he swore it, and still she saved my life. Because she knew she had the stronger claim on him. It was only by her marriage to him that his oath did not condemn him.

I kept trying to remember. I knew that Bassanio stood in the court, that he said to all that he was married to a woman he loved, that he had money enough to pay the debt three times over, but that he'd give up everything for the man he loved beyond anyone and anything. He shouted this, and she heard him. She, dressed in her lawyer's robes, heard this oath. She saw that passion. The very day of her wedding to him, she heard him make this declaration. What kind of woman was this?

We learned what kind. A practical woman of Venice, a woman who required a man and who found one who was pleasing to the eye. Hers was an intellect unparalleled in Venice, to be sure. But vain, I think: a woman who must make sure that her triumphs are known. Surely I could not blame her for that—who does not wish the world to know of their triumphs? What I could not shake from my mind was the way she devised for her husband to know, to be taught, that it was she who forever was to be his master. It was this that so impressed me.

The trap she devised. Her trap.

The decision of the court was handed down. The duke granted me half of Shylock's wealth, the other half the state, in its wisdom, claimed. I could not see the fairness of such a fine, and so I spoke.

"So please my lord the duke and all the court to quit the fine for one half of his goods, I am content; so he will let me have the other half in use, to render it upon his death unto the gentleman Lorenzo who lately stole his daughter." If nothing else I could see to it that my band of no longer wayward youths were well accommodated.

And so the duke ordered.

As the court emptied, Bassanio thanked the young lawyer thus, "Take some remembrance of us as a tribute, not as fee. Grant me two things, I pray you—not to deny me, and to pardon me."

Ignorant of whom it was he addressed, he could not know what he'd soon beg pardon for. And in her—what?—her anger, her pride—this young lawyer spoke with the art we had grown accustomed to hear from those lips.

"You press me far, and therefore I will yield. Give me your gloves; I'll wear them for your sake. And for your love I'll take this ring from you. Do not draw back your hand: I'll take no more, and you in love shall not deny me this."

I'd wager that could we hear her inmost thoughts, we'd hear her say, "Because you love Antonio more than your wife, I'll demand what I know you have promised never to give."

Bassanio was nearly as poor a dissembler as once I was. "This ring, good sir, alas, it is a trifle! I will not shame myself to give you this."

And shame it would have been to part withal, for Portia had bade him never to let that ring leave his finger. And in the heat of his determination to win this formidable woman, so he swore. The trap was sprung. Her husband's loyalties tested. And oh, she knew the stakes. There was no saving a man's honor if he did not give up that ring to the lawyer who'd saved my life, and there was no staying true to her if he did. Only she knew they were the same person, and yet she set this trap. She set this trap for a man she said she loved? What kind of marriage celebration turns into so open a demonstration of power?

That, I know, is a naïve question. A marriage with money at the root is watered by power. Its fruit cannot be love. Such a marriage may bear many things, tests and games, perhaps, which may fire the heart and fill the days. But it makes for a perverse marriage celebration.

And what a poor wedding guest I was. It was true that their nuptials were completed already, but Bassanio's return from court to his wife was to be occasion for further celebration and thus was I invited to accompany him to Belmont. Portia greeted us as if completely ignorant of all that had befallen us. Her new husband introduced us, two people already linked by my rash pride and her painstaking cleverness.

"Give welcome to my friend," Bassanio said. "This is the man, this is Antonio, to whom I am so infinitely bound."

She spoke not with warmth but with the knowingness of the winner. "You should in all sense be much bound to him, for, as I hear, he was much bound for you."

What place was there for me between these two? A narrow one, becoming less and less comfortable, as if a vise were being wound shut, and so I bowed to her primacy. "No more than I am well acquitted of."

With a regal reserve that foretold much she granted me this, "Sir, you are very welcome to our house. It must appear in other ways than words: therefore I scant this breathing courtesy."

We soon learned what it was she would not offer scant attention to. For then the talk turned to rings exchanged and oaths sworn. This was the method whereby she'd humiliate him before me, his friends, before all of us gathered to celebrate them. What else was that test about the ring but a means of humiliation? This precious ring she bestowed on him, and bade him swear he'd not remove it for any reason, as a test of constancy.

The hapless Gratiano, newly married to Portia's companion, walked a parallel path to failing the test it was impossible for these new husbands to pass. His wife demanded to see the ring she gave him.

He squirmed, "My lord Bassanio gave his ring away unto the judge that begged it, and indeed deserved it too; and then the boy his clerk that took some pains in writing, he begged mine; and neither man nor master would take aught but the two rings."

Was this sport for the ladies, to watch their newly minted mates struggle so with discomfort?

Portia turned to the man she had taken to husband. "What ring gave you, my lord? Not that, I hope, which you received of me." Right well she knew it was, and yet she demanded this of him.

All watched him suffer. "If I could add a lie unto a fault, I would deny it; but you see my finger hath not the ring upon it—it is gone."

With a cold vengeance this young wife prolonged her sport. "Even so void is your false heart of truth. By heaven, I will ne'er come in your bed until I see the ring!"

Well it would have contented me that she never did come in my Bassanio's bed. And well it might have contented him. It was only in that mean thought I could wrest some satisfaction as I watched this game unfolding. The depth of the ladies' spleen was only fully revealed when they displayed the rings they had demanded, and told of how they had come into their possession. They claimed that they had received the rings upon lying with that same young lawyer and his clerk. Portia had the icy poise to tell her husband thus.

"Pardon me, Bassanio, for by this ring the doctor lay with me."

All this to see what effect her stratagem might have upon the man she took as husband? To see if it pained him to know his bride had lain with another? Surely this was her collection of another debt, one she invented knowing of the strength of the bond between Bassanio and his Antonio. For that was a bond no woman can compete with. I watched her play out a revenge that could bring nothing but spirals of resentment.

I urged this upon him, this taking of a wife. It was for his safety, a bid for peace in this city that demands duplicity. I knew all of this and still I wanted to know that he might be happy. Surely I was well on my way toward dotage to ask such a question, knowing what I have known and seeing what I have seen.

It is beyond my imagining what words could pass between this pair as the sun rose over the lagoon surrounding Belmont. What kind of consummation could there be? With this woman he has bound himself to, a woman who will save the man her husband loves, and then devise the test whereby she will impress upon her husband just who is the strongest. What can be said between lovers who find their love so corrupted by money and power? What do lovers who bind each to each in trickery, and torture each other with dissembling games, what do they say to one another? Does the dissembling stop? Can it pause? Or would a pause not be a pause at all, but a crack, the flaw that demands noticing, that opens into a tear, then a fissure, then a chasm, then a torrent? Is that what life was to become for my beautiful boy? That is not love. That is an ordeal to be endured.

$\oplus$

For my part, I am glad I do not know. My fortunes rescued by his talented wife and Shylock's overreaching mirror of mine own hatred permitted—nay, demanded—my withdrawal. A wealthy man, it is true, but meager and miserly in spirit. My fire guttered, and it was meet that I was chary of the few embers that remained. Bassanio sent me word that all was well at Belmont, but came not. I knew why but that did not stanch the ache of missing him. And the missing cannot stanch the corruption of the conditions of my missing. The means of our survival rendered survival a questionably desirable state. After all this, after life on the *Black Phoenix*, after life as a comedian, after the rescue of Sebastian, who then rescued me, after scheming with the countess, after mastering the world of Venice, I am master of nothing. A tale told by a cynic, whose meaning is too dark and too plain for any man's bearing, and so must go untold. Until now.

Deus ex Machina

Grief and anger can be hot, or they can be chilly. No longer could I find fuel to make heat within me. I seemed to be made of ice. Rime encrusted my mind as the white invaded my beard, my thoughts ran slow and in well-worn grooves like the tracks of a sledge in a snowy landscape. Rarely straying from that frozen track was itself a kind of comfort, but for me to have known even that would have required a sensibility that could know it was seeking comfort. I sought neither comfort nor feeling of any kind. The icy numbness suited the circumstance. Solitary, gray-headed, and wealthy, I lacked only that which provokes activity. It is desire that spurs action, and I desired not.

Sixteen times the moon shifted her shape, swelled and shrank, drawing her changeable figure across the night sky. Sixteen months passed and it might as well have been a day or a decade for aught I knew.

Marina stayed with me, clucking her resignation as she collected the trays she'd so carefully prepared, meals that my meager appetite despoiled only slightly. I saw few others. Letters came. Marina left these on the desk in my study, where piles of old contracts, old charts of shipping routes, sat and settled under the mantle of dust that thickened over them. I opened the letters, cast my eye over them, hardly noting their contents. Bassanio wrote only the blandest of blandishments in what became a monthly chronicling. Portia brought forth a son, so his beauty will not die, but flourish again in the little prince at Belmont. He wrote not of love but of money. I wrote letters in return, letters written by a frozen ghost, but one who did not have to urge him to remember me.

The heat of a second summer had warmed the rest of the creatures of this earth when a letter with a distinctive seal arrived. The initials "G de N" surmounted by a leaping dolphin. My breath quickened, there was a stirring in my chest as if there was danger near, yet there was no danger, not a soul encroached on my study. Carefully I lifted the waxen seal with my dagger and set it to the side. My heart pounded. There was moisture round my temples and in the small of my back. I unfolded the heavy vellum, and read this message:

My dear friend,
I still count you as a friend, and presume to think myself as one to you. I write with the hope that my paltry missive meets your eye with the beneficence that I intend. Your eclipse from Venice society showed your wisdom, even if you did not know it. Many a time and oft has titillating news sailed a stealthy race up the Grand Canal and stirred the minds of those who frequent the Rialto. Many a time has the political life of our city roused the passions and the yawns of those who throng the swelling scene in the square at Saint Mark's. Loud rumor speaks of others, and fills the ears of the gluttons that feed on such. You are quite forgot in this teeming hurly-burly. You have shown great fortitude. I wonder if you have fortitude enough to grant me the pleasure of your company.
I convey an invitation. It is my hope that you will come to me at sunset on Midsummer's eve. You will recall my passion for collecting what examples of the masterpieces of antiquity my agents can procure. My appetite has been whetted to a nearly unseemly and salacious extent by reports of what arrives on that day if time and tide are with me. Come to my house to be with me as I uncrate a work of singular importance and magisterial beauty. I urge you to rouse yourself and come. It is meet that you rejoin the world.
Gerard de Norville

⊕

All of the stones of Venice seemed to exhale a vapor as the summer heat waned. I directed my boatman to take a circuitous route. It had been months since I'd seen the city, and it is true that the warmth of the air had an effect on the chill in my—I could not tell if the chill was in my body or in my spirit—in both, then. There was a haze over the small canal that branches into two that form the boundaries around the Field of Saint Mary the Strong. As we emerged from under a bridge near the building site of the new Cathedral of Saints Peter and Paul, all the moist and heavy air seemed to change its hue as my boatman pushed us along. At the moment we emerged from under the Rialto Bridge and we could feel the sun bearing down on us from the far side of the Grand Canal, the blue mist shimmered with rose topped by the darkening gold of the dwindling afternoon. By the time we reached the Saint Angelo, the sun was a ruddy orange spun-sugar confection that was dissolving over the rooftops of the city. I felt a quickening—a sense of what I'd missed during my eclipse. Indeed, to know that I had missed anything at all was a quickening. For I had not witnessed a sunset since the day of Bassanio's wedding, so shut up was I worrying out my raveled sleeve of care. The boatman pushed on as the Grand Canal turned east, toward de Norville's palace, just across from the Academy. The evening sky softened, but was punctuated by torches burning at the mooring, and at his door. Soft strains of a lute floated over the water, beckoning. Pleasure beckoned, and I found that I could answer not with scorn, but with the timid curiosity of a young girl. It was not objectionable to find myself so meek, but I did not understand, at first, that I was like a tanned skin that had been frozen, and to regain its former supple softness, it needed to thaw. I was thawing.

Oswaldo greeted me at the door. "Very good to see you, sir. My lord awaits you in the gallery."

"Thank you Oswaldo. And the doctor's health of late?"

"Neither better nor worse. But such consistency is itself a novelty for which we are all, I may be pardoned for saying so, most grateful."

"No need to ask pardon when one is grateful for consistency, I think."

"No, sir. Only that to some it may seem churlish to be relieved that a deal of care no longer is required."

"Only those who have never had to bestir themselves could think it. And does the doctor expect other guests?"

"No, sir." He opened the doors to the gallery and announced, "Your guest has arrived, my lord."

"Antonio, oh—you look nearly spectral." De Norville approached me with his arms outstretched. "This beard, once so richly brown, now grizzled and shot through with gray. A visitor from beyond, indeed. But pardon me, sir, this is not the gracious welcome I intended." He turned and led me into the gallery.

"I trust your most unguarded utterances far more than the silken comforts that fall from your mouth so easily. I thank you. I know quite well my appearance is altered."

"Not so much altered as, well, some might aver that it is improved."

"Now I begin to be wary."

"Refreshment? An excellent Cyprian wine, flavored with pine resin, most cleansing to the palate, good for this summer weather, I think." He poured two goblets, and held out one for me. His hands were thinner, still pink, and still adorned with the rings he favored.

"Thank you. No other guests attend this unveiling, Oswaldo gives me to understand. Surely there are others who would crave admittance to witness this event? I have appreciation for beauty, true, but little knowledge of the craft of creating it. With an addition so momentous, I expected a throng of those who do to congratulate you."

"Ah, I have fallen in your estimation into that category of men who demand applause and adulation. But I assure you, that is not my character. The custom of the low world is not universal, old friend, and if you are to rejoin us, you must stop before you condemn us all."

"A thousand pardons. You are quite right. It has become a habit."

"Only one request is necessary. Yes, no other guests. This night is for you alone to witness."

Oswaldo had set several tall candelabra around a large sturdy crate made of hewn timbers lashed together with leather thongs. It looked as if it could transport a great weight and withstand any of nature's blasts. The crate rested two steps above the floor on a raised platform that was covered with dark velvet. De Norville had conceived of this night as theater, a private spectacle. His breathing quickened apace, and he licked the gathering moisture from his lips.

"Before this treasure in revealed, it is meet that we pause to consider what it is we do."

"What we *do*? De Norville, I must tell you that since my withdrawal from the world, my tolerance for riddles and mysteries, never great, has disappeared altogether. You must speak plainly sir. What it is we *do*?"

"I will speak plainly. I have invited you to see the newest addition to my treasures. But what, I can imagine you wondering, is it? I am told that this is a Jupiter, or possibly a Neptune, depending on whether the raised arm held a lightening bolt or a trident. These accoutrements have, it saddens me to tell you, been lost. My sources tell me it is one of the finest examples of bronze casting they have ever seen. I've been told to prepare myself for amazement. Oswaldo, will you care to begin? Carefully, man, have a care."

I did not doubt that Oswaldo rolled his eyes at this, the thousandth remonstrance of the evening, as he grasped the slender iron bar he used to loosen the front panel of the crate. De Norville wrung his hands with growing urgency as Oswaldo worked his way across the top edge, and down along the sides. The panel shifted, and Oswaldo picked up a blade to cut the lashing. With a gentle but palpable pause, the panel stood a moment, then fell to the floor, raising a small cloud of dust. The candlelight was filled with tiny swirling motes.

Shadow obscured the statue inside.

"Oswaldo, bring the candelabrum nearer—nearer—hurry." De Norville seemed agitated, but rather than approach his treasure, he sat in a chair opposite the platform, as if to watch a play. "Can you see him now, Antonio? Go nearer, regard the work of the ancient master." His eyes gleamed with pleasure.

The statue was magnificent. The virile god stood with his legs planted apart, firmly rooted as his great right arm was raised and flexed, as if about to loose a fearsome weapon. The god's brow was not troubled, but resolute. A full beard curled along the strong jaw, and the god's divinity was asserted by the perfection of his naked body. So perfect was the rendering of muscle and sinew and hair that it seemed to live. I could not speak. It had been so long since beauty such as this could touch me. Now I stood before it, and it wrapped me in an embrace that stopped my breath. How could ancient bronze effect so great an awakening?

"He is impressive, don't you agree? Where do you think I ought to place him?"

I stepped nearer to the god, and pulled the lights closer.

"He is so perfect, he seems nearly to live." Unbidden, tears leaped to my eyes. I blinked them back.

"I see you are touched. The ancient sculptor would be flattered by the response his work evokes, I think."

"Yes, de Norville, all who see this will envy you. This is indeed a great addition, perhaps the capstone of a collection."

"So fitting that it is the prime Olympian. You see, I choose to think of him as Jupiter. The father of the gods is a fitting climax. Go on, look more closely if you wish."

"Perhaps Oswaldo and I can lift the statue from the enclosure that protects it."

"Yes, yes, go on, touch it. Move him into the light."

When my hand brushed the god's flank it felt warm to me. The surface seemed to give, as flesh would, at the slight pressure of my hand, not press against me with the impervious cool of bronze.

"What mystery is this, de Norville? This feels not like bronze, but like flesh." I touched the thigh, then held it in my hands. "This is living flesh." I looked at the god's face, and saw that its eyes lived, that the body breathed. I staggered back and fell to the floor.

"What mischief is this, de Norville, what strange potion have you used to confound me, and why? Why do you mock me with this elaborate masque of unveiling? This is not friendly. Not friendly, I tell you." For some reason that I cannot account for, I began to weep. "This is not friendly."

De Norville approached and put one rosy hand on my shoulder. "Gently, Antonio. If you will breathe a moment and attend, you will find my actions more than friendly. But attend. Watch the statue one moment more."

I wiped the brine from my eyes and watched as the magnificent god lowered his heavily muscled arm, and turned to meet my gaze. With his other arm, he began to wipe the paint from his face.

"Napkins, Oswaldo, napkins at once!"

With each stroke of the linen a man emerged from under the guise of the ancient god. His eyes fixed mine as he descended the steps, bent to take my hands and lifted me to my feet. His eyes filled with tears as he smiled. Franceschino brushed my chin with his finger as he bent to claim my mouth. Warmth spread through me. I lived.

Epilogue

Since I am relating this history you can be certain I was not to be swept aside in the conventional rush to conclusion. That is the problem with comedy—even with romance. Those stories always end with a wedding. Those forms make such stringent demands that figures like me are dispensed with as easily and with as much thought as one gives to kicking the dust from one's boots. This time I have the last word.

The endless wars in Italy made moving west difficult. No sooner was the Treaty of Madrid ratified than the League of Cognac was convened in an effort to gather together a force strong enough to throw off the Emperor Charles's power. Man's favorite pastime found endless grievances and energy. Lombardy, Florence, Milan, Rome, even the Serene Republic were all vexed and vexatious through the endless succession of battles.

Since it was impractical and so sorrow laden to think of heading west, Franceschino and I looked for our fortunes eastward. The Treaty of Constantinople ended the hostilities between the Ottomans and the Austrians. Suleiman even accepted the evacuated Muslims and Jews from a Spain rent by the Inquisition. With the luxury of the passage of time, Savonarola seemed a rather puny despot whose spasm in power was brevity itself compared to the robust machinery the Inquisition of Spain invented. For a time, Constantinople welcomed all gods, and so had no need for such dire interventions. It was a city of traders, the point where empires promiscuously brushed up against each other, and we could be lost in its cosmopolitan chaos. We found a small house halfway up a rise commanding an advantageous lookout across the Bosporus. We could gaze toward Europe and watch the rolling sea where we'd toiled and traveled.

Growing older casts an iron shadow. I could not find a way to recognize the impetuous, proud boy of Florence I was who tasted the first bitterness of disappointment in the arms of this man Fate bound me to again, so many years after that confusing moment. How glad I was that neither my temperament nor any lineaments found correspondence with that boy any longer. The man I became was so much worthier. No longer young, no longer catnip to some, and so much a better man. In Franceschino's company I came to know peace. The losses of Rodrigo, Sebastian, and Bassanio were all part of that peace. Loss gave me peace. What a thing to say to oneself, or to you. Loss gave peace a resonance as deep as the bronze bells of Saint Mark's. I felt my weight settle into my feet. I stood more surely on the earth, somehow. Foreign earth it was to be, but my newfound sureness made all of the earth I would tread on familiar. I lived in a city new to me, but I did not feel foreign any longer.

You will have guessed that Gerard de Norville was the miraculous magus who translated Franceschino and so saved him. His collection of cordials and potions was put to extensive good use. His affection for both of us was never spoken as deeply as the actions that proved it. It was not until we were safe on the far side of the Bosporus that I asked Franceschino to tell me the tale. The asking and telling while abiding in a hostile place felt dangerous to me. Alas, I had grown querulous with the shocks that I was heir to. Once I was as certain as a man had reason to be that I would not lose him again could I ask about this mystery.

De Norville had arranged for him to be spirited out of Venice to Sicily where he lived for a time in the house of one Leonato. De Norville's principle interest in Sicily was as a source of the antiquities he so loved, and in Messina the construction of the new parts of the city yielded many antique treasures. But as the gatherer of intelligences from all corners of all kingdoms, he cultivated many who were worthy men indeed. Noble Leonato was one of these. Leonato kindly kept Franceschino in comfort those many months. But he could never be seen again in Venice, and so another plot, another adventure brought him back to me.

We were on the terrace of our house when I was at last ready to hear all. Time and safety tamed my fear that the telling of the tale might lead to its undoing, a fear so wayward and fanciful that I blushed to confess it. The early fall breeze cooled the heat of the day. We sipped the resinous white wine of the Aegean, looking out on the sun sinking into the sea.

"Franceschino, unravel me now your adventure entirely. Now I can hear it with no shudder of dread. Now I may be able to hear it with the joy that I can feel knowing we are safe."

He set his cup on the wall and kissed me.

"There is no need for fear any longer, handsome one. We are together, and at peace. My adventure?" His smile hinted at more than mirth. "First, there was the considerable difficulty of my removal from a cell that was practically in the bosom of the Duke's Palace. De Norville's web included a strand that led him to the guards there. He brought with him gifts of wine for them, nicely laced with a cordial that invited the soundest of sleep. Hapless men, I wonder what punishment they met upon awaking."

"Their mishap was suppressed," I said. "Your execution was staged and bruited about. Some claimed it was a goat they burnt between the pillars of Saint Mark's. But the rabble had their festival day, and the Council of Ten got their sacrifice. Some could be content. But what of you?"

"That is harder for me to say. I, too, was instructed to drink. The sleep was a sweet one, I vow. It seems I was easier to transport as the contents of an old trunk than as a man. Once out of the Palace and to the edge of the harbor, it was easy enough to load me on a ship. By the time I woke, I was more comfortably accommodated than I had been for many days. We enjoyed a swift voyage southwards. Leonato, noble man, was a most generous host and I bided my time in Sicily."

He drank and shook his head in wonder.

"It was the discovery of the monumental antique bronze of Jupiter near the harbor of Messina that set the plan for my return in motion. When he was pulled out of the earth, de Norville's agents knew they had to pounce. It was truly an ideal resurrection. When arrangements were made to ship the Jupiter to Venice, I could begin my overland trip. I didn't actually travel in the crate, at least until the last night before we sailed into Venice. Another beautiful example of the irony of man's folly: for it was the wars against the despot Charles that caused chaos enough to make my perilous journey back to Venice possible. I had to get as far as Bari overland. There, I boarded one of Bassanio's merchant ships, sent to meet me by our enigmatic benefactor. Yes, de Norville counted on your young lover for my secure entry. The crate to transport the monumental statue was on board, as was the trusty Oswaldo, who brought ducats enough to keep Bassanio's captain content. De Norville is experienced enough to know not to count solely on a young lover's loyalty. Ducats will do it, in the end.

"As we neared the lagoon, Oswaldo demonstrated his talent. He daubed me with the paint that transformed an old man's flesh—"

"—hardly old—finely aged, with the emphasis on fine—"

He grinned and brushed my hand away from his belly.

"—transformed this graybeard into a god. His care and craft brought a dead man home, and back to life, an anti-Charon, making his way back toward his love through Venice's canals."

"I've never understood his devotion, but I've benefited from it more than once."

"We've benefited from it more than words can say. And now, Antonio? What now?

"I desire nothing more than to remain where we are. We've been tossed ashore one last time, and it is a pleasant one, warm for an old man's joints. Bright for an old man's dimming sight. And there is no one I would seek after. The man who launched me into this whirlwind is the man I reach for as my anchor. But will you have it thus?"

"Oh yes, I will have it thus."

"But to remain together, a pair, a marriage, or what you will. Can this content you?"

"I know that I resisted you. I know that more than once I evaded you. Can you forgive a man who could not conceive of a life like the one that is disclosed to us now?"

"It is not for me to forgive." I drank and a shudder passed through me. "What a troublesome boy I was to you, Franceschino."

"Not so troublesome. Just a boy who could hurt a man as boys hurt their lovers—without meaning it, or even knowing that they have the power to hurt. Did you think I would not remember the time when I hurt a man who loved me? Did you think it would not pain me to the core to recall how I failed you? You had to learn, and so did I. You had to turn toward the rough injustices of life and see what you would do, and so did I. You didn't turn away, did you? You had to live the life only you could live, and so did I. And now, you are just a man who is loved by a man who finally has the sense to hold you fast."

He kissed me. I drew a breath and let it out slowly. I felt the sun on my shoulder, smelled this man's fine scent, felt the hardness of his hands, my weight on the warm stones of the terrace.

And so my story wound to an ending ere words enough to tell it could fail me. The pains of love's loss recounted, together we allowed the ordinary pleasures of a life lived in love's company to occupy the rest of our days.

Acknowledgments

The sources for this story are the plays of Shakespeare (attentive readers will note those words of his I have borrowed, to what I hope is a good purpose) and important works of history by several major historians. I am indebted to the scholarship of Fernand Braudel's encyclopedic *The Mediterranean and the Mediterranean World in the Age of Philip II, Volumes I and II* (1973, Harper and Row) and to John Julius Norwich's *A History of Venice* (1982, Random House). I was inspired to imagine what life for men who love men might be like in the Renaissance by Michael Rocke's *Forbidden Friendships: Homosexuality and Male Culture in Renaissance Florence* (1996, Oxford University Press), and Guido Ruggiero's *The Boundaries of Eros: Sex Crime and Sexuality in Renaissance Venice* (1985, Oxford University Press).

The invaluable gift of an introduction to the city of Venice was given to me by my dear friend Jeffrey Bannon.

I was encouraged by the attentive readings of early drafts by the greatest friends a person could have: Wayne Hoffman, Jeffrey Bannon, Stephen Mays, and Kenneth Lewes.

Any meditation on love and loss is indelibly marked by the love of two men I lost, men whose abiding presences will always augment my life: Mason Wiley and Joe Tribbie.

About the Author

Gil Cole is a writer and psychoanalyst in New York City. His first career was in the theater. He graduated from the Juilliard School and acted in several plays of Shakespeare, as well as in many classic and contemporary plays for nine years. He then became a social worker and completed a psychoanalytic training. He is a contributing editor for the journal *Studies in Gender and Sexuality*. He is the author of *Infecting the Treatment: Being an HIV Positive Analyst* (2002, The Analytic Press) and many papers published in psychoanalytic journals.

CPSIA information can be obtained at www.ICGtesting.com
Printed in the USA
BVOW041718030213

312236BV00002B/33/P